MTG

Cover Art by **TranceVizion**

Dedication

My son, I'll lead you so that someday you will as well. And, Mrs. Janet Worsley

ISBN: 0692304746
ISBN-13: 978-0692304747

MINUTES TO GO

CORI D. COLEMAN

MTG

Table of Contents

Acknowledgments

Jasmine, you have always supported me, thank you. Catherine, you gave me direction as a writer, I will never forget your favor. Kelvin, your wisdom strengthened my ability to research. Tj, your artwork is amazing, thank you for the great cover art. Devin, if not for your nit picking, I may have never revised, ever. To every reader, I am grateful to have you and welcome each and every one of you. Thank you to everyone who has supported me in this process.

God bless.

Marked...

Prologue

As the sun settles into the darkness of the clouds, two men in fine suits are seated at a table in a diner. The lights are dim and in front of the two men is a book. A rough brown leather binding laced over it and one strap with a metallic cross at the tip seals it shut. One of the men removes his shades from his face revealing steel blue eyes and a caramel complexion. His suit is silver flavored and thread with expensive material. He slides the book over to the other man and looks away as if he wants nothing to do with their meeting. The other man, with tan pigmentation and of foreign decent is wearing a black suit with red trim. He however has a solid stone look upon his face as he places his hand over the book. He strokes his beard before looking over his left and right shoulders. Assuring there is no one near who can witness him take possession of the book, he then slides it from off of the table. Something is troubling him and he makes it evidently known.

"Are you sure this is it?" He inquires.

The man across from him turns into his line of sight and makes a deadpan gaze. He speaks no words but his expression says everything. The other man rolls his neck as his awareness of his surroundings still concerns him. They are alone in the diner but the mood is an unsettling one. Discomfort is the result of uncertainty, but the man has no time to waste. He needed this book and only wanted to be sure he is not seen with it.

Just as he goes to leave the table the other man speaks, "Stop, there is no other copy of this book. I removed it from heaven myself. Remember it, learn it, and then dispose of it. And most significantly demon, do not cross me. Or I will kill you." He said with sincerity.

The foreign looking man checks his cuff links and allows his accent to take over, "I have a plan. And also a name, thank you."

"I don't care what your plan is, and in fact, I do not want to know what it is. Just do your part."

"You disciples and your arrogance, one day it will be the death of you."

A deep sigh is his response to the demon's subliminal threat. A waitress in a white apron approaches them. She has a pad in her hand and a pen in the other.

"Can I help you gentleman to anything else?"

The demon's eyes transition to an orange tent, and he stands to his feet and replies, "No thank you Julia, Paul will take care of the check."

Out of his pant pocket he pulls a one-dollar bill and hands it over to her as a tip. Disgust takes her face as she accepts the cheap tip. More disturbing is the fact she never gave either of them her name and a gasp of air reflects her shock. Paul looks up to her with his blue eyes and reaches for the dollar. As he applies a single touch of his finger to the money, it transforms into a one hundred dollar bill.

The waitress is unsure of whether to be amazed or pass judgment, but her sense of human nature tapped in real quick. Taking the bill, she says, "Have a good night gentlemen," accepting her blessing.

Just before the demon can leave the diner, Paul issues another statement, "Oh and Edward," the demon turns around insulted and replies, "It is Eduardo."

Paul places his arm above the seat and crosses his legs, "The key will be in Randallstown. The Bengal will find the boy. Do not waste my curse."

Eduardo grabs the door handle sucking his teeth, and a strong smirk hides his irritation as he nods upward and makes his exit. Stepping out front, he stands beneath a streetlight only to look up discomforted by the brightness. One wink and the lamp burst leaving him to stand in complete darkness. Removing a phone from his jacket, he makes a call.

"I have the book, prepare the circus for Randallstown. The chosen one will be there."

A deep voice replies, "Shall I inform Savatir?" Eduardo looks down at the street taking a second to think, and then replies, "No, no need. I have a different agenda. Heaven will soon be ours my brother."

Part 1

Catch a hint

Either you lived in Randallstown or you did not. But if you did, you accepted that this place capitalizes the S in small town. Yet, somehow the ninety-two town folk, in total, managed to keep up with technology. You'd expect such a secluded town to have been shut off from the new age luxuries, but as everyone keeps their cell phones diagonal to their stomachs, fingers cuffing for support, and eyes dropping down like a penny off a mountain top. It is evident they still remain in sync with the growing technological era.

Randallstown is not much of a town as it is a back alley compared to major cities. Although, like any small town– it has perks. And not to mention, it is not your typical small town, which usually has small town limitations. Randallstown is a secluded area maintained by wealthy residents.

Four silent compact neighborhoods is the result of a heavy police force with little to no crime activity ever. There are twenty-three officers in total with a zero tolerance for crime on a daily routine. Most of the officers spend their time patrolling streets while placing bets on who will see some action first. Mostly they cover a neighborhood of five mansions half a mile from the other communities.

The town is a pricey area to live in, and it holds a reputation for eloquent decency. Mostly, this is due to the clean gutters and streets blending into the rich scenery. The grass is greener than the recycle bins posted outside many of the homes and on many of the corners. The street lamps are filled with L.E.D bulbs, which is most uncommon for any area.

The town is fifteen miles from the inner city and to be honest, the people of Randallstown hardly ever take a trip down there. This is likely because of a small shopping district that has every store necessary – a privileged benefit for those who can afford it, to keep the citizens within the town limits, satisfied.

From a pet store to a hardware store the size of a garage, but just so happens to have every tool anyone can look for, business has a cycle. If you need it the town has a store that has it. Everything is on one strip; the diner on the corner, coffee shop, a mobile store that provides every phone carrier, a bakery next to it, florist next to that, and across the street a superstore.

The town folk are not exactly what you can consider out-of-pocket. Most of the residents here like to keep their lives–and their riches, to themselves. However, they also have no problem being friendly when it calls for it.

Like the Gunner mall nearby that receives so little customer traffic, it should be closed down for good. Most of the store clerks stand outside and basically reel in customers with an over toned voice and over expressed cheer. Gunner mall is one level and without the teenagers, not much business arrives until the weekend. Especially, due to the city kids who envision their visit to Gunner mall as a field trip. The facility is beautifully decorated and above average.

It is a fancy looking mall, with chandeliers dangling from the ceiling like the little strings attached to a ceiling fan, and two large marble fountains located at each end of the mall's two main entrances. Incontrovertibly appearance is everything, and for Gunner mall that is all it is.

The town has a cycle, and in order to keep the teenagers from going into the city, parents have no problem giving them their credit cards and letting them roam throughout the mall all spend crazy.

But the owner of the mall has faith in the new community being built a mile over, which host some very expensive looking homes. Only seven homes are occupied but most of the families are new to the town. Majority of the owner's faith goes in his most consistent customers Miley Hargrove, 18, and her boyfriend Tyler, 19. The two are a teenage couple from two different sides of town. Miley is one of two residents who have been living in the new community for years.

Although, Tyler is not much of a customer as much as she is. Often he is dragged into the mall by his undying love for her and her sobbing, which begins most of their dates.

This morning, Tyler finds himself in a predicament highly common for a young guy such as himself with a gorgeous girlfriend. Tyler is not from Randallstown, and actually he does not even live there. He only drives into town from the city to be with Miley but it seems every time he comes, he faces the same issue, some guy attempting to take her from him.

Department store

"Incredible, how much is it?" Asks Miley glaring in jubilance at the diamond necklace she later intends to hint off to Tyler as a gift, which he is soon expected to present her with for Valentine's Day.

The department store is fairly empty, giving one of the clerks the cue to entertain himself. The store clerk, a six foot five male with a neatly trimmed goatee and a posture straighter than a yardstick– applies his charm. But he does so not only to entice his customer into a sudden purchase. Miley favors smiling, and she does so to the point any stranger could misperceive her reflective glamour for flirtatious feedback, which indeed typically occurs. The clerk well attractive investigates this misconception further, and with countless efforts to spark small talk.

A bad move but a move nonetheless. Moving around the glass counter revealing many diamond rings, he strikes a sanguine pose.

"That necklace looks indescribable on you, it almost chemically evens out to the beauty of your smile," he says smirking and folding his arms. For sure his words left his mouth with confidence as he drops his weight to one leg while lifting his shoulder a bit.

Fortunate for Miley, she knows well of her stereotypical influence on men, and she replies, "Thank you, I appreciate your time and assistance."

Before her shoulders could rotate symmetrically with her waist – sending her in the direction of the exit, the clerk speaks deeper and louder to force her returning attention to his persistent invites.

"Is there anything else I can assist you with," he asks, flexing a smile so grand his angel white teeth catches the attention of other women in the area.

But not Miley's, his behavior is quite common and even if it had been rare, his smile is far too aporetic. He notices her shoulder bears a mark that looks like a tribal tattoo, but it is really a blackened scar from her childhood. It is most fascinating and he is unable to disregard speaking on it, "That is a beautiful tattoo," he says [appearing] ecstatic.

"It is not a tattoo," she says aggressively, "And no, no thank you," she replies.

As much as Miley wants to continue pacing and eventually break into a sprint for the exit, her inner self-respect turns her back around. Even though mentally she has already made her escape, yet physically she made light steps back into his direction. The assumption that all pretty young ladies like attention is what he is basing his approach off of. However, Miley is not like all young ladies. And she thinks nothing of her scar to allow compliments to have an effect on her. Over time it has become something she has learned to live with. To her it is just a black mark and that is all it will be. Being rude however has never been her way of handling any situation.

It makes no sense for the clerk to make another attempt; however, in the mind of most attractive men, they are never making attempts but only progress. The clerk then asks, "Are you in a rush?"

Miley thinks that to be obvious being as though he witnessed her back twice in less than thirty seconds. Turning to face him again she smiles and says, "I have to go meet my boyfriend, he is actually probably waiting for me impatiently right now."

"Boyfriend, you do not need one of those," and the look on his face during his statement made the word boyfriend seem comparable to the word Malaria, "you are gorgeous and young and you should be out living life free to mingle with whomever you desire," he says.

"*Wow*," thinks a speechless Miley – in appall at his overly aggressive input and poor choice of words.

However, he makes a very revitalizing point, she is young and she can most definitely be living her life. But, how can she do it is the question without an answer, which she puts off for now. A thought that crosses her mind often as of late is being explorative, but she will wait until later to reflect on such an idea.

It is evidential this guy is one who does not often leave conversations with women empty handed. The audacity of his approach brings Miley to a burst of laughter, mentally creating sarcastic responses for a guy who refuses to take a hike on his pushy ambition. He continues to smile clueless to the true humor behind Miley's laughter, yet as she covers her mouth and leans forward chuckling, clues become colds and he is beginning to catch one.

Seconds before Miley convinces herself last word or not she is leaving, Tyler walks up beside the two of them and ask, "What's so funny?"

The clerk replies, "I am handling," applying great emphasis to the word handling "a customer right now, I will be with you in a second, okay kid."

Tyler, under the impression he just interrupted what appears to be a successful flirtatious sphere of energy, begins to think the worst. And along with the fact, he still has a bit of insecurity about Miley and his relationship. Miley, is beyond beautiful and while Tyler – a handsome young man – still feels he is the underdog who lucked up on Cinderella.

An unfortunate perception but Miley's constant celebrity moments do not lead him to believe otherwise. There are certain times where you have to make a decision to trust someone, but when you are young you either put too much trust in a person, or simply not enough. Tyler is pretty much caught on the limbo line.

Contemplation set in, and it begins to set off a parade of speculations– leading Tyler to respond to this situation how he most definitely should not.

"What the hell is this?" He says glowering.

Miley lowers her head and then replies, "Tyler stop," anticipating his epic expression to follow his previous response. He never reacts with an outburst of violence and anger, but also because he has never done so is why Miley will not underestimate the possibility that he can. Tyler is not a hot head but he also hates looking a fool. In his mind, seeing his girlfriend chuckling away as if she were being tickled and some guy standing as if he were the tickler, kind of makes him feel like a fool.

She knows what is coming next, and this is because this is not the first time a guy made a pass at her while Tyler was around. It actually happened about twenty times before, and Tyler remembers every moment like his own birthday. If looks could kill Tyler's would torture. His eyes are focus and his face tight with aggression. In his mind, it is more of a *not again* moment for him but these are the pretty girlfriend curses– as he perceives it.

Having a gorgeous desirable girlfriend is a burden of troubled situations, or at least Tyler thought so. No matter where they would go, some guy and even girl, is always using their eyes to navigate the perimeter and area of Miley's heaven sculpted curvy body. She has the breast cup size of a twenty-five year old woman, and to even out the etched look men make, her butt is perfectly round and sloping like the side of an orange. Her thighs are slightly thick but in shape and her legs are smooth and slim. Not to mention she is one of the very few popular girls in Randallstown. Except, unlike other girls Miley chooses not to take interest in the younger guys in town.

Someone always speaks and Tyler is always there to announce his claim of ownership – metaphorically speaking on the matter. This time, on the twenty-first occurrences, Tyler intends to handle things differently. He is not going to walk out, which will make him evidently appear weak. Shouting and making a scene is a bit immature, even though being teenagers it would not be all that unexpected of them. Fighting the guy is a bit typical but truly solves nothing, because if he loses than he suffers the embarrassment of Miley, and also he pretty much looks weak, again. And even if he wins, he is going to spend a night in jail, not too smart-which he knows being as the town police experience too much boredom to not make a petty arrest.

Not to mention, Tyler is slim and athletically cut but he does not possess the most intimidating look. Especially, with his naturally soft curly black hair and a face that without a full chin of hair would not help him look a day over fifteen. His height is at most all he has being six-foot-one.

Fortunate enough, Tyler is actually a wise guy. No not that type, the actual wise guy that can use any opportune moment to display his skillful innovation. Which is what he does, "I don't believe this, you have to be kidding me. Every time I go somewhere they always do this," he says ecstatic. Miley's eyebrows fold inward and the clerk looks as blank as she. Tyler paces pass them and stops at the jewelry section, "Every time I buy something a week later it's on sale," he says staring at a selection of watches. He lowers his head and smirks at the feeling of a successful display of feigned anger, and then he sighs deeply before turning around malcontent.

"Welp, hey baby, are you ready?" Clapping his hands and then grabbing her hand while looking towards the clerk, he throws up two fingers up and says, "Ard bro, be easy."

Miley smiles and follows behind him as he walks toward the exit with enough confidence to make a chicken fly like a falcon. She admires his silliness and most of all his ability to control his emotions. In most cases, Tyler is capable of being amicable about Miley attracting guys. However, he tends to look forward to her countering his doubts with an over pour of endearment.

Miley even though surprised, she still is excited to have evaded such an unaccomplished attempt at getting her attention. Yet, the clerk's words are still becoming a thin vine growing around a railing. She thinks for a second as the scene begins to slow down, and as they are walking out in slow motion, she mentally resound his words.

"You are gorgeous and young and should be out living life free to mingle with whomever you desire."

Minutes to go - part 2

Indecisive and loving it

There is little time to stop the loud sounds of anger and revenge entering the airways from Dill's voice box. "Dill you are the worst little brother ever," says Miley.

Footsteps can be heard above, and then the sudden drop of feet onto the ground stomping towards the stairway. Which indicates Mrs. Teri Hargrove, has heard the complaints of her son. In seconds, their mother finds her criminal to the harmless crime committed against her angel eyed junior.

"Miley, why are you antagonizing your little brother?" A disgruntled and ill-informed mother inquires.

Miley responds, "I didn't do anything!"

Favor is not on Miley's behalf as their mother typically sides with Dill. Dill is a mischievous yet sly first grader, who has found using his hopeless sad face to inspire the evidence needed to support his innocence. Without a second try, Miley knows the outcome of this small predicament.

Teri asks, "Did you take the clothes out of the dryer and put the clothes in the washing machine, in the dryer?"

Miley had not done it yet, and she knows well a lie as convincing as she can tell it means nothing to her mother's experienced years of dealing with excuses. Especially, since the divorce from Dill's father Dawson. After they moved into the luxury homes becoming one of seven occupants, Dawson became an irresponsible wreck, and his excuses defined the true meaning of "*Full of crap.*" The divorce ended very ugly as Dawson even at the bench kept his lies well believed by himself.

Cheating was a small issue compared to Dawson's over aggressive defensive behavior. Once, Teri confronted Dawson about simple chores around the house, and he began shouting and using hand gestures not even gangsters could confirm, to express his instantaneous frustration. Either the television had an important subject matter, or he was already in motion to operate elsewhere around the house. Regardless, Dawson was never prepared to do whatever he was supposed to do, and at the moment were being asked to do. Having trouble with controlling his emotions, Teri often found Dawson reacting more physically than socially. It was never his intention so he claimed, but whether it truly was or was not, Miley couldn't deal. Eventually, Miley called the police; who also were reluctant to proceed with any arrest being as though Dawson also happened to be their boss.

On several occasions, Dawson refused to be home and his excuse was that he was out *making money*. The question arose immediately, what a lieutenant and captain are possibly doing after twelve hours of work to make extra money. The specific truth never surfaced, not even one time could Dawson explain his later hours or – in and out – the house activity. The most disruptive response to this was his on and off lingering through hot spots in the city, which also is where most of his officers made arrest for prostitution.

Teri always questioned why most of his calls came down to those specific locations. Dawson psychologically prepared Teri for any and every possible lie or unjustified excuse, and because of this, getting one over on her was nearly impossible.

"No, I did not but I will do it now," says Miley closing her laptop and taking out her earphones.

Her room is as organized as the library of congress. A bookshelf is under the window seal and a book nook to the left of it underneath a set of stairs. Her ceiling is painted like the night sky with white stars sprinkled about. The floor is carpet and she also has her own bathroom with color-coordinated racks for her personal affects. There are some dark drawings of hers however, resting on her glass desk that set her room apart. Also, the books scattered along her desk are young adult fiction stories. One had a picture of a chess piece on the front cover, and many yellow sticky notes as bookmarks peeking from the top. It is her favorite book second to one other. Another book beneath it has a fiery symbol lying on a sky blue cover. These two books are her best reads. Something about figuring out stories and putting pieces together entices her. But mostly it is the freedom the characters fight for that she finds most fascinating.

As she walks through her bedroom door, the strictest pain springs through her foot. "Ow!" She shouts to only look down and see Dill's toys scattered like breadcrumbs along the hallway once again. Dill's actions submerged thoughts of revenge into Miley's overly crowded mind but with Officer Teri protecting him, it is not worth it.

After handling the laundry, she makes her way back up to the kitchen for a drink. As soon as she opens the refrigerator her cell phone sends out the jingle that identifies only one significant individual, Tyler. Before she answers the call, a knock on the door sounds. Small moments of contemplating - yet easily an opportunity to multi-task, she places her phone back in her pocket as her intuition paves a sure thought over her assumption. The front door opens and before she can greet her unidentified guest, a soft kiss leaps onto her lips.

"Hello beautiful," says Tyler who regains his posture with a smile only made by true love.

"Tyler stop, my mom is here," says Miley. He eagerly replies, "So what, your mom loves me. Now let me in." Tyler steps in and suddenly spins three hundred and sixty degrees with style, and he then waves a rose from behind his back into Miley's vision.

"A beautiful rose for someone beyond beautiful," he says taking one of his best shots at being romantic.

Eyes at a glow and glare, she hugs him tightly radiant and smiling. "Thank you baby, you really make me feel special," she says.

But, truly she wishes he did not. It makes it harder for her to remember she has to tell Tyler the big news. Stroking her hair from the front of her face he replies, "I am supposed too," and then with no warning a plastic toy baseball collides with his head. No suspicion is necessary, as he knows exactly his foe.

"Oh okay, someone wants to activate the Tylernator," he says turning around to see Dill ducking behind the couch grinning.

Dill raises his arm and says, "I do."

Tyler races over towards him and clears the couch leaping over it. Instantly, his voice changes and curling over like a dinosaur, he pretends to be Godzilla trampling through the living room in circles after Dill. Miley stands and accepts the welcoming sight of her sudden romance being stole by her little brother, and she then pursues her half-full glass of juice she left in the kitchen.

"WHAT IS ALL THAT NOISE DOWN THERE? MILEY," Shouts her mother from upstairs.

Dill and Tyler quickly pause and look up to the stairs. Teri comes walking down in pajamas and a tee shirt with a scarf wrapping around her hair. She also has facial cream on and an off-flatiron dangling between her fingers. Stopping in mid-step, she sees her vase knocked over and the couches moved out of position.

"Tyler, get your ass up," Teri says as he tries to hide behind Dill, who is standing with the look of innocence he has professionally mastered.

"I am sorry Ms. Teri, I was waiting for Miley and then I see the most awesome little booger in the world," Tyler grabs Dill's face with both hands and continues, "Look at this face, who can avoid having fun with it?" Dill smiles back and show his teeth, and also a space where his one top front tooth should be.

Teri almost cracks a smile but diverges as she feels more attention needs to go to her furniture. You can play with a lot of things but you do not play with or in Teri's living room, and also with her faith in God. Her living room is decorated with biblical pictures and a bible above the fireplace. On the wall is a picture of the last supper and rosemary hanging from its top left corner. The couches are out of place and her antique looking pillows are on the floor. She is stern on those values and keeping them respected is a must. Everything in the living room looks expensive, and that is because it is. After the Divorce from Dawson, Teri was left with a pretty decent portion of money, which is also the only reason Teri can afford to live in Randallstown.

For Tyler this is all new to him. He is from the city and has hardly ever seen a home not attached to another. And the silence is soothing, as he once tried to sleep in his car outside their home – just to embrace the peace before riding back into the city where the noise level leaps. Randallstown's finest however was not allowing it. They arrived as soon as his seat went back, and then after an hour of questioning, they made him leave.

"Tyler fix my damn living room, and oh Tyler baby can you take the trash to the front please," she says soothing her tone of voice at the end of her request. Dill and Tyler reply, "Yes mam," and begin to move the couches back into position.

Miley in the kitchen is unaware of her involvement in this mischief, and quickly her mother makes her aware. Before proceeding back upstairs, Teri says in demand, "Miley come here, why do you have this boy down her waiting for you?"

As if she can hear her, but Teri may have been shouting for general purpose. In the kitchen, she does however hear her mother's over toned voice and begins to shake her head. Finishing her glass, she places it in the sink and long arms immediately wrap around her waist. Warmth set in and she shows her appreciation for his company with a snuggling gesture in his grasp.

"You smell so good," Tyler says.

"Nuh uh she stinks," says Dill passing through before heading into the basement, which is the location of his tomb of toy treasures.

Tyler sniffing her neck says, "Don't listen to him baby, lies they are, just awful lies. You smell good by the way."

Miley grabs his hands and smiles feeling loved more than ever. Yet, something inside is trying to bridge a gap between how he makes her feel– and feeling it. Just as she becomes comfortable in her moment, Tyler says, "Oh, and your mother wants you to take out the trash."

"What? No, you do it," she replies unfolding his arms and walking into the living room.

It is about noon on a Saturday, and the rest of the afternoon is up for grabs. Tyler has plans but he has not yet divulged them to Miley. Usually when he does, Miley informs him of her predetermined plan of action, canceling out any idea he brings to the table. This time, Tyler wants to be more affirmative and knows he is not taking no for an answer. More or so less, because of the incident last week in the department store, and ever since, Tyler has been feeling this need to secure his rightfully earned position. Miley on the other hand thought nothing different of the situation but that it was nothing, and it truly was. In Tyler's mind, it was another fight for his woman and another swing of his mighty blade of confidence.

Pacing behind her into the living room and joining her on the couch, he tells and does not ask, "We are going down to the convention center, there is a car show down there and Paul told me it is really cool."

Speaking in third person, "*Well Miley, because you have nothing else to do today, it sounds like you are going,*" she says [sarcastically].

Miley then offers her opinion in consideration of his own, "How about--," Tyler states quickly, "NO! We're going." A negative answer is not acceptable. He just cannot allow it.

"Master is you surest I have too?" Miley replies. Tyler rolls his neck and sighs deeply, "Look, I already bought the tickets and I cannot return them."

"The car show is free," she says staring bold into his eyes.

"They just changed it due to the amount of visitors they are expecting."

"Baby you lie terrible."

"Well then do not make me lie, or, help me get better at it? So anyway, it starts at three and it is one o'clock now, might as well start getting ready." He says proudly.

Miley never likes to turn down the opportunity of spending time with Tyler, but she already spoke with Amiyah about going to the mall. Tyler does not get rejected nearly as much as his invitations are accepted, but when Miley does turn down his request, it is always something he really wants both of them to do.

Fate in favor for Tyler, Amiyah has not called yet, and this unknown information still forms a window. Miley begins staring at Tyler and then says, "You are really handsome you know that?"

Quick, Tyler replies modestly, "I must be in order for you to have chosen me." And that immediately sparks an entire new debate. Insecurity is a tick and right now that tick is attached to Tyler.

"Why do you always say that?"

Tyler looks at the fireplace and mumbles, "The truth," and Miley pushes his shoulder. A strong gesture of disapproval but even she cannot deny he has evidence for his worries and doubts. Nonetheless, she also will not allow evidence to overshadow the fact she does care about him but not as much as she has convinced him to believe. And, Tyler is actually not stupid enough to think she does not, he is perplexed by her choice. Dating attractive women is never the issue, it is dating attractive women he does not trust to defend constant attention that bothers him.

She then says, "I did not choose you. Besides, you should stop saying that anyway because I am here and you have me head over heels." A lie, but also worth the mental reaction Tyler returns.

"I do?" Tyler says appalled and taken back.
"Shut up boy, you know you do."

He does not, and neither does she, but Tyler takes a second and then says, "I do now, but you did choose me. It is evident you still have options. You choose me every day we are remaining together."

Cannot blame the kid for stating the facts, because she did choose him but that does not have to automatically remain his unmoved perception. Secretly, there is an internal doubt but not for the proper purposes. His basis for his fluctuating motives does not however result in capricious responses, yet Tyler is only behaving like any nineteen years old would, insecurely. His heart, even so young, favors a more committed side of what should be a young free spirited life. A life Miley has lately been conceiving in thought.

Negatively moved by his last comment, she gets up and walks around the couch. "You really think I was flirting with that grown ass man? He was like 40 and I was not flirting with him."

"So if he was younger," Tyler says and Miley instantly knows after that statement she needs to avoid furthering the conversation. Tyler has a way with sarcasm and a slick tongue to follow. He can move a rock the wrong way with his responses if he reacts too soon with his words.

Going to the car show with him is what he is looking for to secure some validation of their relationship's solidness, which as of late has been questionable. Even though going to the mall is pre-set in her mind, Tyler is looking forward to spending time with her. In his mind, every second counts as he always feels the need to show his feelings for her. He believes it guarantees she will focus on him, if ever there is a time she does not. And well, there is. However, Tyler is unconsciously onto something he cannot at the time recognize.

Miley is not and never was the type of girl to entertain multiple men. However, her beauty brought more than welcoming attention any guy could misperceive for attraction to the limelight. Indecisive and frozen in thought, Miley wants nothing more than to show Tyler she is his and he should not have to worry, but she also believes that should come naturally observed and not insecurely proven. Which also brings around the type of thoughts that can make being committed unkindly recollected upon.

Minutes to go - part 3

Black Friday

It is finally Friday, and the sound of cars pulling out in the morning awakens Miley from a sleep pattern with so many gaps. She could go to sleep at ten and wake up at least five times before eight. Yawning and stretching, she turns to look at her clock and sees the time most people read and pull their quilt over their head to go back to sleep.

Friday's are not the greatest of days for Miley. While other teenagers are getting ready to plan out a successfully free day in Randallstown, Miley is probably going to get stuck with chores. This is necessary as she usually escapes on Friday evenings never to be seen or heard from until Sunday morning, which is when Teri would never excuse her for missing church.

Chores are possibly the reason Miley has not latched onto the average unhealthy teenage habits, like going into the city. Although drug use was never a concern her mother has for her. Unfortunately, Tyler is a victim of the influences polluting his lungs like oil spills into the sea, or was. He used to smoke marijuana lightly but he stopped after being pulled over by Randallstown's finest and having his car searched for two hours. A curbside became his love seat as they held a conversation about throwing him into jail, for having a half an inch of a rolled blunt left. The police are pretty stern and evidently overcompensating for lack of constructive utilized time. Experiences like such however– Tyler has chosen to not endure again. The police knew that Tyler did not live in town and that created a tension toward him. That and the fact they knew he was dating Miley, Dawson's stepdaughter.

Miley's cell phone goes off and it never is a mystery who is able call her at 8:30am every morning. If there is anything Miley can truly appreciate about Tyler, he is consistent. He always keeps Miley confident in the romantic part of their relationship. Although, she is not much of a morning person, more like the evil medusa before ten. Yet she appreciates hearing from Tyler, as he is the only exception. Everyone else is likely to be cursed out, possibly even Dill.

Speaking of, Dill burst into her room shouting, "MILEY YOUR CELL PHONE IS RINGING."

"I hear it you little dweeb," she says as she grabs her phone and pretends to throw it at him, "Now get out!"

"Okay!"

The door slams and the sound of the lock sliding into position seals in the secrets of her room. By the time Miley checks her phone Tyler had called and hung up. The frown moves her cheeks into an unsettling position. She tosses the phone onto the bed and runs her hand through her hair fully aware of her objectives this morning. Today is supposed to be the day she lets him know. A part of her cannot though, his company has gained value on her heart, making revealing her secret all too difficult. But, it is necessary.

Change is just as necessary as growth, and both will be on the line soon. It is imperative that she informs Tyler today, but a part of her feels averse to do such.

Her room is usually clean but this morning not so much. Clothes are on the bed and hanging off of her desk chair. Colors are scattered all over her floor looking as if she were playing a game of Twister. She walks over and removes a shirt from off the chair and notices an envelope. It reads: *Join the tour.* It is her invitation to the college tour. She fixes her eyes on the document and pauses. After taking a second she stares at her reflection in the mirror and looks at her shoulder.

Her mark is just a mark to her, and she does not allow it to be any more than what it is. At times, Miley does question the presence of her mark. Many mistake it for a tattoo but she knows it is too awkward for her to accept that. Teri hardly ever discusses how she got it, mark and she avoids the conversation. Just as she avoids the conversation about Miley's father. And just as Teri avoids that topic, Miley is avoiding a particular conversation with Tyler. One she must have sooner or later.

Kind of like her relationship with Tyler, which the college tour reminds her of. Tyler's presence in her life is temporary and for the convenient time being. A thought cycling her mind but always well put off as she has developed an expectation of his attention. A bit selfish but she redeems her morality by giving him the attention he request. Even when she does not directly require it, she accepts his presence gratefully. This mixture of negative and positive emotions troubles her ability to make a decision. Some bonds are chemically put together, but the coexistence of the mixture has an expiration date.

Walking into the kitchen is the easy part. The incontrovertible conflict is the second Teri comes down stairs to fix breakfast. Teri is a stay-home mom who manages to perfectly work the stay home mom businesses advertised on T.V. Much of her income comes from sitting behind a laptop but she also makes side-money doing hair for the local neighbors. Teri is better at hair but after seeing her first check for four thousand dollars, she could not turn off her ambition to see checks of that amount continuously.

"MILEY," Teri screams throughout the house. Teri always shouts when requesting the attention of Miley, and while she never means harm it balances out the reaction she has trained Miley to give her.

"Yes mam."

"Set the kitchen up, I am about to make breakfast. And take the trash out."

No matter what time of day it could be, Miley is always instructed to take the trash out. While Miley grew to not mind the chore, she understood it before tolerance set in. Trash is Teri's pet-peeve. Any signs of hoarding would set Miley's mother off immediately. Dawson was a hoarder. He saved everything like the planet was about to die and he needed every resource in order to survive. The way Miley sees it, the less clutter the less her mother sulks around the house in deep thought of the harsh days being married to Dawson.

Pots and pans are stuffed beneath the counter top in a cabinet. Their kitchen is very heavenly looking. Everything is white from the countertop to the kitchen table and chairs. Actually the only item in the kitchen that is not white is the refrigerator, which has two double doors up top and below a freezer that slides from beneath. Teri does not like her kitchen to have any dishes in the sink and no devices that are not being currently operated, visible. This strictness has caused her daughter to fetch the idea of freedom, as her home is at times equivalent to a military base.

As Miley goes to kneel down, an awkward bump on the patio door grabs her attention. Standing tall she looks upon the glass seeing no shape or form of any person. Still in her bugs bunny slippers, navy blue plaid pajamas, and tank top that reads, "I am a problem" she slowly slides her feet across the kitchen floor and around the counter to pull open the curtain. It is no one, not a soul, and neither any disruption to the loose doormat encouraging the idea someone could have actually been there. Suspicion arrives, and one thing she is really good at is being attentive. But, a sound without cause is a mind bumper. For now however, she will tuck away the thought. Much is on her mind today and going crazy is not on the agenda.

"Miley," says Teri walking up behind her unannounced.

"Ahhh oh my God," she screams as Teri walks in proceeding with the question, "What? Why are you so jumpy this morning?"

As bad as Miley wants to say something, her mother has very little imagination. Quickly, Miley turns to her mother and nods her head to cancel out the process of explaining the misunderstood. Teri is pretty straightforward and disregards any talk of irregular activity. Especially, paranormal activity, which has caused Teri to frequently walk around her home anointing it with oil and prayer. The last thing Miley wants to do is alert her active voice with a spook about hearing things.

"You want cheese on your eggs?"
"No thank you, I just want bacon and a biscuit."

"What's wrong?" Her mother asks dropping bacon into the skillet as grease pops.

"Nothing," says Miley with her eyes wandering everywhere but her mother's face. Teri is a bit strict but Miley's off faces can break the mold. To see her daughter sulk just as she once remembers, similar feelings are speculated and out of pure humane heart, Teri did not want to leave the issue alone.

"Miley what is wrong is this about the college tour? Did you let Tyler know you are choosing to go?" Teri asks tossing some butter into the skillet causing the pan to sizzle more aggressively, which releases a scent only Dill can sniff out for miles away. And in no time footsteps hit the stairs. Miley drops her bottom lip and lets out a gasp. She wants to discuss the matter but diverges. As Dill enters the kitchen, she closes her mouth and the pressure of her teeth pressing into her tongue insinuates her feelings are going to be kept inside.

"Nothing," she replies.

Tucking away inner feelings like a handkerchief before a meal, Miley is becoming very comfortable with putting off the topic, and not just with Tyler but anyone. If she can do so with Teri, it is a reflection of no thought to do the same with Tyler.

Dill places his toy on top of the table and begins making sound effects as if a war is taking place on his empty plate before him. This early, Miley is anxious to begin these chores, as her expected phone call should be received around noon.

It has been a week since Tyler and she went to the car show. Unfortunately for Tyler, Miley decided to try and kill two birds with one stone by inviting Amiyah – her best friend, to the car show with them. It did not go well, if there is any way to describe how last Saturday went, it is the opposite of a good time. Amiyah is not particularly the go-to friend when you need a third wheel. She is more of the go get in there-what are we waiting for type of friend. A mentality she imposed inconsiderably into their day.

Miley spent most of her time with her wrist under the grasp of Amiyah's hand, which forced Tyler to mentally interact in a form of tug of war. Tyler, spent most of his time looking at older model cars like the SS Chevy Nova, which was midnight blue with dark grey stripes soaring over the hood and roof until the trunk kissed the bumper. Exactly his style and taste, but Amiyah had Miley looking at hundreds of thousands- dollar priced vehicles on another floor.

After long hours of fighting for Miley's attention, the day came to a close and as Tyler stood before Miley she gazed back up into his eyes. Surely as he believed her lips were about to touch his, she backed up and turned to Amiyah spreading her arms gesturing the biggest group hug invitational. Tyler's scowling at Amiyah was his way of informing her *if there were a chance to save her from a fire, instead of running in to save her he would probably shout her name from the outside.*

At noon, Miley promised Tyler they can go to wherever he desires. For Tyler, ideas like that are less than enticing. Tyler is the type of guy who enjoys the element of surprise. This, over the plain Jane idea of just saying what it is and getting barely any emotion beyond a yes. But Miley, again attentive, pretty much likes to sight out the clues and piece together the puzzles.

Around 1pm, Miley finishes most of her chores and has already taken a shower and begins getting dressed. Tyler calls and honks the horn twice to confirm his presence and everlasting level of patience. And Tyler is indeed, patient.

Once, he waited for Miley for an entire four hours. Her phone had died of power and Tyler went searching around the harbor place – where getting lost meant being stranded at sea in the middle of the Atlantic Ocean – as Miley was also shopping down there. While doing so, Tyler had to run to the car to get his phone. On his way back a mute man passing out cards, which thought to be free but actually cost one dollar, stopped him. The card explained how to communicate with a mute individual, who apparently took Tyler's dollar and miraculously vanished.

After searching store to store, Tyler had lost Miley and she was neither answering her phone. Evidentially she could not, being as though every one of Tyler's attempts went to voice mail immediately. Tyler walked for an hour throughout the harbor unable to locate Miley. Soon he'd venture to the car and sat tight expecting her memory to act as breadcrumbs leading her back to the vehicle.

Three hours passed and Tyler had not slept neither even attempted to doze. He was alert and at sharp eye cautious that Miley had forgotten of his presence, and thus left without him. In seconds, Miley with more bags than she can carry comes splitting through parked cars inching by. One knock on the window and Tyler popped the trunk. Miley got in the vehicle and as her butt pressed into the leather seats coating the interior of a 2001 Honda Accord, she immediately witnessed the exertion and stressful concern upon Tyler's hardly hairy face. While Tyler stood angry for a day or two, he failed to manage aggression properly as his anger faded the day after, which is when Miley and he finalized their relationship.

The sun is shining like it has some point to prove to the winter season and insinuating it is the boss of weather. It is a nice day and where they are planning to go, it is a perfect temperature for the next ten miles maybe twenty.

Miley walks out to the sidewalk to see Tyler's wide-eyed expression facing up the north side of the block. His vision is taken by awe or shock but his expression is smeared into confusion and his body is frozen in disbelief. He is not moving and from the stillness of his pupils, movement is not an option. His look rushes concern into her heart and she begins to worry placing her hand onto his elbow and asking him, "Tyler, what is up?"

He is still unresponsive, still gazing, and still looking as if death had stolen his soul. What is appearing to be just an awkward moment from him turns out to be an even more devastating realization. Miley looks to her right and as her head turns slowly, sound is removed but sight is still active. And then she sees it; up the block she sees a tiger eating a man in the middle of the street. Blood around its lips and mouth with the man's liver dangling from its single tooth, and the sight removes nerve activity. Fixed on the abominable sight their bodies may have transformed into street lamps stuck in the ground with a brightness of fear above. Coldness from the sight of death stole the warmth from their bodies.

A car, zooming past Tyler's parked car, shoots forward to only apply pressure to the brake pedal with instantaneous fear. Smoke from the tires clouds the streets quickly, and in a blink of an eye the once speed-demon aggressive driver is in reverse doing forty miles per hour back up the street.

Miley screams, and then her handbag falls from off her shoulder onto the grass, spilling its contents onto the sidewalk. Her scream is so devastating and loud her neighbors open their home door, and as they did the tiger gives sincere attention to the birth of the sounds of fear. Tyler still shocked but not physically paralyzed anymore closes his door and sprints around the front of the car. Grabbing Miley, he runs her back towards her house instinctually in effort to secure her safety. Miley's neighbor Mr. Cantwell shouts, "Oh my God! Honey, call the police."

A squeaky voice can be heard from the bathroom window, "I can't hear you what?"
"Call the got damn police," Mr. Cantwell shouts.

Almost like in a movie scene, the tiger jumps Mr. Cantwell's parked Toyota Camry. It is a 2013 model with tent all around and coated cranberry red. The power leap left claw imprints all over the roof and fear all over the faces of Miley and Tyler. Mr. Cantwell praised his car and to see the tiger easily mangle the roof, a bit of dissatisfaction and anger overtakes his ability to be scared.

At the door, Miley turns back to see her handbag on the ground and her house keys lying partial in the grass and on the sidewalk. Nothing could compare to speed at which Tyler's heart begins to race as he bangs on the front door. In the back of their minds circles the thought to question. No one can imagine how a tiger is even possibly in the streets of Randallstown Maryland, a town with completely no wild life at all. There is not even a possum yet along field mice. Regardless of the fact, this is real and every balled fist Tyler plants on the door ensures the reality.

"OPEN THE DOOR!"
"Open up, somebody open up the door," they shout together playing whack-a-mole on the front door.

Mr. Cantwell is a small man and not built for any physical altercation. He is also about fifty-three years old and is a war veteran now retired from the post office. While his physical presentation read less likely to defend against any attack, it has to be instinctual bravery, which leads to his next action.

"Over here you stupid cat, come over here," says Mr. Cantwell who somehow thought of using the flapping top piece of his mailbox to create a noise, loud and irritating enough to steal the attention of this deadly feline.

Not sure if he is innovatively creating a counter move but Mr. Cantwell keeps trying to draw the animal's attention. At this point and time, whoever is home on the block have become eyewitnesses from their living and bedroom windows. One of Miley's neighbors across the street opens his window completely and begins shouting out noises intending to distract or at least confuse the tiger.

The seven homeowners are all fond of each other, and they have a level of trust to even have given each other keys to their homes in case of emergencies. This trust must have also developed some sort of unity and synchronized defense system. Everyone is pitching in, but the tiger is choleric and centralizing its nature of falconry on a direct pursuit. Unfortunately, Miley's keys are too far to make an attempt to retrieve.

This tiger is no ordinary animal; its feet are the size of water meter plates you find cemented in the sidewalk. Eyes sunflower yellow and teeth flexing as if a dentist had instructed it to open wide; Miley watches as the tiger lands from its pounce and creeps slowly in their direction. The tiger has not yet made a move as all the screaming and shouting from multiple directions is causing a great deal of distraction. A plan gone well until the tiger finds focus like a pair of earmuffs has fallen over its ears.

And now, the beast determines its next victims with a growl that translates *I am coming for you*. Noise or not, its eyes are fixing on a new objective, Miley and Tyler. Death is prowling.

Minutes to go - part 4

In the eyes of death

"Come here you beast," shouts Mr. Cantwell.

Miley and Tyler curl up at the foot of the front door with nowhere else to go. From the way things are looking you would expect them to have made an attempt to run, but the tiger looks so obstinate how far can they actually get. The tiger has a straight on stare that is pin pointing towards them as if its eyes are communicating words to their heartbeats. A slow prow, very calm but unflinching inspires the steps of the feline. Teeth are showing like an infant, yet only as sharp as a witty scientist. From the looks here, there is no escaping the destiny of becoming news for the media. Reporters might as well prepare a sad tale for the evening news because death is approaching, and it does not look like it will turn away.

But Mr. Cantwell is finally about to get the attention his heroics are asking for. The tiger turns its head into his direction, almost asking Mr. Cantwell if this is really what he wants. At his age maybe it is, but who can accept going out like that, and why would you want to?

"Come here you stupid cat," Mr. Cantwell shouts now holding a rake in his rattling hands. It is now set in fate as the tiger turns its entire body to him. Teeth reveal as a taunt first but also a warning of attack, and surely as they show Mr. Cantwell closes his eyes sealing in the actuality of his decision. The look on his face is not fear, but his eyes are wider than drapes being pulled open in the early morning. He knows what he has confirmed and as the tiger slowly prowls over towards him, he turns to look at his front door. It is open, *if only I can make it,* Mr. Cantwell thought timing his back peddles. A loud collaboration of sirens ring through the streets but a look of relief is not evident on the face of Miley's bold neighbor.

The police are showing up and squad cars are swerving through the street into dead stops. Officers jump out of their vehicles like swat ready to make a raid. The tiger growls louder than ever heard before; the sirens have put it on alert and in the blink of an eye the beast begins dashing over to Mr. Cantwell with its mouth gaping. A leap away from transforming him into a corpse, Miley's voice captures the air.

"Tyler," she screams in fear.

Tyler takes off sprinting at full-speed, and this is the type of fast that could impress any Olympic runner. With just enough distance to prance onto Mr. Cantwell, the tiger let out a roar that shakes the windows enough to crack. Fear immediately takes over and turning his skin paler as he is clinching the rake so tight splinters slide into his palms. A massive shadow covers the sky above him and he can feel the energy identifying the presence of the beast. He closes his eyes sure of his last seconds, but as quick as they shut, Tyler spear tackles the tiger with just enough force to disorientate the attack.

It was a bold move by Tyler and very unforgettable, especially for his body build, which is not bulky or buff. However, the tiger recuperated much quicker than Tyler, and is now facing upward, eye stalking him as he lies with his hands behind him and his legs flat out on the grass. Tyler does not even have enough time to think about what he just did. Adrenaline pumping he grips the soil tight. This time there is no growl and no hesitation, the four legged carnivore moves like dust in wind.

"There it is," a cop indicates by pointing his rifle.

Gunshots ring out causing Tyler to close his eyes and curl up fearful of being struck by a stray bullet. Mr. Cantwell still in shock stands gazing at the beast taking severe gunshots to its body. The beast falls from the force of the gunshots rendering it disabled. But just before its eyes laid rest, one last swipe of its paw is made in effort to be remembered. Tyler screams in pain as its thick claws dig into his thigh and gush out blood from his wound. Blood stains the grass and pours from his wound heavily as large abrasions are left on his leg. Adrenaline intensifies as one of Mr. Cantwell's lights, which stick into the grass to light the walkway, is in Tyler's sight. He grabs it and without hesitation he sends the sharp end straight down into the Tiger's sides finishing it off. He leaves the device inside the tiger while a black liquid blending in with the egesting blood excretes. Next, he falls back onto the grass and agony moves in like a roommate.

Tyler is screaming so loud Miley cannot move. She is stuck and the feeling is that of being cemented into the walkway of her home. Mr. Cantwell surely thankful – dashes over and falls to his knees placing his hand on Tyler's back. Teri rushes out of the house and identifies her daughter's safety right away. The pressure on her heart is pumping like a runner in a bull race. Miley faces her mothering quizzical as to why the door never opened. Teri's wistful look creates no sympathy. Before a moment can unravel into inquires, Miley turns back towards Tyler who is no longer capable of looking at his leg.

"Son, are you ok?" Asks a cop who sprinted over as soon as the gunfire ended. Tyler continues to scream as more blood pours from his leg. Other officer's gather around in amaze, and then in short time the sounds of an ambulance can be heard nearby. Tyler's pain is surging out in his expression. He begins to feel the regret; thinking, *was it worth it,* to have gotten the results of his leg nearly torn off. Such a feeling isolates him, and it is as if he is lying in a dark room with no windows and an off breeze - as he bleeds out. Had Tyler made the smartest decision, he cannot determine at the moment with the results of his actions, but from the looks of facial expressions on the witnesses around, Tyler did something he should never feel sorry for, which is saved a life.

Two days later...

The next two days are nothing but smiles and hand claps as Tyler sits up in the bed watching the news stations broadcast a video someone captured from their cell phone. Miley watches in amazement as the last thing she can recall is seeing Tyler surrounded by blood. In her mind, the tiger had swiped his head off and removed her boyfriend from life. Hardly the case, Tyler is being praised as nurses check on him every ten minutes, which is an appreciative effort for his diligence. In a way he feels the comfort from the speculators, but the memory is daunting and dark. At this point, all he has is his sarcasm to counter act the brain thumping memory. Mr. Cantwell however is honing the light. He has been featured on a few news stations explaining the story and giving Tyler a reputable face.

A bizarre circus show was passing through town, passing through, and it had been reported in the next city that the ringmasters had lost a tiger during a training session. Because of the death of the tiger, the circus had pursued a lawsuit against the Randallstown police department. Fortunate for Tyler, the lawyers said because he had suffered injuries and a video went viral of the attack, the circus is dropping the suit and offering to cover Tyler's medical bills. As well let's not forget one man had already lost his life.

Tyler watches as a rerun of Mr. Cantwell's interview plays on the television.

"It was incredible, that kid is brave one possibly braver than some goonies I served with." The reporter asks, "Does it still feel unreal?" Mr. Cantwell replies, "Honey, I have been through 3 tours, whether it was real or not doesn't matter, what amazes me is that boys actions."

He turns off the T.V. and looks off to the window. Hero or not, he does not like the thoughts that resurface, like a war vet, and Tyler is receiving some uncomfortable flashbacks. Pain shoots through his leg every now and then but the nurses make sure Tyler is well treated with morphine. A kite often resembles his height of alacrity, although for dosage they deliver the effects are minor. Tyler has a history of heights that makes coping with the drug a walk in the park.

"Tyler I am about to go to the cafe, do you want anything?"

"No, I am okay," says Tyler sitting up trying to secure a position of comfort.

"Are you sure? I know you Tyler, you will let me go down there and come back, and then finally figure out what you want."

"I am okay Miley."

"I am going to get you a snack anyway," Miley says as she exits the room. As calm as she sounds her hands still shake every now and then. But she does not have it as bad as Tyler, who tends to have bigger problems.

Just as Tyler sinks back into the bed, *which is unbearably uncomfortable to lie in*, a tingling feeling begins to set in his thigh and his eyes grow as he anticipates the worst irritation he can suffer, an itch. The itch begs to grow consistently and causes him to throw his blanket over. His room is a freeze box and without that blanket, he feels like he can catch hypothermia.

Leaning over, he stretches his arm to reach for his blanket lying on the floor somehow impossibly far from his capable grasp. No matter how far he reaches, it seems he continues to push the blanket further down. It is hard to get frustrated because his leg is also hoisted up - extending in the air. Weirdly noticed, as Tyler reaches more and more he is also stretching his body just enough to use the cast to scratch his leg. As it begins to feel good, Tyler adopts a routine he begins over and over. Soon the itch finds its soothing point and Tyler's next objective is to retrieve his blanket before he turns into an icicle. While he could wait for Miley to return, the tiger may have injured his leg but it did not injure his pride.

But just as Tyler's fingertips touch the blanket he hears a growl. Looking up very fast and there it is - the tiger. The same tiger is back yet silent and staring with vacancy. Tyler freezes as the beast is lying over the bed and under his leg. A stare down begins and Tyler begins to sweat. His hands get shaky and fear makes a home on his nerves. Screaming for the nurse could not possibly save him with the tiger being this close. The same wounds from gunshots are covering its body. Tyler's heart pulsates sporadically and his exhales get deeper. Fear has taken over.

He closes his eyes and turns his head to grab his covers, as soon as his eyes left, the tiger growls louder than he remembers. As he turns back around, and just like that the tiger is gone. A sudden knock on the door and Tyler jumps again nearly removing his body from the bed.

"Hello, Tyler is it?" A man asks walking into the room. Tyler nods his head up and down but says no words.

"I am Detective D... Dennis. I am here to ask you a few questions about two days ago. But first how are you doing?"

Detective Dennis steps back to stand in the doorway until Tyler speaks his first words. He has not been talking to anyone other than Miley. Ever since the video of Tyler tackling a full grown tiger had gone viral, news reporters and celebrity talk show reps have been bum rushing his hospital room, and mostly for questions and insight on the latest scoop.

"Um is any of this going to be recorded?"

"No. None of it will because this is completely off the record. What is discussed between you and I is only between you and I."

Dennis wastes no time crunching into Tyler's long-term memory box. Tyler gives him straight on eye contact and then asks, "Sir not to be rude, but have we met before?" Asking but already assuming they have because his face is too familiar. Plus, Tyler caught his pause during his introduction. But he gives Dennis a chance to prove his title, and after all he has had a few reporters lie about being the authorities to get into his room. Randallstown finest was not having such foolery. They now looked upon Tyler like a citizen of the community and not just an invader from the city. One of the officers, sophomore recruit Benny Booter, keeps close watch over Tyler. Every now and then he may step in to check on him, mostly because Mr. Cantwell is his grandfather. Benny is forever grateful for Tyler's heroics. This time, Dennis's pay grade had Benny take a fifteen.

"Are you asking me have I ever arrested you?"
"Not quite, you just look really familiar." Tyler says.
"So you do not remember me?"

Tyler looks off to ponder a thought. He snaps his finger and looks to the ceiling before releasing a deep sigh as nothing comes to mind. Even if something had of, Tyler would not have said anything. "No, but you do look familiar."

"Well, let's just say you are not as innocent as the reporters may believe."

"But I have nothing to do with the tiger thing," says Tyler sitting up as much as he can. By this time Dennis has entered the room and found a resting in the single chair to the left of the bed.

"No son, no one thinks that. However, I never forget a face. At least not the ones I had to keep my eye on through my squad car's rearview mirror. That's beside the point, how are you feeling?"

"I am okay. Leg itches every now and then but I believe I figured out how to end that misery."

"Yeah those things," knocking on the cast around Tyler's left leg, "are not the best of smiles. I know you have been through a lot within the last two days with the media and all, but I just need to get these few questions answered and I'm out." A nurse knocks on the door and walks in smiling stopping at the foot of the bed. Grabbing Tyler's chart, after examining it for a second or two, she then progresses to the right side of his bed and smiles big.

"Tyler, are you doing okay?" she asks with a voice soft enough to put you to sleep.

"Yes I am fine, just..."

Before he finishes his sentence, Miley re-enters the room. She practically walks around detective Dennis almost like he is not there. Had she noticed him she may not have remained in her skin.

"Hi," speaking to the nurse as she drops a handful of snacks and a Styrofoam container onto the bed.

"Hello, so Tyler, are you hungry?" The nurse asks with her eyes wide over the amount of snacks brought in. "If you do get hungry, you can order from the menu next to the phone," the nurse says tapping the phone with her index finger.

"I'm okay. Plus, the food they brought this morning was terrible, no offense."

"None taken, I did not fix it," the nurse says sharing a laugh.

Dennis clearly is not getting the privacy he believes capable. A small chuckle into a cough and everyone turns their heads to give sight of his presence. Miley's eyes grow into suspense, her nerves begin to jitter and veins begin to show through her skin. Her cheeks become redder than tomatoes and her long pause makes Tyler double take. A once dull memory now resurfaces with a bright circle of light surrounding him in his seat.

"Miley what's wrong? You know Detective Dennis, he wanted to ask me about the other day," he says, and she says nothing but her lips separating insinuates she has much to dispense. Words are supposed to leave her mouth but for some internal nerve pausing moment, she is not speaking.

"Miley!" Tyler shouts.

Detective Dennis looks up at Miley and before he can say a word. Teri walks in with Dill. Dill is sulking as if a hospital could have been the worst field trip ever. Dill looks to his left and sees Dennis, and Teri looks down and sees Dennis now leaning back into the chair. His demeanor is reinvented instantly into a smearing shameful smile.

"Dawson?" Miley and Teri say simultaneously as Dill follows them with an outpour of screaming joy, "Daddy!"

"Dream and now stop." - Unknown

Minutes to go - part 5

Quick as sand

As quickly as Dill runs over to Dawson arms spread and with an everlasting smile, Teri and Miley regain recollection of every lost question they've been asking throughout the entire duration of his absence.

"What you are you doing here?"
"Where have you been?"
"When did you get here?"

"Why?"

Miley and her mother begin to tear down Dawson with questions he has not prepared answers for. Imagine being in a courtroom and the jury is granted the opportunity to question you instead of the lawyers. That is the heat Dawson is facing with no shaded area for miles. A bias nurse sucks her teeth staring at Dawson, insinuating he at least flatter them with an answer to one of their question. Although, answers are just like his family history, he does not have any.

"I..." Dawson takes a pause and then looks at Tyler. His eyes grow arms and begin reaching in Tyler's direction for some form of help. In what way Tyler can help is completely out of thought even to Dawson. Innovation is not his best approach but the thought also crosses his mind. Leaving is a possible avenue for escape, but he is not interested in evading his family as much as he is intending to stay.

"No dude, nope," says Tyler pushing down Dawson's psychological reach for help.

Tyler has been around long enough to hear of all Miley's unstoppable raging explosions about Dawson. Maybe if it were a tiger raging at him Tyler's defense can serve purpose. But then, his escape comes, yet unlikely to his expectations. The nurse turns up the blinds and sunlight obscures Dawson's vision. Tyler covers his eyes as the sunrays take sight from him as well. The glare is brighter and full - lasting for but ten seconds before a flash takes Dawson and Tyler.

Miley and Teri are facing the opposite direction, so they only feel the warmth of the beaming rays on their backs. As for Dawson and Tyler, the sunlight has taken them from the room and from the hospital completely. The entire surrounding scene is white, and nothing exists but for a moment.

Until they remove their hands from their eyes and they both stand in an open room with all white floors and no visible ceiling. It is cool and feels as if they are standing inside a cooler with a momentarily two second warmth flash. Dawson's suit transitions white and his shoes as well. Tyler's tee shirt is now plain white and his jean and sneakers are now pearl white as well.

Looking around, they began to feel over their bodies, patting themselves up and down from their chest to their legs. Everything feels real so it is difficult for either of them to believe they have died and moved on, but being as though the switch happened so fast, who is to say they are not dead? In addition to that reality, begs the question how did they die?

"Are we dead?" Dawson asks.

"My leg is fixed. Yes, my leg is okay, thank you Jesus." A voice deep and clear as water replies, "You are welcome."

And then silence adopts the sound of their thoughts. Disbelief is a virus that begins infecting their reality. Not for a second can they fathom that hearing a direct response to Tyler's praising– can this possibly be who they think it is. It will be impossible to accept, plus there is no way that they both suddenly dropped dead. *Right?*

"No damn way."

Dawson looks at Tyler with a serious stare and says, "Way or not, if it is, do you really want to be cursing in his presence?" Tyler thought it over and as foolish as he feels to say it, he has no choice but to make it a reality, "Jesus?" He questions.

"Yes?" Answers a voice in a tone calmer than the seas after Jesus relaxed the storm his disciples feared.

"Are you really Jesus or is this like a dream?" Asks Tyler, who is now looking up to a never-ending ceiling of pure white openness.

"The answers to your questions are yes and yes. And Dawson, you are here because my father has called you to be," says the voice of Jesus. An unreal but expected ability that Dawson's thoughts are readable. For a moment, he almost tries to deny this is not some weird black out affect from being in a difficult position back in the room. If this is real, and it is, Dawson ought to have also considered the fact he is actually in the presence. After all, his track record is not politely introduced in any conversation Teri has had to deliver his name in.

Dawson lowers his head and a deep depression set in dramatically as the word called leans on the word dead. Tyler sees Dawson's pale expression and captures the doleful look himself. And he too allows the axiomatic assumption to take over his state of mind.

"So... We are dead," says Dawson more as a statement than a question. Jesus voice speaks even clearer, "Why do you put more faith in death than in life?"

Tyler takes initiative to speak on Dawson's behalf as he witnesses Dawson's demeanor sinking lower, "By called you mean we have passed away? Like permanently? Because truth be told, I am not going to be too pumped about being dead either."

"By called I mean exactly what has been stated, you have been called. Do not fear death, even in the event you feel you have surpassed it. Allow my voice and presence to be charitable in light rather than the absence of my voice in darkness. This is a good calling so do not fear my father's request."

One of the hardest things to do at the moment is comprehend the reality of their own presence, and at that before the Son of God. Tyler begins walking around the emptiness hoping to explore something other than open nothingness. Dawson folds his arms trying to hold in a devastating cluelessness, which is eating away at his perception like termites on a log cabin. God has called them both but for what remained a mystery. Evidentially, they were not called to die, however, in the presence of the Holy Spirit, who could deny the only doorway in, is death?

Tyler cannot hold his expressions in, "Jesus, I know I haven't talked to you much but I am sorry, and I know I smoke weed but I cannot help it, its harmless right? And I feel so focus," Tyler pleads, "Can I go to hell for smoking weed? Is that a sin?"

"Kid, I don't think we are here to convince God we are not sinners," Dawson expresses with a smirk of sincerity.

An incredible sound of bolts unlocking and chains being removed from, "A door!" Tyler says having more craze than Dawson. They turn around to see an enormous door with a handle too far up to grab and a height too tall to fear hitting your head on the way in. This door is massive and great and white. The design incrusted in the frame is that of some abstract art, yet with symbolic value.

"Do we go through?"

"Jesus, do we go through?" Tyler asks.

"Yes," says the voice of Jesus the Christ with epic clarity. Dawson leads, feeling like even though they are somewhere where his title did not serve much authority, being a skilled and trained leader, he would likely be more pre-cautious than Tyler who every second or two is letting his legs wander just as curiously as his eyes, even with nowhere to go.

Jesus continues, "Dawson and Tyler, my father has a purpose for you both. First, I want you to choose what you value most, as it will become the bargain of your efforts." Both, Dawson and Tyler look bewildered. Yet, Christ still speaks informative, "Tyler, you will have a choice. Dawson, you will have a choice. Your time has come to defend the light."

After those last words Tyler cannot help but express his inability to have understanding. He looks at Dawson and says, "Dude, WE...ARE DEAD!"

Impatience begins to settle with a mixture of anticipation. The door is so massive and huge; one can only expect nothing less than its description behind it. As they step forward, another voice is heard only much deeper and more powerfully driven out.

"Go on, with me. Do not forget I am here– with you."

Dawson and Tyler spin quickly as the voice transitions from a distant sound to brushing pass their ears like a small leaf flying through a breeze.

Minutes to go - part 6

Big past mistake

As Tyler and Dawson walk back through the hospital room doors, Dawson is greeted by Dill, again. Miley is smiling and staring at this moment to be captured as if the tension felt not but seconds ago, was not any short of hatred and confusion. Tyler walks from behind Dawson still firmly being embraced by Dill, and then through the door. Miley's smile strengthens as natural attraction begins to run its course through fate.

"Hello," she says soft spoken and hesitant into Tyler's direction.

His face nearly falls off as he identifies how Miley's eyes are wider and more fluorescent. The moment is for sure one to undergo revision, as Tyler begins to vividly envision the days when Miley barely took a look at him.

Harbor 09

Rain had just stopped and the sounds of police sirens echoed beyond the waterfront. Tyler was working hard to get off but found no outlet as more customers poured into his store as if every item were free of purchase.

"Excuse me do you have these in a size ten?"

"Hello sir, can I get these in a size seven."

Request came over and over and all Tyler could envision was his slender, yet athletic build passing under the exit sign, which was posted over the entrance of the athletic department store he was employed at. And then, a breeze swooshed through the store as if someone opened a kitchen door in mid-Autumn. Tyler just finished giving a customer the most specific and quickest help ever provided in retail history. As usual, the clock behind the register read the wrong time, which was a combination of numbers far from his designated time to get off work.

It was summer of 2009, and Tyler took a deep breath as his board shorts imprint a bulge, due to a very fine defined grown woman who made her way into the store, she was switching almost perfectly– hypnotizing shoppers. Her thighs were thick and smooth but her waist was as slim as a runway model on veggie parfait diet. Her skin complexion was that of amber. She walked up to Tyler passing every other sales associate who appeared to have lost the bottom half of his or her mouths, except him.

Tyler was staring but not at her butt. His eyes were fixated on her eyes, which were deep and black.

"Hello, I am looking for some sneakers that just came out yesterday, and I had a pair on hold."

He swallows, and then she had to do it, she smiled at him. Well not directly at him but okay she smiled at him. Tyler broke into a dash and wind gathered through the clothes as he took off to the back. He was excited but more so flabbergasted to have been selected by her royal beauty to receive her undivided attention. When he had returned, he did so not alone. A pair of unique sneakers that were limited edition was in his hand held firm. The smile on the woman's face sent out so much charm, Tyler was convinced he misplaced his words for his routine response to customers after he satisfied their wishes.

"Are these the shoes?"

Tyler kept staring at her eyes but remained a bit unresponsive, actually silent as if he instantaneously died standing up. She stepped forward and waved her hands in front of his face twice and he remained absent mentally. Next, she snapped her fingers by his ear and Tyler jumped back into the storefront regaining attentiveness, "Hey, hey I found the shoes. We have them in for you," he said shaking the box up and down.

"Thank you, I will take them."

"You do not want to see them?" Tyler asked. Feeling over the box of shoes she replied, "You did not look at them, is something wrong with them?"

"No not at all, I mean yes, I mean no nothing is wrong and yes I did look at them. I mean I did look at them but nothing is wrong."

Tyler walked toward the counter and sat the shoes down on the edge, where for a moment they stayed before falling off the counter securing the routine of his clumsy behavior. His manager shook his head because he had witnessed Tyler fumble orders before but not like this, his behavior was just comically irreversible-social-disorientation. Just as Tyler smiled and turned away from the woman, he bumped directly into someone with his elbow.

"Hey!"

"I am sorry, so sorry," Tyler pleaded as he seen juice had spilled all over her side, "Oh no, I am sorry I did not see you."

"Clearly you didn't," she said brushing down her side. She looked up at Tyler and he looked down at her. Being as though he was about 5"11' and she was 5"3', he kind of hovered over her. They locked eyes and the entire room became black as if the night had taken over and hid the moon from the sky. While captivating, anger took forward action.

"You should relax and stop getting so nervous around women," she said looking at him as if he had stabbed her with a knife in her side.

Tyler laughed and then straightened out his smile as he realized what she said before he replied, "I do not get nervous around women." He did get nervous around women, in fact if there is one thing Tyler gets nervous about, it is being around women.

She rolled her eyes and sucked her teeth and replied, "Whatever dude, you almost forgot you were alive with that lady over there, and just now you caused me to spill my very good drink all over my pants. Clearly you aren't paying attention," she said patting the side of her pants while mumbling, "I like these pants."

Tyler lowered his head and a light bulb struck a fuse as the darkness cleared out. Light returned to the store and within one circling view, the store had become crowded, "I can buy you another drink," Tyler insisted shuffling his hands in front of her anxiously.

This was actually his sporadically convenient plan of escaping the rush of customers. The store was not under staffed so he pursued his plan further, but to be sure he skimmed the store checking all the sections for a staff member. Nerdy Zack, who looked like a mimicked image of Steve Urkel, was helping two customers in the men's section. Tierra, whose hair and nails were longer than jury duty, was kneeling down helping a kid in the children section. And lastly, Darius who kept a shape-up sharper than blades to cut diamonds, and also red eyes that indicated he was higher than the U.S. debt ceiling, kept customers laughing at the back of the store.

Tyler looked at his manager and said, "Josh, I am taking my fifteen." Looking back at the young lady he said, "I am about to take my break I can buy you another drink."

"You are such a get over. So instead of staying and doing some work you are going to take your fifteen when the store gets packed?"

Tyler's face was completely dismantled with confusion. And even stronger questions formed like why was she even paying attention so well. She caught onto his plan right away, so Tyler began to really find some sense of regret. He was never good with communicating with attractive girls but he would try if ever the opportunity presented itself. Mostly because he knows how to communicate with others very well, but dealing with girls has always been a troubled area.

"Um okay, so can I buy your drink or not?"

"I do not need you to get me another drink. I can buy my own. How about you just start paying attention to what you are doing."

Even though she had an attitude in her tone of voice, she still spoke clearly, and this hinted off to him that she has some sense, even acting like someone without any. Or at least, Tyler thought so because of the scene she was making. He stepped back with his eyebrows raised, as he was unexpectedly being served up a fresh course of *tell me how much I suck at life*, "Whoa. Okay what is your problem? I just want to correct my mistake."

What Tyler had not realized was that this young lady obviously had some back history tension he had just set off. She took a pose and grinned while her arm hung from her side like it was broken. Whatever was on her mind, Tyler was about to know every thought.

"You guys are all the same," she fixed her posture as her tone of voice simmers down, "...you make mistakes and try to fix them instead of trying to not make the mistake in the first place." Tyler dropped his jaw and replied, "Are you crazy?"

His biggest offense, and possibly far bigger than spilling her drink, "I have to be crazy for thinking that men should be more careful and stop womanizer ways from causing them to hurt people? No you are crazy for not seeing the logic in that."

At that point, Tyler had no idea of why he was being attacked like he was. The barking at his every response and all because he spilled some juice. *Is she crazy* – or had Tyler really tripped some wire leading back to the bomb attached to her nerves. But then, he seen something, something he could not ignore as her shirt hung a bit off of her shoulder. It was black and covered her shoulder. She must have been trying to conceal it.

"Didn't your mother tell you not to stare?"

Tyler thought about it as he continued to stare, but as he came to, it dawned on him. "No, my mother actually doesn't tell me anything."

She sensed a deepness that caused her to retract a bit of her aggression. Yet, she still felt inclined to cross her point, "Well, you shouldn't stare, it is rude."

"But, is that a tattoo?" He couldn't help asking. Her shirt slid over her shoulder as she looked away and back before she replied, "It is nothing."

Customers looked upon but also tried to continue shopping, as Tyler and she both looked young enough to have been a young couple fighting. He gathered her point of view but was he truly being a womanizer, of course not. This young lady was releasing some tension built up and Tyler began to catch on. He then decided to redirect his approach and figure out what is really boiling her pot.

"Okay, what is your name?"
"What does it matter?"

The ceiling holding up his efforts almost collapsed on his head, but he thought quick and with persistence remained keen. "Well, if I call you anything other than what your name is, and with how you have been lashing out on me – over what clearly is not because I spilled your drink, I am sure you would be offended. I know I am not a womanizer and truly cannot even remember what that word even means. So, what is your name?" He said as a last effort to calm the storm.

She sulked, and then stopped to pace the thoughts of anger as she paused to envision Tyler's point of view. Quickly, she turned her head as if she wanted to walk off, but the sense of feeling like she was wrong persuaded her to stay.

She began to realize why she started blasting off on him. This conviction brought her to some sort of subtle response. And like a sterno losing its flame, she regressed and found a moment of peace to cooperate.

"My name is Miley."

Minutes to go - part 7

While you were gone

Tyler snaps back into reality and finds himself facing one of the most beautiful young ladies to ever confront his eyes. The only sad part is he is already in a relationship with someone. The even more confusing part is that someone is Miley. She is acting as if she is seeing Tyler for the first time ever, but only this time she is so much more admirable as she is embracing his appeal. While he can definitely grow to cherish it, it is yet weird and surreal.

Looking over, he sees Dawson basking in the mystery as Teri is smiling from ear to ear and Dill is playing around with him. Last Tyler heard of Dawson, Teri was not so fond of his presence, his attitude, and not even his facial hair, which is hardly ever trimmed.

What is going on?

Tyler thought to himself, and ever since they left the white room - everything has changed. Miley begins to pursue her interest stepping closer to Tyler wrapping her hand around his waist petting his side. Yet, she still smiling raises a question that ensures something about this scene is disheveled.

"How do you know Dawson?" she asks.

A puzzled Tyler looks to Dawson and shrugs his shoulders, and Dawson's bland look gives him no help. He then replies, "Miley, it is me Tyler. I am your boyfriend."

Miley smiling just nods her head saying, "You sure can be Tyler, you are handsome."
"Miley, seriously it is me Tyler. What are you doing?"

Dawson catches from the corner of his eye the awkwardness of Tyler's conversation with Miley. At first he thinks it is her unusual ways of making Tyler feel better about almost being tiger chow. Tyler looks at Dawson and then at Miley, who has her hand placed onto his chest smiling as if she is dreaming the most beautiful part of some well-dreamt lifestyle. Even the nurse watches in confusion, which made Dawson, raise a question, '*What is going on?*'

And then it hit him, the words he needs to be voicing and the individual he needs to identify. Everything appears far too surreal to be well– *real.* This is either a too good to be true dream or some fantasyland made up all in his mind. Perhaps they are dead, and what they are experiencing is the everlasting longings of their deepest desires.

Dawson while hugging Dill looks out of the window and mumbles, "God..."

Immediately the room spins and a flash of light takes the room-blinding Tyler and Dawson. They are now back – in the white room, and cloudlessly isolated again as if they never left. Clueless to the madness, if it is safe to call anything God is doing, which Tyler and Dawson did not completely understand – madness. They look around; and being as though everything is white in the room, there is not much confirming necessary. They are definitely back in the room. That is what they think it is, with no ceiling and no walls, and who can really consider where they are located to be, a room?

"Back here," Tyler takes a pause and sarcastically sighs out the word, "again."

Dawson takes a seat folding his arms over his knees. Tyler remains standing while his head tilts to the ground. "Why are we here?"

The mystery is surely composing more confusion but sub-consciously there must be a motive behind this shimmery. Rational thinking gives Dawson a clue as he begins to raise his head. And while he catches a clue, Tyler looks at him and points like a witness trying to identify a thief in a line up, "This is all your fault, you walked in the room and started asking me questions," Dawson unfolds his arms giving Tyler his undivided attention and says, "Go on..."

It takes a second, but Tyler thought of the reality in his statement, preposterous thinking leads to daft reactions. How could Dawson have inspired any action that has taken place or is taking place, he could not and cannot. As bad as Tyler wants someone to blame he never thought that after he excludes Dawson and himself, he would be blaming a specific someone, and then God's voice drops into the room like an atom bomb, "You are here because you chose to be Tyler. And so are you Dawson."

Tyler replies, "I did not," spoken with aggression.

God speaks again, "My child, I gave you the evidence of your wishes. It was your lack of belief that decomposed the manifestation of a reality by thought, which you only created yourself. You have shown your true values."

Tyler cannot catch it all at once, so he replies, "What?" showing every wrinkle in his young face.

Dawson intends to keep reserved but an inquisitive conscious reveals his intention did not last but a second as he has to ask, "So because I desired to see that," he gets a bit tangled with words, "scene, wait so that was real?"

A strong chuckle invites them to God's sense of humor, "Did you believe it was real?"

They both thought the same thing *it felt real.* Everything about it felt real, but their realities are so different. Tyler began to wonder why Miley had behaved so awkward. And then, a dark but revealing sense of groundbreaking truth hit him like a straight jab from a professional boxer.

"You," Tyler turns to Dawson pointing as if he were a kid watching a balloon lift to the sky, "You were never there."

"Yeah, I actually was kid. I looked right at you," says Dawson as Tyler snaps his fingers and turns to speak to an un-presented God, only to turn back to Dawson continuing, "No dude, you were not here, I mean there. Everything changed. Well for you, I mean for me too, but for you mostly."

Dawson flexes a small form of humor, "Dude. What are you talking about?"

In a way, the confusion Dawson tangles with brings Tyler more perception. "Okay, listen you were not around for your family."

"Watch it kid," Dawson taunts.

Tyler continues as he is on to something, or at least he thinks." He crosses his arms and says, "No man, like you were not around really but in the manifesto thing," Dawson corrects him, "Manifestation."

Never mind, Tyler is on to something for sure. His choice of words may not be his best but nonetheless what he is about to say needs to be said, and will be said, mostly because Tyler wants to say it. He is also not shy on the tongue. If ever a thought crosses his mind, regardless of how cruel or beautiful, he will share. A sense of humor usually removes the insult from his directness but often he tells it exactly how the thought crosses his mind.

Tyler now smiling because he put all the pieces together, "Yeah that, Miley did not know me because you were around. She didn't have time to meet me because you guys were a family."

Whether Dawson wants to hear it or not, Tyler made another point. This point however is as sharp as a thorn and hanging like a chandelier above his head.

A revelation begins to sink into Dawson's realm of belief like heavy rocks in mud. Dawson's theory, side swipes Tyler's moment of certainty like a speeding bus. All Tyler requests are that Miley show an adorning interest in him, which now becomes the hammer hitting the nail.

"Miley only favored me because it was what I believed in my mind. But, without that thought, she... she would have never known me."

Sadness runs down Tyler's face like rain on a leaf. Dawson cannot completely determine how much Miley meant to him, although bits and pieces of his worries are connecting a pattern that designs true love. It is never Dawson's intention to interrupt, but Dawson truly wants his family back and if that meant breaking Tyler's poor little heart, so be it. Tyler is not thinking as demanding as he, which puts Tyler directly into the pawn position on Dawson's chessboard.

"Look kid," walking over placing his hand on Tyler's shoulder, "I can see you must care for Miley, and a lot. But, I miss my family." And that was his vision, to attain his family back.

Tyler looks up disgruntled and furious, "You miss them? You miss them? All the time you had to be there and you miss them? Really, were the bad guys giving you that much trouble with the hand cuffs, you could not find time to lock down your own house hold?"

His frustration speaks through his words and although Dawson is well more mature than Tyler, such a rant only promotes his hidden anger for his own mistakes. Dawson drops his arm quickly from Tyler's shoulder and deepens his voice, "Now you listen to me kid, I am a man who has responsibilities. My responsibilities are not debatable and neither understood by some homebody who wants to cook and clean to live off of my money. I ran that household. I built that place and sustained it incontrovertibly with extreme efforts applied and pursued. No one and not even you can question my absence. What you call absence, I call dedication. I made that home," Dawson shouts tightening the tips of his fingers into his palm. Anger pulsates through his body.

"Yeah you made it, but you didn't make it being a man of the law now did you?" Tyler steps closer to Dawson, at this point his size and authority meant little to nothing, "Miley told me. She told me how you brought evidence home and how it never made it back to the station, and how that evidence just disappears but you come up with money you hid from your own wife. And for what reason did you hide it? Not because you were sustaining a home, but because you were creating another home elsewhere – with Veronica. You should have stayed away you coward," Tyler says thrusting the palms of his hands into Dawson's chest.

Dawson recovers his balance and swings, hitting Tyler so hard he falls six feet back. Light flashed like a light tower searching over the seas. It becomes so bright nothing but glare smothers the area. Tyler flies through the hospital door back into the room and lands on the floor before Miley and Teri.

Dill shouts, "Wow!"

Miley goes down to comfort Tyler, "Oh my goodness, Tyler are you ok?"

Blood runs from the side of his mouth and he swipes his finger pass his lip to catch it, and then turning his finger over looking at the blood, seeing the redness, and feeling the warmth it brought him down. Tyler looks up and everyone is gone. Everything is silent and blood is all over the door to his room, and the walls are covered in black slime. A cold chill creeps up his arm as he looks down at his leg, which is now badly bruised as blood begins gushing out. He places his hands onto his legs and tries to stop the bleeding by covering the wound. He cannot stop it, blood just rises between his fingers and down onto his hand. His heart begins racing, pumping harder and harder and his breathing speeds up. Inhale after exhale after inhale and he begins to go into shock. Just before he arrives, a growl strong enough to shake the floor brings his eyes from his leg to look up over his head.

Blood drips from the ceiling but he sees nothing. He continues to look up not sure of what is happening. He rolls his eyes forward and lowers his head to look straight and when he does, the tiger leaps at him. Tyler begins screaming louder than before and Miley grabs him shaking him out of his hallucination, “Tyler, it is not real! Tyler, wake up!”

He regains consciousness and begins breathing heavily. This is the fifth time it has happened since the attack. Sleep is a gift he cannot receive due to irreversible patterns of confusion. Still breathing deeply, Tyler is however back and the moment becomes worst for Dawson. They all look up and see Dawson with his hand cocked standing in the doorway. From the looks of things, everything is back to normal, or, in other words Miley and Teri are back to hating Dawson. And from the position he is holding, with an additional good reason.

"I can explain," says Dawson lowering his hand as they look upon him with stares that can kill flowers like winter chills.

Minutes to go - part 8

Facts

"What did you do?" Teri shouts helping Miley pick up Tyler.

His leg begins to bleed heavily and as he throws his hand over the bandages, the nurse rushes over grabbing a handful of gauze pads. Dawson is clueless. His mind begins running a thousand and one thoughts and the first one being, *'how did we get back?'*

"I didn't," pausing in bewilderment, "we were talking and next thing I know we are here. I did not hit him for any old reason," Dawson pleads.

Teri sitting Tyler on the bed replies, "What good reason is there to punch someone Dawson?"

Dramatic he replies, "Have you heard what comes from that kids mouth, he had that one coming."

Truth hurts but not the teller of it. Words are words until they mean something that can actually turn a stone on your path. One thing that is hard to understand is how to the truth is coming out at you. But, that is where Dawson continuously makes his mistakes. Truth is the truth no matter where it comes from or how it is delivered. It may have been in his best interest to accept it. And then again, who really has mastered the art of embracing the truth and keeping it cool?

Tyler while a talker, he is also a young man who knows how to accept what is going on. The trouble comes with letting things go. Doctors have been working with him to remove the idea that he is still under attack. In that moment, before he allows his thoughts to return to the environment he questions, *is the price of being brave, the removal of your sanity and the intake of pain and frustration?*

A thought that begins to sprint through his concerns is why, why was it him that had to be in that situation, at that time, and to make that decision God must have known he would make? Time tells tales and over time Tyler speculates if the hands of the hour will tell his. Just as the thoughts arrive they leave and he focuses on Dawson.

The nurse immediately dashes out to get him an icepack and a rag. On her way out, she stops before Teri and says, "If you know this man, I am asking you to make him leave before I call security!" Dawson smirks and Teri puts her foot down once again, "Dawson, I think it's time for you to go."

"Teri I am a captain and lieutenant, no one here can make me leave," Dawson says in sure confidence flexing his rank. While true, the atmosphere is filled with resentment, so Dawson can feel the energy becoming his escort.

Tyler's voice comes up stronger and louder, "Well how about you be the bigger man, and just choose to go."

Miley holding Tyler's hand makes a firm grip and Teri pulls Dill closer to her. Dawson looks at them picturing where he should be, which is exactly where Tyler is, even though Tyler is in no way shape or form filling in for Dawson. It still feels that way, and such a feeling can make any man feel like his home is not lost, but taken from him. As the energy set in the room, Dawson shakes his head left to right. It is a gesture never mistaken for anything else but disappointment, yet who it is for is for now unclear. The presence of a strong energy relieves the tension in the room as it exits from the area as Dawson leaves.

Five months later...

The sun shoots through the window and Mileys' eyelids open like a mouth gasping for air. She jumps up and Tyler jumps up next to her turning to see sweat drenching her tank top and forehead. He could assume she has a fever but her skin is cold. Yet, her skin is as soft as satin, and as she lies on her back he gazes at her. Tyler is most appreciative of her looking over him. He values her presence and the more he stares at her, the more his heart warms over the fact he has her in his life.

Even at the sight of her discomfort he fails to find discomfort with her. Mostly due to the fact he finds her beauty to be a fireplace and his heart a lone young man in the midst of the cold.

"Miley, what is it?" He asks admiring the scar she has over her shoulder.

It is unique and to this day still unclear to her how she received it. She has had it since birth but Tyler never saw it like he sees it now. It runs down her arm and with it, his fingers gliding down gently before resting a soft kiss onto her shoulder. Not a word is said as she lowers her head and closes her eyes. Something is different, and her shoulder begins glowing but then suddenly stops. Her illuminating mark is not foreign to Tyler, as he has seen it before. But ever since the attack, she'd let him know the nights the glowing would occur. It does not trouble her as it could, but nonetheless she mentally inquires its existence every so often.

Her quilt is half off the bed and mostly on Tyler's side of the bed. He can be a bit stingy when the open window sends a breeze overnight. She shakes her head replying, "Nothing stingy."

Tyler acknowledges how most of the blanket does happen to be hanging off his side of the bed, "What? You threw them on me in your sleep. I thought you thought I was cold and were looking out."

Miley turns up her face, "You are a liar and you snatched them from off of me, and then rolled over like you always do." Tyler stops to think and then says, "Always? This is my seventh time spending the night over here."

Which it actually is, and also the first time he ever spent the night in her bed. Most nights, they are lying on the couch watching horror movies until the movies begin to watch them. Those moments he took pride in, every night he made sure to hold her as if she'd slip away.

They used to spend hours making out and wait until mid of night to actually try and watch the movie. That never worked out. But last night was Tyler's first night home from the hospital. After hours of rehabilitation and lying uncomfortably in the bed watching reruns of some 70's television show, he became tired of rehearsing the lines and predicting the scenes. Movies were a relief, especially after his hours of practicing the habit of walking again.

Miley wanted to be home, in a way home has become her sanctuary after the attack. Much rather preferred over her previous perception, which she was not so keen of today. Tyler received his invite when the doctor instructed he would need someone to check up on him. Teri approved and also thought well of Tyler for standing up to Dawson. Most grown men do not even do that. More significantly she knew of Tyler's inability to stay at home by himself. It was no question that he had spent so much time around Miley, and enough that Teri realized his emotional dependency upon her daughter. Possibly the only reason today she has warmed up to him.

Suddenly, a loud knock can be heard from upstairs and it gives Miley the shakes while Tyler jumps out of the bed pacing to the bedroom door. Miley's reaction makes Tyler more precautious and alert. Before he exits, he turns to Miley and pauses, and yet, seeking out his curiosity in the form of a common question asked when things go bump, "What the hell is that?"

"I don't know. The only person I know who beats that hard on the door is you." Tyler smiles, and replies, "Yeah I do," looking coy.

"Shut up, go find out who it is."

"Alright you got my back?"

Miley shakes her head up and down and grabs her shorts from off of the floor, as she begins to slide them on Tyler stares at her as if she disappeared. "Baby you are sexy."

A louder bang on the door comes again and Tyler wastes no time dashing down the stairs. As he gets to the door, he looks out of the peephole but no one is outside. It is still morning and early, too early for anyone to really be awake, actually no one is awake. Most of the neighborhood does not come alive until noon, but in town most shops opened at about eleven o'clock.

Another fact about Randallstown, everyone pretty much operated on a similar schedule. Storeowners and employees all opened and closed together. This helped the police department, as there is less crime to be committed with several witnesses. Dawson thought of a plan like such, in order to reduce his presence in the county.

The sound of the banging makes Miley cringe as she stands at the top of the steps, and awaiting Tyler to say it is some advertiser or neighbor. But, Tyler remains puzzled and equivalently cautious.

Glass breaks in the kitchen and Tyler dashes in with his guard up, fist bald and his elbows square. One of Teri's fancy wine glasses had rolled out of the dish holder and broken into several pieces on the floor. The look on his face is priceless as his eyes scroll around the kitchen looking for an explanation. None available, his assumption of coincidence withers into ignorance. This however is not the first time it happened. At the hospital, strange things happened. His cups moved or rolled off the table with no one present. His blanket would get pulled off of him at night, and he would awake again to no one present. While he had much time to speculate as he laid in his bed, he found that putting off the curiosity spared him of the anxiety.

At this moment, he recollected those events and is taking nothing for façade.

"Tyler what is it?"

Tyler walks around the counter and sees no evidence of any sort to explain anything. "I don't know, I..." His first thought is an absurd idea, but with no other identification, he feels inclined to assume the impossible. A spirit, one has to be in the house, yet his thought is challenged by his knowledge of Ms. Teri's anointed home.

Immediately the knock on the front door comes again, but this time only one big bang, and enough to make his and her nerves rattle. He grabs a knife from the silverware drawer and runs through the living room to the front door with a killer's intent. However, Tyler is not going to kill anyone, at least not in reality.

Miley is now at the bottom of the steps gripping the banister as if it is her only support for standing. As Tyler reaches for the door handle, another glass in the kitchen breaks. They both turn away from the door with a haunted expression. Their hearts are pulsating and before they can even react, another glass breaks.

"Miley come here quick," Tyler instructs as he prepares himself to swing the blade at any moment.

Slow and cautious steps guide him back towards the kitchen. It feels like the door is a million feet away. Every step is made in hesitation. Just as they step through the kitchen doorway, another combination of knocks hit the front door. This time the knocks are calmer and less aggressive but still impatient. Tyler fed up turns around and paces towards the door raising the knife in hand. He grabs the handle and turns it too quick to rethink his action, and as the door opens he shouts, "What do you want?"

His eyes are spread wide and adrenaline pumping like a v8 engine. Before him stands one of the ring masters from the circus, who throws his hands up frightened jumping back from the door step, "Oh no don't," he shouts, "I just want to talk."

"What the fuck man. Oh God," Tyler says lowering the knife and breathing heavily just nearly missing the opportunity to use it.

Minutes to go - part 9

Fair warning

"What are you doing here?" Miley asks.

The ringmaster replies in a very distinctive foreign accent, "I am Eduardo, my apologies for the early awakening my friends. I am only here to help."

Help? She thought. *Why would he be here to help and with what?* The question quickly runs circles around her mind. Tyler steps back as to send off the gesture Eduardo is welcome to come in, although it is his curiosity that sends out the gesture more than his manners. Mystery begins to run its course, and as Eduardo enters through the doorway a deep feeling of gloom fills the room. It is like someone instantly died– and they feel it.

Keeping their senses at an alert, Miley and Tyler remain skeptical of his presence, however if curiosity truly killed the cat, we already know bullets and many questions killed this one.

Eduardo extends his hand, "Pleasure to meet you my new friends," spoken as if their meeting is not but the first time.

Out of respect Tyler extends his hand and shakes, although he is not overly fond of these moments locking eyes with a man and making a firm grip in some sort of ego test. Yet, fortunate for Tyler he feels no worry as Eduardo's handshake is non-aggressive, plus he did not stare long. Awkward moment number one avoided.

"I have urgent news, very unsettling yet urgent and," exhaling, "very imperative nonetheless. Five months ago you my boy did something highly unthinkable and remarkable. However, it resulted in the loss of life."

Tyler replies, "You mean the tiger?"

"Precisely, and while I understand the circumstances you both endured to survive such a tragic happening, it is not so logically thought out for others."

Miley steps forward, "Others?"

"Yes others, well one individual in particular but others in the spiritual dark." His words may have killed them both. Their jaws drop and their faces cringe in confusion. In what way possible are they supposed to accept the last two words of his sentence, especially after he just informed them he is issuing a warning? Nothing good is about to come from this conversation.

"What do you mean dark? What are you saying?"

Tyler speaks before Eduardo can continue. "Wait, are you insinuating," Miley cuts in, "Good word Tyler," and he continues, "Thank you baby; that something is spiritually after us?"

"Precisely," he says holding up his hands with his index fingers touching his thumbs.

"Why? I mean what did we do?" Miley asks looking into Tyler's eyes and then back at Eduardo who continues, "The tiger was no ordinary creature, it was not just a tamed beast of the wild. That animal was protected by the spiritual elders of Ziga."

Ziga?

The wonderment taking over their facial expressions is galactic. Both Miley and Tyler are steadily attentive while it could be a fool's decision that their interest is not highly supported by fear but curiosity. Either way, Tyler wants to know more while Miley is more concerned about other matters. The typicality of teenagers to not respond with a sense of alert, fixed in his direction they await the continuation of his explication.

"Is that why glass has been breaking all over the house?" Miley asks stepping forward quickly in desperate need of an answer but also showing off her attentiveness and ability to connect dots. She is so inquisitive that it is a compelling feeling for Miley to figure out what is going on.

"What has happened?" Eduardo shows great concern making fast gestures as if he is more surprised than they are.

Tyler unfolds his arms taking a breath from deep thought to follow up, "Basically shit has been breaking. You know paranormal shit, which if you think about what you are telling us, it really is kind of normal [now]. But wait, dude is you even serious right now? I mean you do not show up at someone's door talking about spirits and stuff. Are you aware of how crazy this sounds? You can freak people out like that. I mean we could call the cops."

A thought Tyler begins to dwell on. It is not that he does not believe Eduardo but after what happened in the hospital, anything pertaining to something spiritual – his interest, is gravitating towards in the conversation.

"Tyler how is any of that normal?" A now mentally moved and disturbed Miley asks.

"They say paranormal because it is scientifically unexplained occurrences manipulating perception, but he basically said spiritually protected, meaning if shit was breaking it was spiritual, making the glass breaking explained, therefore it is normal," he explicates arms folded and confident.

Miley disappointed in Tyler's logic replies, "Tyler, no just stop."

Eduardo takes charge, "Okay listen, my co-master, Vitriolic," a slight pause as the name being sounded out brings in an unsettling insight. Nothing about that name sounds positive. In fact, it takes a second for them both to accept that is what Eduardo had just said.

"VITRIOLIC," Tyler and Miley say simultaneously. "His name is Vitriolic," their voices merge as one as their words are spoken in sync.

"Yes," it is evident that Eduardo has a knack for dropping informational bombs. Not but a second after his words, thunder clapped stronger than ever heard before. But, no rain is pouring outside. Miley, grabs Tyler's arm gripping through his skin feeling the shape of his bones. Fear is nearly running a perfect lap throughout this untimely introduction of their mysterious friend. Funny the use of the word friend as the question begs is it his urgent warning that is to value, or his demeanor, which is nevertheless not as frightening as the message he delivers.

"So what's going to happen to us man, are we going to be haunted by some ghost tiger?" Tyler asks sarcastically refusing to show fear before curiosity. But fear is present, and it is in the part of his mind where he stores all his embarrassing moments. That part of the mind usually has about three thousand locks and a deadbolt.

"No. The demons that possessed the creature are going to be after you, and if they find you, "he pauses, "If they find you they will kill you. The tiger was a demonic relic to the order and they will seek vengeance."

Miley looks at him and her hand drops from his arm, Tyler notices but ignores it briefly.

"Wait, you said spirits protected the tiger, now demons have possessed it? This is just is insane. *Demons?* Like Supernatural TV show demons or actual Bible revelations demons?"

Hands over his head and eyes rolling, Tyler begins to inhale and exhale excessively. The story is becoming more than tolerable, and then a second thought crosses his mind to *ask Eduardo to leave*. Almost, and then a third thought crosses his mind and as stated, curiosity is in the driver seat. He is not about to take this lightly but nonetheless it sounds completely absurd.

Miley turning her back sighs and before she weeps, an ear for love notices the cries of an unexpected flash back. When she turns around she sees Tyler breathing like his lungs had been locked inside his chest and determined today, the day they will break out.

"What is wrong with the boy?" Eduardo says stepping closer and kneeling as Tyler falls back first. He slides over the side of the table and shouts, "No, No!"

His hands slide along with his feet across the floor. His eyes widen and bear the look of shock. Miley grabs his hand and palms it firmly. Another hallucination, and this time more automatic and casually but then Tyler loses his expression.

"Tyler! Tyler wake up, it is not real."

"I do not think your love is sleeping my friend," Eduardo says pointing to Tyler's facial expression, which has gone blank. As if his body has not the anatomy of a human, his eyes can be just as rocks used for a snowman's eyes. Keys jingle at the door, and she remembers it is Teri and Dill coming back from Dill's morning summer camp classes, which starts far too early but ends way to fast. Miley panicked knowing Eduardo will offset Teri with his presence, and talk of demons. Not to mention his absurd reason for being there that will be impossible to explain.

Miley looks at Tyler and shakes him by the shoulders but no response. Turning to his direction, "Eduardo, pretend you are the..." She turns around completely and searches for an absent Eduardo. He vanishes and cannot be found by current search of eye. Just as her suggestion to import him into a master lie is made, she is mind blown and struck with confusion while turning to face Tyler. Her hands went up to her chin pressing against her skin in appall as if a bee just stung it. Tyler is gone.

Is this some magic trick or is she hallucinating, and if so, why. She looks left and stands to her feet. More confusion arrives as she checks the kitchen and walks through the dining room. Tyler is nowhere to be seen and neither is Eduardo. The topside of her hand is placed between her fingernails. A pinch ought to determine the legitimacy of her current bewilderment. The pain arrives but Tyler does not. She falls to the floor by the couch in sadness, a deep sadness as her emotions begin to resent her ill-hearted intentions.

Teri and Dill walk in and she immediately can see Miley looking more broken than a glass cup dropping into a washing cycle. However, it does not disconcert her ability to observe. Miley's face gives away the inexplicable moment. Magic is fascinating on television but in person, it raises some concern when your eyes send a sight to your brain that it cannot comprehend.

"Miley, what are you doing?"

Miley looking at the floor legs bent and hands in her hair, "He's gone."

He might have meant a male cat but they do not have a cat so Teri does not quite inherit her point of view, which she can match with her expression to understand what is going on.

"What? Who is gone? Where is Tyler?" Teri asks.

"Ty... Tyler disappeared. He is gone."

Minutes to go - part 10

Perfect for me

Teri drops Dill's backpack as the redness in her face insinuates she has no time for games. If Miley could explain she would have, but right now the fear and instantaneous feeling of being alone is spiraling around her mind, not to mention how incredibly outrageous the information she just received sounds. Tyler has always been around Miley, she made sure of that as she had come to realize how different his presence is compared to past situations. He is always around her and enough that he should know Miley's dependency on him shows like red wine stained into a white blouse. But at the moment, it is not just a feeling of loneliness that stalks her. Actually, Miley has been preparing for that feeling for over two months. Instead, Tyler's disappearance is awakening some desire to confess a secret.

Sudden moments can at times produce sudden truths. Of all their time spent together, it is not quite loneliness that is the spark to her hidden convulsion.

Attention has always been a personal craving of hers, and having elected Tyler for a time now to provide it, his sudden absence still startles her into her realization. But, for now she will fight it in effort to also express her concern for his wellbeing, which is apparently being threatened physically and psychologically.

"Miley stop playing around and get up off of the floor."

Teri is not taking Miley serious, but how could she when her daughter's long-term boyfriend has been known for pranks and jokes. One time, Tyler decided Dill and he were going to pretend they had been kidnapped. Teri ended up calling the police who began an investigation, which later lead to them hand cuffing her as she nearly strangled Tyler with her bare hands.

And that is not to over shadow the time when Tyler and Miley broke into her car, and then parked it on the next block pretending it had been stolen. They both went to the library three times a week to watch online videos about breaking into cars. Every day they did, they would walk through the parking lot at the mall to practice on old vehicles, which more than likely did not have an extensive alarm system.

Stealing *2010*

The day they actually broke into a car they did more cheering than actually considering the fact they did break into a car. Mall security was poor but every now and then they would swing through on their go-cart. Like hearing mice in the night, the security guards stopped their cart immediately. Dark and hardly lit was the parking lots on the lower levels. Such an unpopular Gunner mall rarely received as much traffic as the five parking levels would have made possibly assumable. As they convinced themselves that it must have been nothing, they continue to circle around the parking lot.

Tyler found a video on the Internet instructing how to use a hanger to get into a vehicle. Well descriptive, he had begun his process of imitation as he pried the wire through the window. The parking lot was so dark and empty they almost believed they heard their hearts beating. Click was the sound that brought much confidence. Tyler turned to Miley smiling and she looked back gazing. Unfortunately, as they began jumping up and down fist pumping, security pulled around again, and this time Miley took off running faster than Tyler.

They ran back into the mall, which was not the best cover for them being as though no one was in the mall. They stood out as it was early in the morning and seniors treated the mall like a track, and walked around it for good spirits.

"Quick run to the restrooms," said Tyler smiling but also breathing heavy. He was out of shape.

Miley's face was reddened as she replied, "You are so out of shape, and Tyler that is stupid and we'll be cornered."

"Miley trust me. Let's go," he said grabbing her hand as they ran for the restroom sign that actually looked like a get out of jail free card as they approached it.

As they ran into the stalls of the men's bathroom, unconsciously they realized they went into separate stalls.

Not but five minutes later as they stayed inside with their feet up on the toilet, the door cracked making a noise that only with their type of nerves jittering, sounded like doom turning a tune. Tyler looked down to see if he could see whom it was. No luck, but Miley in the stall before his – had a vivid view, and this was no security guard, this was an actual police officer. He walked to Tyler's stall and tried the door. With no luck, he then knocked on it again for good measure.

Tyler quickly grunted as if he were straining and then mumbled, "uh sorry occupied," his voice went deep, deep like a man hoarse of shouting instructions from years of service.

"Sorry about that sir," and the cop moved on to the next stall. As he entered he took no more than seconds and then proceeded to exit the restroom, and also without have washing his hands.

Miley whispered, "That is disgusting."

"Like you never did that?"

"No. No Tyler I have not. Wait, you have?"

"Heck no, I was asking you because it is disgusting. Sickens me to know people go out and just don't wash their hands. People are sick."

Miley had a brooding expression, "You have done it, and you are nasty." Tyler a bit guilty but still in denial gets very dramatic, "What, whoa no I have not."

The door cracked open slowly, the sounds of silence filled the room. They were not sure if leaving was the best idea but at the moment it was not an idea at all. The faucet ran and then quickly shut off. Wind from the hand dryer could be heard and within seconds the door slowly opened again. If someone had left, they were not sure. Tyler wanted to know so he slowly peaked over the top of the stall door, where he saw no one was there.

"Miley, we should probably leave."

"Leave? We just broke into a car and they are going to be looking all over for us."

"We broke into a car not the bank vault. No one really cares. Plus this was your idea," Tyler said sitting down on the toilet trying not to wet his shirt in the water filling the bowl.

"Okay first of all, your ass decided to break in my mom's car. Then you said 'oh Miley let's get some practice in.' who practices how to steal cars Tyler?"

"Uh car thieves maybe," Tyler said opening his hands into the air.

Miley got off of the toilet and walked out of the stall. She then knocked on Tyler's stall door, but Tyler more than melodramatic turned his back to the door. He made his voice thicker and replied, "Stalls taken buddy, now go crap elsewhere." His humor was always a bit over the top but their chemistry was building even in that moment. Yet, Tyler at times did not know when to quit.

"Tyler, open the door," he turned around and peaked through the opening between the wall and door. "Mam this is the men's room, I am not sure how you got in here but vagina's are down the hall on your right," Tyler said comical.

Miley smiled and replied, "Asshole, open the door, I think someone is coming." Tyler opened the door and Miley rushed in closing it quickly behind her. Her back faced Tyler while she peaked through the opening to see if anyone were to walk through. As she searched, he moved behind her and up close, so close his pelvic pressed against her butt. His arms wrapped around her waist and he placed his chin between her neck and shoulder.

"Don't get any ideas," she said. A late request because ideas already began to entice his hormones.

He squeezed her tighter and pressed closer, "Ideas like what?" She smiled and lowered her head as she felt him getting strong below, "Ideas like that Tyler."

He laughed and replied, "It is a bathroom stall, and you think I would try something here?"

Miley turned around and said, "Yes you would mister, I know you," as she gazed into his eyes. They were locking in a moment, still cautious but yet young love was taking over, young love and the urge to be mischievous. A sensation tickled up her spine as he leaned in and gave her a soft kiss on the neck. Young but not dumb, Tyler was always good at being sensual and affectionate. Most of his delicate gestures he actually searched online. Research is a good area for him but unfortunately applying what he learned became his troubled areas. But, after practice in many failed relationships, Miley was getting the best of his emotionally expressed replications.

"Tyler, I said not here," but Tyler knew his advantage and he had grown on her too strong for her to say no to his face, no matter how much she thought she could. Their love was still fresh and spontaneous, which opened a lot of opportunity for them.

"I am not trying anything–I am just kissing you," he said as he continued to kiss on her neck. As soft and enticing as his kisses were to her, she found some control as her hand palmed the back of his neck, and just as he placed his last kiss she pushed into his chest pushing him back. When you are young, you know what you want but you just have the worst time determining when it is the right to give it to yourself.

Right time or not however, Miley knew a bathroom was not going to be the place their first time together would happen. It was not that he did not respect her, he was thinking like any young boy would. But, teenage boys will be boys and that meant a lot of fervent impetuous behavior.

"Tyler, not here."
"Okay, but you were thinking it."

Miley smirked and said, "No you were thinking it," looking down at his bulge. Tyler sat on the toilet and relaxed his urges as they both second-guessed leaving the bathroom in fear they would be spotted on sight. Two hours passed by and Miley with her back on the stall door was losing the ability to remain standing. Every time he offered her to sit down in exchange he be the one to stand, she insisted she would not be sitting on a toilet seat. And, she could not conceive how Tyler brought himself to do it.

"Baby, sit down," he said as he grabbed her hand gently and pulled her over.

She rested her bottom in his lap and leaned her head into his shoulder. Comfort set in as she closed her eyes and he placed his arm around her backside. At this moment, Tyler's presence was her safe house. So much attention she receives from boys every day, it was moments like these that she knew why she chose Tyler.

"So why do you like me?" He asked taking opportunity of the time they had to spare.

"Are you really asking me that right now? Tyler you know why I like you." He sighed and said, "I know that you do, but I do not understand why. You are like super beautiful and I know what type of guys you can attract and do attract. I just question sometimes why you chose me. I am not trying to sound weak but I don't know, I thought the day we first kissed was unreal, like I must have done something really good for God to have let me have you."

Involving God in early love experiences sounded nonsensical, especially for Tyler who still smokes marijuana and prays less than a predator. But, faith is faith and back in the store when Tyler met her, he prayed for his chance to actually know her. And there they were, hiding in a stall in a mall conversing over their young love.

Miley did not like sharing her feelings with anyone, a past of bad experiences led her to believe as soon as you reveal how you truly feel, guys take the big head float and soar off into the abyss of over confident. Tyler was not like most guys though, although he did something's most guys never do– in fear of looking weird or strange, he was still a delicate soul. Most of what he did came natural. Holding doors, pulling out chairs, walking on the curbside allowing Miley to walk on the inside, Tyler never thought about what he did, he just knew Miley is the one he should be doing it for.

"Tyler I love you, and you should know that," Miley's words froze him in place, his face went blank and appall shaded his skin like a tan. "You do?"

A speechless Tyler just could not fathom words like ***I love you*** leaving the lips of Miley, an overly gorgeous and well desired young lady with little to no known flaws. Tyler did not see her as just perfect but more or less like even her few flaws were beautiful qualities accustom to her beauty.

"Tyler you have this thing about you, I mean not a bad thing, even though it does make wonder how you ever had a girl friend with such an awkward way of being funny. I mean I find it funny because I know for sure that it's who you are. And, that's so much better than dealing with guys who are always being someone else," Miley expressed as she looked up into his eyes.

It was that moment she captured the beauty of his gaze. His eyes dark brown and shiny, average but yet, they stood out. Looking at him brought her hope for something a young teenage girl does not receive at her age. The opportunity to completely use all of her natural emotions without feeling restricted. For a young girl, it was an urge she craved the moment she realized she could feel something other than anger, which is what she expressed in school avoiding the rudeness of ignorant teenage boys.

Tyler smiled but still to understand clearly where she was taking her point of view, he felt like he needed clarity. Regardless though, he felt so encouraged hearing her elegant voice touch base on his major concerns.

The lights in the bathroom were automatic, which meant if no one was moving the sensor would not recognize a presence. The brightness of the room left quickly and Miley scooted closer into Tyler as if to find comfort – in – what in light would be her knight in shining armor – in the darkness. If ever he felt the ultimate level of confirmation about her presence in his life being real, this was surely it.

"I am used to being called weird and crazy. I just knew when you said it and smiled, it was not for the same reason," he said tightening his fingers in hers.

"I am not perfect Tyler. Don't think that, please. I know you think so but that is what bothers me– yet keeps me so attracted to you. I'm not sure if your tolerance is completely strong but I know you see my flaws, and I know the way you look at me is never a look of shock but glamour."

Their conversation was so mature one may have mistaken them for being anything but teenagers if they were heard but not seen.

"If you saw what I have seen every day, I am blessed to see you," he inhaled, "you would never find beauty in another person, place, or thing. You are like the perfect noun." As he spoke, his fingers rolled down the left side of her shirt and off of her shoulder. And there it is, Miley's skin from her lower neck down to her elbow, and her upper back – a life lasting imprint of her mark, which illuminated like the behind of a firefly correlating an orange glow.

He gazed upon her skin and rubbed his fingertips over her shoulder as he said, "You are so beautiful," disregarding the acknowledgment of her scar for the countenance of her beauty.

"Don't forget to have faith..." – unknown.

Minutes to go - part 11

Nature of a smile

"What do you mean he is gone, Miley where is he?" Teri asks now witnessing tears roll down her daughters face. She wants to keep calm but it has only been five months since Tyler almost became food for a tiger. Her nerves are bad and she hates how much her emotions are flowing all over her, like water drenching the soul from the showerhead. It is at most a mystery to them both where Tyler has gone. But then, Dill walks around Teri and jumps back as his eyes spread and fingers clinch his pants.

A mother on alert notices her child's demeanor and without have even seeing his facial expression she inquires, "Dill what is it baby?"

Dill turns around and says, "Tyler... He is right there. But there is some guy holding him. He just said 'be quiet.' Now he is waving hello, and he just said 'stop talking.' He looks confused. I don't think he knows what he wants."

Teri confused looks at Miley and asks, "What is he talking about?" Miley on cue cut the water works and tries to explain seeing as though there is no other outlet, "Mom, a man showed up about an hour ago, he said he was from the circus. He said Tyler and I were in danger. He came to warn us or at least I thought so, and then he took Tyler."

Teri's eyes burst with offense feeling the insult in Miley having the audacity to create such a bizarre explanation. And then again, she has to also take into consideration Miley knows her zero tolerance for excuses ideology, *so why would she lie?*

"Miley, where did he take Tyler?" Teri insists she share but still staring in disbelief.

"I don't know mom, he was right there and then I turned around and they both were gone."

Teri finds it hard to believe but Dill continues to laugh and giggle, which he clearly is not doing for any odd reason. The moment when sanity meets delirious is an uncomfortable position, but Teri's brooding begins to permit her ability to reason. He is staring at the wall with a big smile and laughing. Teri starts to become very convinced, as Dill laughs, she can only think of one person who spent that time getting that type of laughter out of her used-to-be isolated voiceless child.

"Tyler?" Teri says in an impugnable tone of voice.

In seconds, an invisible force field burst into visual sight as Tyler and Eduardo reappear. Teri screams and shouts, "Who the hell are you?" She says reaching into her purse for her can of mace.

"It is me Tyler!" Tyler shouts.

Removing her can of mace from her purse like a gun out of a holster, she aims it up and says, "Shut up Tyler I know who you are," aiming the mace at Eduardo she reiterates her question, "who the hell are you, and why did you steal my daughter's boyfriend?"

He jumps back and throws his hands up gesturing he wants no confrontational interactions. Tyler is back to normal and standing on his own, but he is scanning over his body after being invisible - trying to figure out how.

"I am Eduardo and my apologies but I had to, Vitriolic is my brother and he can sense when my nerves show signs of strong interruption. But, I am here to help." He pleads before thinking to vanish again as to escape further discomfort.

The thought crosses his mind but it also will raise a major question as to why he would be leaving a situation he created. Dill being able to identify him however is causing him to second guess that option and also what causes him to stay a bit longer and apprise his warnings.

"Help? Who is trying to hurt my daughter?" A bold mother insists.

"Not your daughter, but he will take her life if she gets in the way." Teri rushes to the typical defense mechanism society has prepped us for, "I am calling the cops," she threatens.

Eduardo shows no signs of fear of the Randallstown police, and actually the statement sort of went over his head or through his ears– as he responds unmoved.

Pointing to Tyler, "The boy," Tyler interrupts in offense, "Uh Young man, thanks," Eduardo pauses and then continues to elucidate the circumstances, and "My brother will be after the boy."

"Dude, I am nineteen years old. Respect that. Respect that."

Eduardo ignores Tyler's simple cry for respect and issues a warning on a nail none of them are prepared to have the hammer dropped on, "If your daughter is to be safe, as well as you and yours," he says pointing his finger to Teri and Dill, "You must leave this boy to fend for himself, unfortunately." Miley cannot even think of any other words but "No I am not going to let him do anything." Her secrets begin to pour, or perhaps tip over.

Her anger is fiery as her face displays the type of disturbance some usually result to violence in. There is no doubt more than a few traits from Miley's mother are directly installed in her. A fierce attitude still does not rock Eduardo's warning. Tyler, a bit disorganized priority wise, completely tunes out Eduardo's caution for Miley's defensive forwardness. Never before has Tyler ever heard anyone say they had so much concern for him. It is in that very moment Tyler remembers what Miley said the first time she ever kissed him.

"I love you, I know you are perfect for me, I know we are going to always be together. You are perfect Tyler."

Words so sincere and so felt, still as Tyler comes to, Teri butts in with an opinion of her own.

"No, Miley I do not know what is going on but if what this crazy man is saying is true," now looking to Tyler, "I love Tyler too," and now facing her daughter, "but you are my responsibility. I cannot let you see him anymore," Teri said lowering her tone of voice as to insinuate her difficulty determining the decision.

"WHAT!" Miley shouts stepping forward. Not exactly the support she is looking for but what can she expect from a parent, her parent. Perhaps it is her years of wisdom making such a choice, or her true nonchalant feelings towards Tyler's dilemma. After all, she didn't even open her front door during their attack. Something Miley questions even to this day.

Tyler feels let down and a bit shocked due to the fact his jaw is vacuuming the carpet, his iris is spinning in his pupils, and as much as he knows he wants Miley with him all the time, reality is irrefutable. Only due to the moment in the white room can Tyler consider any of this to be real. But it is, and whether Miley or Teri is prepared to accept it, Eduardo has shown no signs of this being a game. At that, who plays with the thoughts of death?

"Miley, she is right– I could get all of you hurt," he pauses and turns to Eduardo, "Look, why do we even believe this? This guy could be making this up." Eduardo looks at Teri and unblinking he replies, "This is not a joke, a game, or an act," and then facing Tyler he continues, "I am serious my friend."

Miley turns to Tyler, "That makes no sense, how do we even know this guy is telling us the truth and he isn't some weirdo?"

"In his defense, he made me disappear, I mean like gone," Tyler pleads waving his hands over his own body for demonstration.

"He runs a circus, and he could make this house disappear."

Tyler exhales and continues to explicate, "Miley don't be sarcastic," Tyler turns to Eduardo, "Wait, could you make this whole house disappear?"

Eduardo crosses his arms and takes thought before nodding his head up and down. Humor in the midst of misunderstanding a serious predicament is likely the inspiration of Tyler's sprightly demeanor. Again, a natural reaction at time he needs to revoke.

Shaking his head Tyler says, "Miley still, we always talked about what if this and that. What if and how we would react? This is that what if moment. This situation sounds so idiotic and crazy but for some reason weird things have been happening and as crazy as this man could be, what if he is right? What if this is those moments in movies where someone warns the victims, and they do not listen and," because Dill is still present, Tyler uses his thumb as an imaginary knife going from left to right across his neck, and then tilting his head left while sticking his tongue out.

Miley, feels guilty but little does Tyler know, she is playing her best role and not only to convince Tyler but to convince herself. Something teens do but never wisely is tuck away emotions inside of emotions, and then they misunderstand how to open the door when it is time to let them out. While Tyler was in the hospital, Miley grew panicky and could not focus. She had a new job interview coming up and as well she was preparing to go school touring with Amiyah along the East coast. After Tyler's accident with the tiger, she canceled her plans. The idea of leaving him made her feel narcissistic, therefore she stayed.

Miley also felt like she could not talk to Tyler about her decisions. She did not want to talk to him about her worries because she feared in the position he had been in, she need not make her problems bigger than his current one. Alternatively, Miley rescheduled months later – her interview, her school touring trip, and as of today she was one month from setting off to her scheduled trips. But this entire time, she has never said a word, and for what reason even she is unsure.

Tyler looks at Miley and says, "Miley I love you. Mrs. Teri even though you kind of just threw me under the bus, I love you too."

Teri softens her voice, "Tyler is this real?"

In seconds, she has taken Eduardo's word for right. No doubt her reaction is a lot calmer but this Christian woman hadn't even started a prayer. Almost like she knew what was coming, or she just knew something.

Tyler's imagination places him into position to believe something like this. Miley having spent so much time around Tyler and all his what if questions, adopted his capability to accept the not so normal. *Did Teri know something?* Or had so many sudden crazy events occurred she put nothing past anything or anyone. Regardless, her decision developed rather quickly. And her attentive daughter catches wind of her skeptical drift. Her eyes cut in her mother's direction and silently divulge suspicion as Tyler notices.

Tyler looks at Miley and as he gazes into her eyes he then hugs her tight squeezing her as if she is a stress ball. Miley means so much to him, and he actually needs her for a lot. Miley keeps Tyler on track and pushing towards his dreams. While some of his past life is a mixture of distraught ruins as far as relationships goes. She made Tyler feel so involved. That type of love should not be separated. But, in Tyler's mind, Miley's safety as well as her families, he understands. And, that is why he looks at Eduardo, and asks, "Is this real?"

Etched, he inhales and exhales and then replies, "More than I wish it was not my boy."

As Miley began exhibiting her frustration her shoulder begins to glow. Eduardo stares in amazement gasping with his eyes popping like kernels in an oven. Thunder roars as Miley is playing her role well, indecisive yet fairly aware of her intention to discover her personal opportunities, to reveal what has been hiding in her head. Everyone stares at her as her shoulder illuminates, except Teri, who looks more stone like than amazed.

With her hunted look Teri mumbles, "No. Not now."

Minutes to go - part 12

What does this mean?

Miley begins to cry because inside she knows regardless of the decision Tyler is making, she has one of her own to make. Tyler rushes over placing his hands on her arms. He is a good comforter when he can be. Over the five-month period of Tyler being hospitalized, while Miley remained present, she and Tyler were not spending time as well as her presence presumed. As tears begin rolling, Miley thinks of the truth. Dwelling on the thought her love for Tyler exists, she has other plans, better plans than Tyler.

One day, back in Tyler's hospital room, Miley sat and thought about that day in the department store. The words the store clerked voiced, "*You are gorgeous and young and should be out living your life, free to mingle with whomever you desire...*" She envisioned his facial expression as he spoke to her back thoughts.

Why is she playing a role? She could not bear the words vocally as she thought over them, but the truth is that

Miley since Tyler, sub-consciously felt bound. His incident five months ago solidified her appearance of loyalty, and also her uncomfortable self-sought reality.

Everyone begins tucking away amazement as her shoulder returns to its normal form displaying only a scar. Eduardo looks at Teri, lip dropping, attempting to inch out his curiosity in one question. Teri shakes her head left to right so quickly, even Tyler looks at her with his eyes popping in suspicion, again. Returning his bottom lip to his top, Eduardo reserves his speech.

"Miley, it is okay. I am going to deal with this and I will be back for you," Tyler says.

Eduardo notices the stronger emotion, yet he senses the defeat in Miley's heart, at his appeal he cannot help but share this secret after evidently just hiding another, "My boy, she does not love you. She cares for you a lot but she has lost interest in you and she will not tell you because she knows how much you care for her," Eduardo says looking a bit wolfish.

He feels as though knowing this can make it easier for Tyler to understand why he must leave, and however, it made it harder to tolerate why. Teri grabs Dill by his hand and they slowly walk into the kitchen as discrete as possible. She knows the feeling of heartbreak, and did not want Dill to witness the break coming between Tyler and her daughter.

"What are you talking about?" He asks.

Eduardo grins and then sulks, "I can read her emotions and they spill the secrets of her mind."

"What are you doing?" Miley says calm but looking bereaved as a tear rolls down her lips.

"What is best, you say you do not want to leave him but truly you do. Your mother and he want your safety and that only happens when he is away from all of you. Tell him what you feel and remove this ghastly tension and confusion," he insists gesturing with his fist.

Tyler steps back, "Tension? What you feel? What do you feel?"

"I don't know. I am confused. I know I care about you but..."

Almost like facing the tiger before its last pounce to slay him, fear reawakens in his eyes. He can feel the truth at this moment, and then more reality dawns on him. What is taking place is the beginning of endings and Tyler knows it, "What is there not to know, this morning, the time we spent last week? Everything was good, but I don't understand what's wrong? I mean wait a second, is he even right?"

"TYLER! I do not know what to say," Miley weeps in frustration. Eduardo makes his way past Tyler and to the door, and then he looks back and says, "Say the truth," just before making his exit. He stands outside the door and smirks, feeling the success of making a perfect effort to separate Tyler from the closest thing he has to family.

Back inside the house, the mark on her back and shoulder grows in luminance again, and it has become so bright that Teri and Dill can see the reflection on the ceiling from the space above the door. Miley is no saint and neither is she a villain, but the time to stop hiding is now.

"Tyler, I was devastated and scared five months ago. I was worried, having nightmares and confused. I couldn't talk to you. I also missed my job interview that I waited all summer for. I was supposed to go on a college tour but missed that too. I have things I want to do and I couldn't because I had to be there for you."

"But why didn't you tell me this? You could have talked to me because that is what I am here for. At least I thought so. Am I not who I thought I was?"

Tyler is so confused and it does not help that regardless of what he feels, the weight of reality is about to collapse over his head. Miley swallows the opportunity to lie. Instead, honesty is something she always told Tyler she had been big about. Her back falls against the wall and Tyler steps forward but she raises her hand gesturing him to stop, "Tyler, I really love you a lot, just with the attack and me missing my job interview, Dawson, and school – I have to get things back on track. Our relationship is very important to me but I'm just not sure if..."

Tyler lowers his head and then raises it to the ceiling in one motion. As angry as he is confused, he is more hurt than anything. Hurt is a lite word compared to a more detrimental definition of how he really feels. One thing about Tyler is he always prepares himself mentally. Although, this is left field and completely a bad time to hear bad news, and from a young lady he allowed to convince him that their relationship is some unstoppable, immovable, and solid freight train pushing forty miles of power – taking no stops across the country. This news is just emotionally disturbing.

"You need time? And this is on time now, so I get it. I don't know what's really going on, or why you are instantly throwing on the E brake, but I know how things like this go, I know how 'Breaks' work. I'm going to go figure out what I am involved in, you take all the time you need, I am sure you will anyway," Tyler says with a sullen appearance while also looking like he is an organ transplant patient, who just got news his organ is not coming.

Miley looks at him and feels a bit more gratified she did not have to say what Tyler said, she knows it would have felt like a break up. And right now she is not sure if that is the image she wants Tyler to try and forget her from. He does not want to waste any more thoughts on something he cannot control and is so suddenly unexpected. As his hand wraps around the door handle, he opens the door – head low, stepping out to meet Eduardo who is gazing into the dry sky with clouds looking like steel wool.

"It is never easy to see things we want most fall before us, especially when we most want to see the fruition of a future one has promised us. But you are a young man, use that to your advantage," Eduardo boldly says.

Tyler is a bit down about the reality but it never takes long for him to push things away. Most of his thoughts eat him up for a while but in random moments he tends to fend off feelings fairly well, or bottle them up. But, this is why Miley and his break are so heavy, because he never bottled up a thing about their relationship. He looks up into the sky and as if gravity is to be reversed tears of confusion will lift out of his eyes into the sky.

Fortunate for Tyler, there is another agenda to focus on. "So, am I going to die?"

"Well, I don't think so and I do not want that to happen but I can tell you more later. I do want to help you, but I need you to trust me." Eduardo says.

Trust is an uncomfortable word to hear after just leaving Miley's house. Tyler drops his head quickly to look over at Eduardo who is now staring at the ground, "My brother and the tiger were bound together. His practice of dark arts is an adopted passion but it may be possible to untangle this curse." His words sound like hope but his warning, which is recycling in Tyler's mind, is less than hopeful.

Curious to ask, he does, "Then why does he lead a circus? Why is he not running some secret society plotting to deprive the U.S. of all its resources or something?" Eduardo chuckles and replies, "He is not always dark, or was so dark minded. Apart of my brother still finds happiness, to be happy. It really is not my brother you have to worry about, but truly the curse."

"Who is cursed again?" Tyler asks and Eduardo looks back to the sky and softly puts his words into a sentence, "The curse is a force of power, a lot of power, with a life source provoking it to act as an identity. It seeks the darkness in an individual's mind ripping through the thoughts like a lion picks apart its prey. Vitriolic made the curse."

The curse is still a piddling concern for Tyler. His confusion with Miley has his entire mind thrown from actuality. While he remains aware that Eduardo is real and this strange curse is becoming more real to him, his life is a bit less debatable without Miley in it. Tyler places his fingers into a grip, raising his hands to his forehead he begins to pray. What is on his mind, evidentially the sour reality is hanging from his windows of opportunity like black drapes.

God, I know I haven't spoken with you much. Okay, that sounds cliché, God can I start over? God ever since speaking with you, I have developed a new fear. And that fear is a fear of losing. I do not like to lose and my entire life I feel like that is all I have done. Until, you gave me Miley. I am not sure why she is leaving, but I need her back. Please God.

And God, I am not sure how to ask for help but I do not want to die. Not today and definitely not by demons. But if they are real, I believe you are too. Please, protect me. Protect Miley, Mrs. Teri, and Dill. Oh and even Pete, although we don't talk anymore.

"So what am I supposed to do now? Do I just wait and die?" Tyler asks.

Eduardo's sardonic look as he hovers over Tyler, as he prayed, can kill a rose on sight. He still answers his question even facing the feeling of disgust as Tyler prayed, "I fear so," Tyler tunes in quicker than an audience at a taping, "Really? Like, you could not have said anything more hopeful."

Again, he is not the most favored when it comes to delivering information. "My apologies, however I have a curiosity, one with irreversible interest. Why does your girlfriend, well, ex-girlfriend – why does her skin illuminate?"

Tyler does not want to say much because of how personal it is to Miley. But, his mood persuades him to void any feeling to hold back. After all, they are on a break. In Tyler's mind, withholding information is less of a loyalty value at the moment. "She was struck by lightning, and...It lasted for five seconds like something was being shot into her. Or, so everyone said. That was the rumor. Actually it still is the rumor. No one knows what it is or how she got it, not even her. It is just...there. And it glows when she gets emotional." Eduardo takes to reaction, "You do not sound surprised?"

His emotions are all over his face, "When you love someone you accept everything. Even if it does not make sense, you accept it because they mean that much to you." Eduardo surprised replies, "That is wise words coming from such a young man," and Tyler responds chuckling, "Yeah I heard it in a movie once. Plus, I don't know how she got, and it is really just a scar."

Minutes to go - part 13

Are you really trying to help?

Dill drags his fork through his string beans. A tasteful tongue for green beans has now lost a flavorful craving for his favorites, chicken nuggets. He let his nuggets sit in ketchup sauce and left his juice towering in a tall glass on his dinner mat. Dill is bothered and Teri has a hunch but she is not quite ready to roll on it. His palm under his chin, he drops his fork and picks it back up to drop it again.

"Dill, what is wrong?" Teri asks placing her glass of wine down on the countertop.

Without removing his eyes from his plate, he says, "You wanted Tyler to leave." Teri in shock at Dill's claim walks over to the table and pulls the chair from under. As she takes a seat Dill asks, "Can I go to my room?"

The sadness in his voice can open a speech before a funeral service. Teri knows Dill is hardly ever down but he barely frowns unless Dawson's name comes up. He misses Dawson so much. Some connections made between father and son are chemically synced. During his father's absence, Tyler and he bonded very well. As his little feet swing back and forth beneath the table, Dill awaits his mother's words dismissing him.

"Dill, Tyler is in trouble and he doesn't want us to be in trouble, Tyler wanted to leave to keep us safe," Teri says.

"That's not true, Tyler likes us and he wants to help us. You just do not like him because Miley does not like him. You both were being mean to him." A strong perception coming from a six-year-old boy is not so easily replied to. She is lost for words with no counter statement to force the leading perception out of Dill's mind.

Inquisition leads his growing mind, "Mom, what's wrong with Miley, is she sick?" Even Dill makes it his business to inquire about Miley's special mark. Still, Teri is disinclined to acquiesce his request.

"No baby, your sister is okay. She is just growing up. You can go to your room now." Dill gets up and glues his eyes to the floor, waddling his way out of the kitchen. As Teri watches him leave she places her face into her hands. A deep sigh identifies her baffling morning. She gets up from the table and pushes her chair in, and Dill's too. A big deal would have been made, but at the moment Dill is already bothered by Tyler's absence. Teri does not want to bother him anymore.

Walking over to the cordless phone lying on the kitchen counter, she reaches for it and a voice startles her. The tone is not foreign to her, in fact, she knows exactly who it is. Placing the phone back down and turning to acknowledge her guest she says, "I was just about to call you."

A man in a thin grey sweater and slacks stands tall in the doorway. His eyes are steel blue and his smooth brown face is hairless. From the door way he sends a gaze that instructs Teri to come closer. She is still unsure of the trust she can place in him. The dinner table is as close as she can approach. Positioning a table between them will not physically stop him from anything, but it creates some form of barricade between who he is and what he is capable of.

"Teri, you did the right thing. Your daughter will help us." He says stepping closer. Just one step forward makes her grip the top of the chair. Teri keeps her eyes on him as she returns her inquiries, "I don't care if she can help, will she be safe? What is going to happen to Tyler?"

A strong stare off to the window and then to the ground implies a negative response to follow. Instead he does not respond at all. Teri demands his attention, "You keep her safe. You are one of God's trusted disciplines. You keep her safe dammit. She does not know what she can do and she doesn't need to know who she is."

He marches around the table and into Teri's personal space. Fear leans her back against the table as he stands over her. "Our agreement was that you tell her of her history, she must know who she truly is," he says.

Teri shivering replies, "She was not ready. She has too much going on. Her power will kill her," pausing in sadness, "her powers can kill Tyler."

Walking back to the doorway, he turns his head over his left shoulder and says, "It's too late to determine now. I will do what I can, but if Ziga figures out who they both are, death is certain."

Four days later...

The phone rings sudden and quick. Tyler is seated on the steps of his apartment complex, his cap backwards, head down, and arms hanging over his knees. Nothing is crossing his mind more than how to deal with his losses. What he cannot control cruises a course around his sea of thoughts. Cellphone in hand, the same jingle longs a tune once more breaking the repeating sounds of silence.

He cares less to answer and even lesser to see who the caller is. Footsteps can be heard from ten feet away. Crackling leaves beneath every step are due to someone who is walking up on him, but Tyler still negates the sounds. Emotionally battling feeling anything and feeling nothing, he fails to find concern enough to bring his head up and acknowledge who is approaching.

"Moping solves nothing for a sore heart. If one wants to see a sunray he should let the shade be as lonely as the last leaf on a tree during a season of fall."

Tyler refuses to look up but verbally responds, "Are you like full of these Shakespeare quotes?" Eduardo snaps in disappointment, "Hardly the remnants of such a visionary. These wisdom words are lyrics of my own song."

The sun keeps the shadows of the trees shading over Tyler, and he looks around to behold his shadow absent in the shade. "Did you have to say she didn't love me?"

Pulling out a deck of cards, he replies, "A lie would have not made you any more grateful. Eventually, she would have showed you every sign of disinterest."

"Why did she lose interest?"

Not just a question but also a reoccurring thought preoccupying his mind. He feels this darkness weighing over his heart and it will not stop peaking from behind a curtain he keeps trying to close. So many questions are at the peak of his brain. *What did I do? Is it my fault? Is there someone else?*

"It happens because many of us are not trained to value what we love." Eduardo says.

"What? That's stupid, and at that you only love something or someone because you value it."

Smiling Eduardo responds, "It takes a wise heart to speak that to life. However, many hearts are far too scarred to feel value. They only long for settlements."

"You mean like we settle for what we want in order to get what we need?"

"Possibly, or we settle for what satisfies quickly, maybe too quickly, to ever care to realize we have not discovered any value for what we have settled for."

Tyler lifts his head to witness Eduardo in a three-piece suit, which looks like it may have cost his rent per month. His shoes are snakeskin and his cuff links can catch every glistening affect from the sun. His hair was covered last Tyler seen, but this time he has a very cool cut, and facial hair trimmed like a front lawn.

"You live alone?" He asks Tyler.

Tyler looks off ashamed to reply but he does, "Yes. I

have lived on my own since I turned 18."
"Where are your parents?"

He has a wistful expression as he replies, "and I haven't seen my mother since I was sixteen years old. I lived with friends until I was old enough to buy a scratch-off. After that, I pretty much got lucky and hit for a couple grand. I have been living off of it for the last year and a half."

Eduardo looks wide-eyed as he speaks, "I am sorry and happy for your progress."

A cool breeze is within the warm weather and it throws falling leaves around with a well-kept balance on the temperature. For some reason the wind appears to whip around Eduardo like a funnel.

"So you are a magician?"
"No, I am help."
"Like you did four days ago?"

Smiling still, "Tyler, I do not take pride in my ability to read emotions, I truly dislike this but your pain would have grown had I said nothing. Plus, the curse would have caused you to get her killed her."

Slapping his hands on his head, "Dude do you have any chill? Is there anything you say that is actually good news or even sounds good?" Tyler cannot take another bad news statement, although he knows that Eduardo is just keeping everything as up front as possible.

"I am not trying to steal the stars from your night sky. I just know you can handle the truth."

Tyler stands up and brushes off his pants. "I can handle the truth and it is day time anyway wizard of Oz. Look, what am I supposed to do; I do not have the one person who cared about me and plus I have all these questions I have no answer for. Some tiger, how it got loose beats me, tried to kill my ex-girlfriends neighbor, who I risked my life to save and this is what I end up with. A curse and no girl, in the movies this is not how the good guy turns out." Tyler is nearing that moment where he is beginning to realize nearly everything is out of his control.

"Everything is out of my control," he says. Then again take that back, he has reached it.

"Sometimes those moments we wish we had control are moments we best are without it. No one is perfect Tyler, and do not fool yourself into believing if you could control every situation, you would make the right decision doing so."

Eduardo places his hands in his pockets and strolls into a deeper thought. Something can be done but his hunch may not fit the occasion, especially since Tyler is emotionally shot. "Come with me," he says waving his left hand towards the street.

"Where are we going?"

"For a ride," Eduardo replies.

"To where..."

"A place..."

"Called?"

"I do not quite remember just yet."

Tyler steps back, "This sounds like the moment when a kid is faced with a stranger pitching a tale of endless candy handouts, and the kid goes with his better judgment as he ask the stranger who he is." Eduardo laughs and takes Tyler's sarcasm for what it is, his defensive mechanism. "Just come, you will understand."

As Eduardo walks to the curb, Tyler's eyes turn to grapefruits, the car Eduardo is driving and the style, the luxury, and the confusion on Tyler's face as Eduardo lifts the door handle up to release the door. They are standing before a half a million-dollar car. It is smoke black and full of abstract designs. The rims are black as tar and the interior looks as if the night sky has been placed in the vehicle. Everything is operated on a touch screen panel from the sound to the windshield wipers.

"Are you coming?"

Tyler still shock that he is before a car he barely ever sees in his neighborhood, he replies, "Hell yeah."

Meanwhile...

Miley is seated in a cafe four blocks from Amiyah's home. Just as she swirls her spoon through her caramel frappe, Amiyah enters with a smile stretching like the red sea. She weaves through other customers and flops down in the booth as if her seat is an enlarged beanbag. While most friends tend to console – with the intent to calm – any favored emotion, Amiyah devotes her support to being shown through rash truth.

"Are we moping? Pause, whom are we moping about? Tyler? Come on Miley, you dropped the dead weight. All successful young people do when we are focused on bigger and better. I mean let's favor this moment, one you are free to get your job you never but almost had back. Plus, you get to go college touring with one of the most remarkable young ladies you have ever called a friend, me." She gloats poetically.

Miley is not ordinarily persuaded easily but she knows what it feels like to have to allow herself to be won over.

"Miley, for as long as you have been with him, it is about time anyway. What were you just coming out of a situation with Chant little over three months before Tyler?"

Amiyah knows no trenches; she plays on the war field and with the bullets dancing around the soldiers. Her personality is that of a brute defense, her reaction to any action is defense and most inquisitive, and her knack for being brutally honest is residual. Miley has a mind of her own but sometimes you need someone to take over your thoughts for a while. The waiter comes over and brings her another frappe. As the mood set, for sure Amiyah intends to persuade Miley out of this dump full of feelings she feels she cannot use.

Amiyah sips her drink and puts some style on her every action, and in a way you can say she is very extra. "Hey, on the bright side, you get to focus on your life and you can do what's best for you. We are young and relationships come and go, and not to mention we are girls, we have options. We can explore everyone or anyone when we want. Do not give up your vagina power," said Amiyah always sounding four years older than she actually is.

It is the television that has captured her mind and given her this food for thought, or, venom for prey.

"Vagina power... We are just lucky that people like to be around us. I don't know, I feel like I knew Tyler was not going to last but I could not let him go."

Amiyah sipping her drink while examining her well filed nails replies, "Miley it is because you still needed that feeling. We girls know we aren't going to keep a guy but we still need that feeling. That *I have someone* feeling and after that you know, drop him," she said dropping her fist like a gavel, "Guys are guys they do not care after a couple days anyway." Amiyah cannot be more wrong. Tyler cares, and nothing is on his mind but Miley, and Miley is in a bit of a departing state of mind, which she is paving a path towards.

"I do not know, I mean I need my time and a relationship is a concrete block strapped to my feet," Miley states.

"Yes and you need more time for other men."

"Amiyah!"

She giggles and eyes-down a young man seated at a table in the back, "What? Really, you have options, you are pretty, smart, and need to take advantage of your bag of goods."

"I can't with you," Miley says turning her phone over still in thought of the idea that she has time to herself. *Is it what she needs*, who knows, however, like any single teenage girl – she intends to manipulate the opportunity.

Minutes to go - part 14

That just happened.

Wanting closure is always the case during the acceptance period. This is the point where Tyler is losing nearly half of his mind trying to erase Miley, like she has been erasing him. Like a piece of hot coal resting on his skull, the thought of her leaving was a burning mess. Heat is prying through his skull every second he tries to remind himself to forget her. He cannot stop thinking of her. Miley was all Tyler knew when it came to something serious. And they were serious, so serious, enough to have caused Tyler to shut out his friends.

He begins to think of his last one true friend, and like the universe heard his thoughts – Pete calls. He digs into his pocket and pulls out his phone, and then he looks at

Eduardo who is vitally focusing on the road. Pete is not as significant in Tyler's life as he used to be. Ever since he met Miley in the city, and she brought him out into the county, Tyler was disconnected. Nothing about the city stood out anymore, it was just a place he lived in.

Pete stopped calling after he stopped talking to Amiyah, which in fact is how Miley even made her way into the city. Her best friend and Pete grew up together. Tyler never met Amiyah but he always heard of her. Pete would never shut up about the girl that broke his heart. The last time she and he patched things up, Tyler had become the median to a confusing web of lies.

Amiyah later moved into Randallstown and Pete stopped hanging in the city. He spent less and less time around Tyler who found that working was all he had to occupy his free time. In a way, they traded places in two years. But Tyler had lost contact with Pete a year ago, and ever since they haven't spoken.

"Hello, what's up bro?"

Pete answers, "Are you alive? Or is this an automated recording set up by the android that has taken over Tyler's body?"

Tyler smirks replying "Shut up dumb ass. What's up? Long time no speak, it's been almost a year."

"I know, we should hook up man," Pete wastes no time conversing as if he had seen Tyler just yesterday. He then shot straight to the point, "Are you busy tonight? There is a concert in town down the Ram's Head. Devin bluffed me and Veronica is bringing Brittany with her. I figured you might want to come."

Tyler replies strongly, "Are you serious?"

A deep sigh and Pete knows of the frustration he just caused him. Brittany is Tyler's "*one that got away*." Tyler was a lot worse than he is now as far as self-esteem. Brittany is a gorgeous girl just like Miley, but more relaxed and less glamour. She was the perfect match and accepted Tyler truly for he is, or was at the time. Practically and orphan and introvert.

Whether Tyler was broke, carless, friendless, or weird Brittany did not care. She really had it out for him emotionally. But, Tyler being Tyler refused to see past his self-thought unfortunate state of mind and struggling city life as well as hardly seeing his parents. At that time, he was not in school, and not working, and hardly had much at the age of 16. All of his peers where headed off to college or picked up a trade, while he spent hours of his day contemplating financial moves he never intended to make. By the time graduation came around, he'd been the only one in his class who did not attend a higher institution.

However, Brittany cared less and probably not at all about any of that. She just loved him for who he was. Because of her, he gained the state of mind that brought him to get a job, become socially confident, and activate his confidence in his own characteristics. But again, before that came to pass, Tyler pushed her away.

His worrying and mental breakdowns over situations he could not control, occupied the volume in his mind more than Brittany's words or actions. In time, those thoughts produced actions that resulted in the type of negligence that packs up emotions, and then calls the cab of impatience to pick up opportunity. This cab of impatience later drives that opportunity off into a sun setting in another season of life.

Deciding to hang out with Pete is not the most difficult decision, and the true alternative is to consider that he would be back around Brittany. Tyler may not have had many friends but he valued the ones he made. Pete's decision to disconnect with Tyler created a gap in time that one phone call does not and will not fill. Seeing Brittany again is an act of restoration. He is well aware of the irresponsible behavior he is about to commit. His cognitive ability recycles his days with Brittany, a much more relieving thought than heartbreak. This is why Tyler gathers incentive to determine he will meet up with him tonight.

Pete has created a confusion Tyler cannot bare sustain at the current moment. Remnants of Brittany and ingeminating thoughts of Miley's dismissal congest his mind like sardines in an aluminum rectangular canister. Anything to take his mind from these pernicious thoughts would suffice, and so Tyler seeks to abandon his state of mental distress. One second he is calm and soothed, and the next he barricades his brain with memories of Miley and he.

"Cool, I will call you back and let you know," he says not even waiting for Pete to confirm. Pete, a good friend, would have inquired why he ended the call so quick, which a good friend should do. Yet, Tyler avoids such characteristics of true friendship, as they will be over shadowed by his recollection of stress and his lack of faith. His feelings rotated even though he had not spoken to him in a year, his current situation prevented him from regaining any connection.

Windows up, Eduardo has the air conditioning system on full blast. Tyler can see cold bumps arising on his skin and has to ask, "Kind of cold in here you think?"

Eduardo without taking his eyes off the road replies, "Oh sorry, where I am from the heat is so uncomfortable. Cool air is like a massage to me." Tyler sits up and turns to gaze back out into the world. But, only seconds before

Eduardo makes car conversation mandatory with a particular question.

"So many girls are in *this* world, why do you weep over one...Or two?"

"Because..." Tyler answers too quickly. He pauses to realize he has no answer at the moment. After a three second silence he then replies, "Sometimes when you find the one, you get caught up on them. And no matter how many people you meet in life, they will never be that one or two." Spoken In thought of Brittany– and Miley.

Eduardo uses his index finger to tap the steering wheel. He finds Tyler's response a bit more interesting, also leading with the fact Tyler did not give him the cop out answer he was expecting from him.

"So this caught up feeling, it bounds you to them? Why? Is it a curse?" Eduardo asks.

Slouching in his seat, Tyler gazes out the window with no intent to return his thoughts. At least he feels like he does not want to reply with his thoughts, but his lips breach and his voice flows an explanation Shawn White could surf over.

"It feels that way. Like no matter how you much you do not see or speak to this person, they are always felt. You always know you want to speak or be around them, even when you know you shouldn't be. It is hard to explain, plus I feel like a little bitch having this heart to heart with a stranger." The car stops fast and Eduardo removes his hands from the wheel placing his palms over his thighs.

"Stranger? You do not consider me a friend?"

Tyler a bit on the hot seat replies, "How could I, I don't know you really. Plus people don't make friends that fast."

"It takes time?" He implies.

"Yeah, no one meets up and just bam we're friends," Tyler adds.

Eduardo staring out the front window looks puzzled. He does not quite understand completely what makes friends just yet. Tyler begins to ponder as to where they are actually headed. They are still at a red light and traffic is picking up.

"Why not? I gave you a ride, isn't that what friends do, they exchange favors," Eduardo says.

Tyler gives an off-look before saying, "No. First off, that is not how you make friends. People think that favors make friendships: well they don't. That is why a lot of people don't have real friends. You make friends by knowing someone, actually learning them," Tyler begins using hand gestures as he speaks, "like taking time to find out what makes them happy or mad and what they do and do not like, or what they laugh at and their favorite foods. And then you have to spend time with that person. Friendships, true friendships just happen, mostly when two people unconsciously just have an interest to learn each other."

People are crowding over the sidewalks, and Eduardo and Tyler are passing through downtown near the Gallery on Pratt St. So many people are around it made Tyler begin to ponder. The car begins to move again and Eduardo begins to read Tyler's mind. *"I wish people could see me in this nice car. It must be nice. Someday I am going to be the one."*

Eduardo pulls the car to the curb fast and zooms into a perfect spot at about forty miles per hour, and just instantly stopping on the dime. The doors lift up and he says to Tyler, "Get out."

"What? Why? Dude I didn't mean you weren't a friend. I mean you are pretty cool actually. You can't just kick me out downtown," Tyler pleads as everyone stops and looks at them. Humiliation strikes again, it is as if it is a jacket he wears often. Tyler gets out wishing he had kept his explanation unheard, and Eduardo removes himself from the driver seat without further words. He walks around the front of the car, gliding his fingertips over his luxury toy.

"Here, I want you to drive," he says holding the keys before Tyler's eyes, which watch the keys swing back and forth between Eduardo's fingers.

"Bullshit"
"Excuse me?" He says.

Tyler corrects himself, "It is a saying like when you think someone is bluffing. Like not serious. Because you must be joking," Tyler points to the car and continues, "You are going to let me drive your car? I don't believe it."

He responds, "But I am serious, I find driving terribly exhausting and exasperating. So you can drive, I will show you the way." Everyone is still looking, and Tyler has no clue because his eyes are glued to the car keys. He looks at Eduardo and then the keys. He takes another look at him and then back at the keys. Tyler grabs the keys and shouts, "Get in," as if the vehicle is not owned by its previous driver.

He runs around the back of the car and hops in the driver seat closing the door in one motion. Hands firm on the steering wheel he looks at Eduardo who is smiling, and observing how Tyler's excitement is exploding through his flesh vessel. In his mind, comprehension of Tyler's thoughts is a bit fair. Is he doing this for the thrills or has Eduardo simply elected himself to be the example of a true friend. At least Eduardo thought so as he gets in the car. He did not see this as a favor; instead his mind conceived the idea as caring for what Tyler felt. This is his sympathetic, yet, effort to bond and fill any gaps of misunderstanding between their ideas of friendship.

Tyler shifts the gear into drive, smoothly relaxing his foot as the engine catches every witnessing eye and ear. His smile smooth's off of his face into a solid display of confidence. Eduardo presses a button on the dash and the roof removes itself disappearing into the rear of the vehicle.

Everyone is looking and Tyler feels this energy surge throughout his hands and feet. They pull off quick – and immediately, Miley becomes a thoughtless topic beyond significance and without relevance to his joy.

Minutes to go - part 15

Keeping secrets... Or not

The fear of being caught lying can damage the mind. Proof is in the experience of facing the sudden moments, when determining whether or not you are prepared to speak the truth. Miley and Amiyah walk into Double Delight's restaurant, the host approaches, "Hello everyone, how many today?"

Teenagers flooded the establishment before and after convenient hours due to the concert tonight. Concerts and festivals always brought the young adults into the city. Those events are the two things that Randallstown did not have, and to this day are still absent. The town gratefully condoned to peace but after the incident the town committed to it. If the police are to remain above standard, they cannot and will not permit any interruptions to the civil resolutions.

Benny made sure of that as he cruised through town in his cruiser noticing that for a weekend, the town's renounced spots for teenage mischief are empty. This piqued his curiosity and later led him to actively inquire why. A phone call is made to Dawson.

"Table for four please," says Amiyah clutching her purse before she begins rambling through it searching for her phone. Miley follows the host as she escorts them to their table located in the far left side of the establishment. This restaurant is famous for late night hook ups between club goers and party wrecks – which have become drunkenly famished. Nights like so, Amiyah usually has a pair of pointless conversation with *gets straight to the point* young men awaiting her arrival. Tonight is no different, as a young man tall and possibly into sports due to his rough big hands, which he has extending in Miley's direction. Her facial expression can fill a funeral home.

"Hello, I'm Thomas"

For a bit Miley freezes, but she regains her perorate ability and replies, "Hi I am Miley," so she thought she said. Thomas, Amiyah, and the unannounced friend stand in awkward silence as they all heard, "Hi, I am Tyler."

"Okay Tyler," Thomas says a bit confused. Amiyah butts in and corrects her, "Miley, her name is Miley," almost stepping in front of her not to feel embarrassed. The other young man remains seated and has a harsh look to him. Leather jacket with zippers ripping through the seam, and he also has on some black boots you usually see in sci-fi future war movies. His leg is hanging out from under the table, stretching in his own gesture of completely relaxed and nonchalant comfort.

"Yeah Miley, come sit down," he says winking.

Miley directs her sight to him and in his face are piercings and a tattoo in front of his right ear. "Who are you?" She asks.

"I'm Mack, like the Mack truck. But you can call me Mac, you know with one C and without the K."

"Is there any difference?" Miley says protesting in her response by tightening up her face.

"Yeah babe, see the K makes the more profound sound of Ack, but without the K it is smoother like Mah. You know what I mean?" Mac without the K replies. Amiyah scoots into the booth tucking her dress beneath her. Miley slides next to her and places her bag between them. Thomas waits for Mac to slide back over but he did not notice Thomas because he is staring at Miley as if she is edible.

"Dude..." Thomas says nudging Mac in the shoulder. Mac slides in; the waiter walks by and turns back around eyes ringent. The lighting in the place is so dim outside the booths. The feeling is set to give customers a sense of privacy, and possibly at the same time a short scare, as most customers never see the waiter approaching.

Seats in the booth are leather, the real kind and have a sloping cushion. The seat kind of scoops you in while the back leans you over. It feels awkward for most until they realize how perfectly they are positioned to enjoy their meal.

"So ladies, what are you gals up to tonight?" Amiyah flips her hair and replies, "We are waiting for you to tell us."

Thomas smiles, "Well there is a late concert rocking out at the Rams head. I took the liberty of purchasing four tickets."

"And there is four of us," Mac butts in to add, smiling like he just drop the biggest punch line in cool guy history. "We get it," says Miley sarcastically.

"Attitude, I like that," Mac sends back.

His ego is at the right tempo, but in the hunt for the wrong person, her. Miley raises her eyebrows simultaneously and places her hand on her forehead. She begins to catch the drift of tonight's mission. Amiyah has plans with Thomas and Mac is the tag along friend to comfort the newly available Miley. However, Miley has undisclosed thoughts she should have shared before allowing Amiyah to create an environment less than reasonably comfortable.

"Cool. Who is playing?" Amiyah asks.
"You'll see and you two will like it."
Mac again dropping in his two cents, "Yeah, you ladies are going to love it."

Miley chuckles and straightens out her smile, "Are you even aware of what's going on here?" Mac has no clue what is going on but he does not care. His ability to be aware of the obvious is barricaded within his ego.

"Miley it will be fun," says Thomas who pulls his dreads from the side of his face tucking them behind his ear. Next he runs his hand through his hair and smiles in Amiyah's direction. Miley rolls her eyes and they land on Amiyah who is captivated by Thomas's gesture. Figuratively speaking, she may have just thrown up in her mouth as she cringes. Thomas is not adorable but he has a decent appeal. However, neither Mac nor he is her type of guy.

The setup is in motion, and spontaneity is no stranger to Miley, especially when it comes to accompanying Amiyah on her promiscuous – hormone raging, obligations. Her phone rings and the screen read *Benny.* Excusing herself from the table she makes her way to the darkest area of the restaurant, near the restrooms. One tap to the screen and she activates the call.

Benny goes straight in, "Where are you?" Miley replies, "I'm out, what do you want?"

"What's going on?" He asks progressing in his cruiser towards the city. Dawson may not have been welcome in their home but the streets are his, and he made sure nothing was to happen to Miley ever again. Placing Benny on the job for double the pay made sure of that.

"Nothing is going on, and you can tell Dawson it has been five months. I do not need a protection detail."

"It is not for you, it is for Tyler."

She pauses, a slight gasp of breath and she responds, "It is not for Tyler it is for me because he thinks Tyler is always with me, and Tyler is not with me anymore." Benny raises concern, "Why, what's happened?"

Miley refuses to engage on that topic with him, especially because of who he is. Anything Benny knows, Dawson does as well. He is not a bad guy and far from a bad cop, but he also respected his work and the values of protecting the community with firm commitment. She respected that but now is neither the place nor time to recollect on dread thoughts.

An inclination to end the call moves her toward her abrupt ending, "I have to go, bye Benny." As she swipes across her screen, ending the call, she begins to hear commotion in the ladies restroom.

"I hate you. I hate you. You are nothing but trouble. And trouble must be punished Teri."

The moment she hears her mother's name she rushes into the fancy room. Two sinks are made of silver and the counter tops around them, granite. Black walls are as dark as the depths of the sea. The stalls are crimson with chrome accents around the door handle and bolts. Four burning orange flames lit the room like an old tavern. A creaking door is released as she takes slow steps further inside. A jitter is the result of the door slamming shut behind her. No windows are present in the design of this room, yet, however a gust of wind strokes the flames.

A moment is taken, as the silence becomes a waiting room. No more voices can be heard but the doors on the stalls begin simultaneously tapping the hinge holders. Fog rises from a circular drain about four inches in diameter. It covers the floor like mist can hover over the ground of a pumpkin patch. A loud scream then comes from the last stall like a sudden boom of thunder. Miley paces over intuitive but as the tips of her fingers press against the door, she begins pushing it open. There is a woman, she is covered in blood and sitting on the toilet with her face buried into her arms crying. The rotten smell hit her nose like stale fruit.

She asks, "Are you okay?"

A sharp sound of glass crackling and Miley turns around cautious. Her nerves create a haunting rhythm underneath her skin. Her look is no quicker than a second and when she turns back around the girl is gone. She gasps–and then she walks into the stall unsure of her sanity. With no further investigation necessary, she thinks to leave in suspicion. A loud scream and bloody hands storm towards her as she turns to the mirror. The girl rushes at her and her eyes are on fire as blood runs from her sockets. Miley frantic tries her hardest to remove the girls grip, but she is too strong. She leans in towards her, hands bleeding all over Miley's shoulder.

"The key, they want the key. Give them the key," she whispers into a shouting manic depression.

Her body burst into flames and she vanishes as ashes fall to the floor. Miley storms out of the stall and heads for the door. Her fingers wrap around the handle and before she can pull the door towards her, she stops. Illuminating is her shoulder, the mark, which she has had since birth and no explanation as to how. Quickly she pats her shoulder with an open palm as if it is on fire. The scar flows with energy and a feeling of power overcomes her. In stress, she pulls away from the door and snatches the handle off without resistance. Admiring her ability and sudden jolt of strength, she becomes stone in shock and awe.

Amiyah rushes through the door and sees Miley standing with the silver handle in hand. "What are you doing?"

"Nothing, I am doing nothing."

No words are capable of saving her story from sounding anything but lunatic. An explanation is reserved as an awkward moment of silence comes between the two. Amiyah then insists, "Well let's go they are ready."

She exits and Miley goes to follow, but before she leaves a look over her shoulder is her effort to ensure what just occurred, happened. But, nothing is there and all is still.

Rock out... Ok that's enough.

As they enter the concert, lights blind them instantly. Blue, green, and purple lights waving over the crowd, and then the bass drops as music takes over the atmosphere.

Everyone begins to shout and scream like money is falling from the sky. Miley shoves her fingertips into her ears ducking her head below, to avoid losing one of her senses. Mac throws his hands in the air and begins jumping up and down like he is grabbing multiple rebounds. Thomas grabs Amiyah's hand before turning to Miley and saying, "We are headed up front." Nodding her head she still has her ears plugged. Mac confidently salutes Thomas and replies, "Don't worry, I got this situation handled."

That is what he thinks, but Miley is not an easy bargain, especially when she has already discovered reasons to disregard any man's presence. Mac is going to have to try a lot harder, but not that it will make any difference because she has an agenda developing. It can be seen in her eyes, as they spread she bites her bottom lip before sprinting through the crowd. All Mac can catch is a glimpse of her hair vanishing through the jumping bodies and swinging arms.

As he takes off after her, Miley begins smiling, a good chase suffices any girl's perception of persistence thus transitioning into some form of appealing. She weaves left then right, maneuvering like a snake through tall grass and Mac almost loses her. He continues to brush shoulders with people of the crowd, and in the blink of an eye she is gone. Mac throws his fingers through his hair and sighs deeply as his eyes could not keep up with her legs. After a full spin and surveillance of the crowd, it is almost time to give up. Suddenly Miley appears behind him, she is smiling running her finger over her face removing a strand of hair from her eye.

"Alright you got me," Mac submits.

"Surrendering are we?"

"I did not know we were at war. I know your kind," Mac replies clapping his hands as if he has come to an irreversible conclusion. Miley drops her shoulder and awaits his explanation.

He looks off to the side and says, "See you are the kind of girl," and as he turns back to look at her, she is gone again.

He places his hands on his waist and lowers his head grinning as he again falls victim to her sleekness. Miley is playing a round of hide and go seek through a roughly jam-packed crowd. Any guy in his right mind would hang up the coat and call it a night. Not Mac, his ego forces his actions over his thoughts. And because of that, he lowers his head under a guy's arm that is waving his four-dollar beer like an American flag on the Fourth of July, and he then continues searching for Miley.

Meanwhile, Miley finally reaches an opening and she walks through excusing herself pass many well-intoxicated individuals. The music is still loud so she walks further towards the gates intending to still preserve her hearing. Typing in her phone, energy hits her like an invisible force field. Something about the feeling is dark and heavy. The music instantly goes silent and it feels like time has frozen sound. People are still leaping, conversing, and too busy dancing to appear coherent with what Miley thinks is going on.

Her eyes become video monitors overseeing the audience. No one is observant enough to give her the impression she is not losing her sense of reality. Hair rises from off of her skin as she feels the electric current shift around her. Her hair begins to lift from off of her shoulders and she looks to her feet to see dust from the ground blowing to the front of her boots. The silence is symmetrical to darkness as she begins to feel that feeling of isolation.

In seconds, Eduardo's entire warnings loop through her mind. The words death and spirits begin to ring the bells on her nerves and fear begins crawling up her body like a million spiders coursing along a web. She slowly raises her eyes to look forward, and standing not but six feet away, is Vitriolic, Eduardo's brother.

A black suit with a red tie made his form. He is big and brute and standing just over six feet four. A grizzly look to him taunts Miley in addition to his deathly stare. She closes her eyes as if she knows exactly why this man stands before her. A loud boom resurfaces as the music returns and she opens her eyes to see he is no longer standing before her. As the music plays and people continue to jump around her. She turns around and her body is frozen in place, as Vitriolic is standing before her.

Minutes to go - part 16

Failure to Communicate

"This is awesome," Tyler shouts as the wind rushes into the car while they cruise into East County. Every house they pass by begins to get bigger and bigger. Nothing compares to what Tyler is letting out right now. The environment is soaking up his joy and the tail pipes on the vehicle are letting out his worries. For a moment, he just stares out the front window taking in the intoxicating rush of feeling control. It is his outer-body experience in a car, and mostly his *look at me now* period of time.

"Turn here," Eduardo says calm but sterner. Tyler can feel the mood change, it is no longer jubilant, and while the scenery reflected many flower beds and steel fences lining the perimeter of nearly every home. He feels the energy decrease from positive and hold steady at a strong medium just above negative. Eduardo's face is emotionless and he looks as if his soul has been snatched right out of him. *Why do such moods change?*

Just as Tyler feels great, Eduardo's tone of voice abducts that feeling from his home of comfort. Every home has a driveway extensive enough to make the yellow brick road seem like a parking pad. Most homes are well lit from the sidewalk up to the porch and inside. They approach a home towering over them all. It is dark and every window looks as if it is sealed with steel shutters. The siding is bound with metal pipes bent into an abstract design appearing to make the sides of the mansion look coated with hieroglyphics.

"Turn in here," instructs Eduardo.

Tyler turns the steering wheel and suddenly it turns itself. He jumps back, "Whoa, what just happened," he says as the steering wheel rotates turning the wheels into the curvature of the path. A smooth stop and Eduardo takes a deep breath. He inhales and then exhales and says, "We are here my new friend."

Something about the way Eduardo said friend set Tyler on alert. It is as if he meant friend like Tyler is not even actually there. To be honest, Tyler thought for a second he might have been talking to the car. Their seat belts undo themselves and the doors remove. As much as it can be said this car is considered a luxury vehicle, the feeling of everything being taken control of by – well nothing – is inexplicable behavior. Unless, you have a great memory like Tyler's who has not forgotten about the fact he has spirits after him.

It is windy, not so much chilly but windy enough to make Tyler shiver. As for Eduardo, the breeze feels relaxing, Tyler can tell as Eduardo rolls his neck and sighs before making eye contact with him. Energy decreases below the median and has dropped to a sure negative. The feeling is deep and dark, and Tyler can feel it in his hands and feet. A heavy feeling creeps up his legs and the more he looks at the house, his entire body is taken over by gloominess.

Eduardo straightens out his tie and collar before telling Tyler, "This way, we go now, inside and set a sail."

His metaphor is misleading at most but at least connecting dots as to why they have actually arrived at this vast mansion. Tyler takes a look around and the entire yard is occupied by flowerbeds made of stone, with dead plants resting between the broken stone sculptures alongside them. The front yard is big and has a lot of burnt looking trees hanging over as if they have been hacked through but never fell. On the branches, the leaves flickered like a lamp in a thunderstorm. Unusual but not surprising as Tyler is beginning to welcome in the weird.

Approaching the front door, Eduardo stops and places his hands into his jacket pockets. He looks to Tyler and says, "You are strong, and I can see that. And if I can then he can, which means if you are going to be strong then you can leave no vulnerabilities."

'Vulnerabilities?' Tyler thinks for a moment and then the reality walks into his mind, "Oh you mean Miley. I am not thinking about her, at the moment I do not care to."

Eduardo feels the depth of Tyler's heart. Tyler is trying to break loose of his emotional bond with Miley but it is not yet possible. The love buried within him is strong enough to fuel Cupid's bow. Since the car had stopped, it was only seconds before he began thinking of her.

The door is tall and black and the knockers are made of titanium, and they are comparably big enough to match the size of car tires. Eduardo stands before it and mumbles some Latin, "Aperi."

The sound of the world's biggest lock unlatches itself and the big doors creak open. There is a small space to stand but there is a black place mat beneath them, and before them black curtains. Eduardo waves his hand left to right and the curtains spread wide in both directions. A light takes Tyler's vision away, which is brighter than gazing directly into the sun. He throws his hands up and covers his eyes, but momentarily, and as he lowers his hand he witnesses his presence in a great hall.

A massive golden chandelier hangs above the well-lit room. On the walls are gold lacings along the seams of the doorways and alongside the floor. Enormous pictures and antique objects decorate the perimeter like some grand mansion from the 1920's. In the middle of the hall is a white piano, bigger than any Tyler has ever seen. The bench placed under the keys has a hard top with the legs bending inward, and it is big enough for the Hulk to rest and find his calmer side. The floor is marble black with paintings of people and what appear to be angels and demons living about freely. It is like the floors tell a story about the characters in the paintings on the wall. Tyler looks in amaze but curiosity piques and Eduardo can sense inquisition.

"They are all leaders. Well at least at some point and time. Many of them are well known by many religious extremist and were led by a specific power you all here call God," says Eduardo walking slowly next to Tyler who is admiring the paintings.

"Why do you say 'we all here,' like there is somewhere other than here? And you said we call God. God has more than one name?" Tyler asks.

Eduardo smirks and replies, "Nothing is what it seems my friend. Everything has a place and is placed somewhere. For humans it is earth, for angels it is heaven, and for others less comfortable environments."

"You mean hell?"

"Hell is another word for it. Others call it home."

"From what I hear about hell, I'm not sure anyone but one person would find that place a comfy confine," says Tyler. Just as he finishes his words his head begins to thump. The room begins to spin and he throws his hands on his head. A voice whispers, "*Go on with me, do not forget I am here.*"

The spinning stops and the thumping sound slows down instantaneously. "What is that? Did you hear that?"

Eduardo raises an eyebrow, "Nothing," he replies shrugging his shoulders. "It was a voice. I know the voice," Tyler proclaims.

"*What did it say?*" The room begins to dim and Eduardo looks forward to a hallway. It is dark, and with the exception of a white and gold six-foot vase, nothing else can be seen. Creaking of wheels can be heard from a far. He can hear an awkward sound, and it is comparable to a dresser dragging across the floor scratching a path. A single light illuminates over the archway and a voice deep and very sinewy breaks the silence.

"Hello friend of a friend."

Tyler looks at Eduardo and then to the archway. A pair of black shoes, shiny and expensive looking are in the balance of the foot rests. Slacks sharp enough to cut through a bone and creased with perfection, rest seated beneath a black jacket buttoned over a white shirt, also with the collar unbutton. His hair is long and grey and his face aged with scars and wrinkles. He is wearing shades as black as a cold night under a full sonar eclipse. The wheels on the chair are rolling by themselves slowly progressing forward. His hands are resting in his lap folded over a strange looking cane. "What is your name?" The man asks.

Tyler looks at Eduardo who nods toward the man insinuating he has directed his question to him. "My name is Tyler. All due respect sir but who are you?" He asks freeing his hands to his side skeptical of his new environment.

"I am Savatir," says the man as the wheelchair stops just as he pronounces the last syllable. He places the foot of his cane on the floor and taps it twice quickly. Physically, energy takes the room and Savatir stands and begins walking towards them. Tyler is trying to set in place his perception, but is it magic when someone asks you to pick a card and guesses that same card without ever seeing the card? Or is the real magic trying to understand why a man who can walk relies on a system of unnecessary support. Riddled in thought, he attempts to keep his business minded, however, like Eduardo – Savatir can sift out thoughts.

Cane balanced, Savatir stands four feet between them. A piquing curiousness develops in his mind as he looks upon Tyler. Tyler is not scared, neither nervous and he knows it. He can sense it, but it is the reoccurring thoughts keeping Tyler from being controvertible about this peculiar man.

"Who is she?" He inquires as the thought had been giving off energy since Tyler stepped into the mansion.

Tyler looks off and sighs. Savatir looks to the ground and then back up, "Do not worry, I will not ask. Your mind is troubled, I am sorry. And your heart, it is marked. What have you done?" An incriminating tone of voice insinuates foul play.

"I did not do anything, which is why I am here."

Eduardo moves his hands behind his back as he looks to the floor. Something rushes his mind, a quick thought. He can sense a removal of permission taking place. Tyler begins blocking his thoughts; he can sense that their asking him questions may be an overly kind gesture instead of curiosity.

"He has killed the Ziga beast. He has been chosen. Virtiolic has sought out to recover the Deagel child," announces Eduardo. He sulks regretfully, impeding on the investigation of Tyler's presence. Tyler in disbelief replies, "Wait, chosen? By who and for what?"

Savatir chuckles in his verification, "Yes, chosen. No one can just kill a Ziga beast. The mere fact you have accomplished that task makes you man number one. See we need something and if what I hear is true, you are our guy. And the tiger you have killed protected by a curse, it is a curse that marks its victims with an obligation."

Too much information too soon Tyler's hand gestures implied. "What obligation?" He asks, "How is this even possible," pausing, "spirits and curses or whatever?" Tyler asks also demanding answers with a straight on stare.

Savatir replies, "Because Vitriolic did the curse himself." Thunder claps like a volcano erupting, immediately the ceiling cast out a red light. Lit is the room and bright red the ceiling shines. A beam of energy shoots to the center of the room and Vitriolic appears with Miley in his grasp.

"Yes I did, and tonight someone will return the untimely favor," he says.

Tyler leaps to defense, "Miley," looking to Eduardo he asks, "What is going on?"

Vitriolic holds her tight as his grip increases in pressure. Savatir teleports over to Tyler and begins a rant, "For a long time we have been searching for a device, one that will free those enslaved and forgotten." As Savatir speaks, the grand lobby mesmerizes Miley, and it takes her a second to restore her attention, as she has never seen an interior so enormous. The gold on the paintings and walls are glowing just like that of her shoulder and arm where her mark lies. She feels like she is in a place of a royal stage, she likes it, but unfortunately there is no time for her to appreciate it. Vitriolic is fierce and furious and his grip is demanding death.

"Boy, have you any idea the trouble you have caused me?" Vitriolic says shuffling the mystery more. Savatir continues, "Your presence here is not without history," looking to Miley, "Neither yours, which is a mystery to be solved later Deagel. For now, you my boy are the one who will help us."

Tyler wide-eyed is stunned but darkened in thought. Savatir speaks but he cannot yet interpret his words. "What are you talking about? Eduardo said we are here to clear me of this curse."

Laughter fills the hall, as Vitriolic and Savatir know truly why Tyler is standing before them. Dimness enters the lobby and Eduardo's eyes glow orange, just as well does Vitriolic. Savatir begins to recollect the history, "When God created the heavens and the earth, he did separate light from darkness. But, before the light there is a lack of detail before the tale." He fiddles with his cane and begins walking along the wall of the hall, defying gravity as he passes the great paintings.

"Satan was not cast out of heaven but instructed out. It was an appointment of punishment, sentenced to govern the dammed and foreseen to sin beyond repentance. We were neglected before trial, far before we ever knew our ability to sin. Your God dammed us to a burning pit without ever pleasuring us with the chance. And that is where you come in– Tyler. For long we have searched and begged for forgiveness at our ignorance. But also, long we have been ignored. No longer will this negligence persist. See heaven has a gate, a door. Our father who art in heaven, has sealed the gates from us with a key. A sacrifice you know as his son."

An impatient and confused Tyler inserts his objections, "I get that, but what the hell does that have to do with me?" Looking to Miley he restates his question, "What does this have to do with us?"

Vitriolic's voice speaks fierce, "EVERYTHING," and Savatir aids his words, "You will help us retrieve this device, as chosen you will help us breach the gates of heaven and seek our own judgment."

"And how do I do that," Tyler ask.

Eduardo steps forward from the darkness of the hall and replies, "Death."

"Miley," Tyler shouts ignoring his words. She turns quick – hair flipping over her shoulders as seeing Tyler make an attempt to escape is a relief, or at least it would have been. That is before Vitriolic waves his hand up and walls of water form from the floor rising to construct a cell around her. *Magic, more magic* thought Tyler unsure of Vitriolic's plan. His intentions seem to be pure revenge. Yet, why would a cursed tiger be of any help to him? Tyler ponders before raising his own concerns.

"What is this really about, and what does she have to do with this?" Tyler asks.

Savatir finally breaks silence snapping his fingers once. The wall of water falls and the ceiling returns to its normal setting, dim. Secrets are all around the room, Eduardo knows more than he speaks, Vitriolic has yet to disclose his true dissatisfaction with Tyler's actions, and Savatir is evidently more involved in this madness. Tyler wants to know it all, but being as though he has no leverage he takes to improvising. Something about that tiger is more significant than demonic possession. And if he is to uncover what exactly is going on, Tyler is going to have to worry a lot less about a cold memory heating up for the presence of Miley.

Minutes to go - part 17

Look who showed up

Tyler bolts over towards Miley and Vitriolic raises his hand revealing his palm. In the center is an imprint that had been branded into his skin. He begins speaking Latin, "vos mos intereo" and in the quickness of a blink of an eye a force of energy pushes Tyler back. He slides across the room and crashes into an antique table, bursting a vase at the top into pieces.

"Leave her alone," shouts Tyler picking himself up holding his side.

Vitriolic chuckles and removes his smile as he says, "Your weeping for your broken love is pathetic. She does not even love you anymore, why is it you still care? The dread you must suffer to be human."

"He is lying to you Tyler," Miley utters quickly before Vitriolic teleports over to her and places his hand around her neck. At the moment, Tyler cannot form any thoughts that can help him take control of this situation. Confused and unable to assure himself that Vitriolic is lying about how Miley feels, he chooses in the moment to ignore whether it is true or not. Nothing bothers him more than any thought pertaining to Miley and how she feels about him, however as Miley gasp for air there is no time to debate.

Tyler looks to Eduardo, "Can you help us?"

In a cold stare, he looks to Tyler and replies, "Boy, no action or words of mine can be made or said in your favor. How is it you think you have come to be in this predicament?"

Anger forces its way into Tyler's unstable emotional state. "You lured me here? What the hell? Giving his attention to Vitriolic, he pleads, "Release her, and just use me. Whatever you are trying to do use me instead and let her go," and Vitriolic releases his grip dropping Miley to the floor. A feeling of control crept into Tyler's thoughts. Still he is baffled and shy in his effort to be creative. Evidently, these three men are in possession of some powers that wit may not be the best defense to.

Savatir walks to the center of the room hands in the air as to congratulate Tyler on his submission, "And it has been settled. The boy will be our sacrifice. Take him to the chambers."

The way Savatir said chambers raises Tyler's eyebrows. If sacrifice is not enough to break his spirit, the thought of being in any room called a chamber – will. He can only envision chains and torture devices like such of medieval times. If there is anything he finds more discomforting than losing Miley, it would be ideas of endless torture and death soon after. The feeling of death becomes a stalking horse. A chill compresses to his skin, and his hands begin shaking.

In this very moment, he considers that he may truly die. Trying desperately to conceive some form of faith, the thoughts of escaping are now more prevalent than ever. Alongside such an idea is the inclination to know why he must die.

"Why? Why me," Tyler begs to know for the sake of constellation.

Eduardo had been a mute for nearly their entire experience. However, this is his cue to fill in any grey areas. His footsteps appear louder and firmer. Every time his foot hits the ground Tyler hears and feels a thump. But what he thinks to be Eduardo's march of death turns out to be his own heart beating like a steam engine. As he stands five feet away from a kneeling Tyler, he speaks with clarity, "Just as the time during Christ, a life must be offered up for the evil. This life will pay for the weight of our demonic nature. You are a special boy, and you have a special purpose."

Unable to find closure through the truth, Tyler begins to wish he never asked. Fortunate for Tyler, his fear becomes his spark of innovation. A hopeless mind becomes a strengthened heart as Tyler seeks his last resort, prayer. In seconds, he remembers his time with Dawson in the white room, and then he also remembers speaking with God and as well God's instruction.

Tyler mumbles, "Go on with me, and remember I am here."

A hole burst through the center of the ceiling, and an enormous light takes the entire room blinding any and every open eye, except Tyler's. Vitriolic, Eduardo, and Savatir all fall to their knees defenseless and confounded. Their hands cover their eyes, as the shine is far too bright to risk peaking at the source.

Tyler, with visibility, dashes over to Miley and grabs her forearm as if he has acquired super strength. His slim build takes her to her feet in a light but focus pull. Quickly he turns to look for an exit, but no door is visible. His hands begin shaking in confusion, knowing they entered through a door but not sure as to why he cannot see one.

The birth of light still filling the room keeps the three demons in an immovable state. Yet, Tyler cannot waste any more time being confused as his adrenaline is supplying his athletic body with confidence. They do not want to still be present when and if the light fades out completely. Left and then right his eyes check for an exit but nothing is within line of sight. He feels a bit blundered knowing that when he arrived, there was a door. In fact, there were many doors, but as of right now, the room is this big dome. The only thing he can see is the paintings and stained windows. And then, an idea crosses his mind. It is an insane thought, but up against dark forces, he feels no inclination to refuse to see his thought into fruition.

"I hope this doesn't just work in the movies," he says clutching Miley's hand firm in his own. He sprints like a cheetah and just as he does the light begins to fade. Savatir shouts in anguish and Vitriolic growls in gruesome pain and frustrating rage.

"Jump," Tyler yells as Miley leaves her feet but a breath after he leaps. Into the air they go jumping towards the glass window like some action packed movie scene. About one foot before they hit the glass, it cracks on its own, almost as if something hits the glass before they even make contact.

And then, a loud cracking filled the room and they both scream as they begin to fall two stories into a pond on the side of the mansion. Water floods the garden as they land and splash like two boulders landing into a lake of ice. Drenched and gasping for air, Tyler smiles leaning over with his hands on his knees after climbing out. Of all things speculated in movies, in this very moment Tyler believes anything is possible. His satisfaction with his movie like escape is interrupted by nearby bushes, which begin to rattle uncontrollably. Vines grow in size and the thorns alongside them thicken in width. A sound of branches snapping correlates to cracking knuckles. Darkness has tainted the green life and set it upon a rage.

Tyler turns around kneeling to lift Miley out of the water. A long branch with thorns – at least sixteen inches long, ferociously swings above their heads just barely missing a kill point.

They dash through the garden as thorns graze their limbs leaving abrasions all over. The vines whip into the air and grab Miley's ankle wrapping her leg like a roll of thread, and next, they begin to tug her into the ground. As if things cannot get worst, Tyler leaps to her aid. He grabs her arm and gives in just enough before forcing his entire weight in the opposite direction. As the vines rip from place, he pulls her away from their ravage intentions. Every speculation about magic or supernatural happenings is of evident reflection.

Unable to yet enjoy their escape, they both still fight for their chance to remain in one piece. However, in this garden of hell it is becoming less likely to remain hopeful for life, especially when something is giving every effort it can to capture and kill you. The vine snaps immediately but thorns have already pressed painfully into Miley's leg. She screams and uses her free leg to push away just in time before another thicker vine noxiously swipes for her ankle. Darkness would be surrounding them, yet the moonlight is brighter than ever noticed before. In a way, as Miley looks up in agony, she thinks for a second, she sees the moon lighting up a path through the garden as if it is a guiding light. But her eyes lose focus as Tyler scoops her up.

"We have to get the hell out of here."
Miley is exhaling in agony and stress, "How?"

"There," Tyler points to a wall ten feet away. Sprinting for it, the ground shakes as if an earthquake suddenly hit. Stumbling over their own steps, it is evident escaping is being optioned alongside death. Dead plants surround them sending out a hint of hopelessness. Moonlight hovers over their efforts to escape, coincidently in their favor. Reaching the wall feels like cold water soothing an aching burn, and as hope arrives – Tyler grabs Miley's waist and lifts her to the peak of the wall wasting no time to look back. Following behind her, they jump down to the sidewalk and sprint up the street gasping for oxygen.

Stopping beneath a street light and relieved of fear for the moment, they reflect on the actuality of what happened. If anything is to be certain, it is that this is more than real. Panting over their knees, nothing for a moment is taken for granted, like their ability to run some more. At this point, they are taking no chances and making no stops until they are far away from any street that connects them to the idea of dark and unpredictable.

After walking for a mile and a half they begin approaching a gas station, which is poorly lit. Tyler has his arms wrapping Miley like a beach towel, and even though he is not the hulk, his arms are long and his back is wide. Miley being short, she fits comfortably in his arms making it easier for her to relax. However, Tyler is a bit uncomfortable having to lean down over her. They are still drenched but the night is without wind and at a warm temperature, still, Miley shivers but only out of shock and not a mild climate. Her thoughts are racing trying to piece together what exactly is happening.

Many thoughts are at the top of Tyler's mind, and one being the fundamentals of survival. As the reality of Vitriolic's efforts is evidentially embedding in his perception, Tyler cannot determine what exactly Savatir means by "*You have your sacrifice.*" Even as lucidly as the statement was made, it is still controvertible.

First a tiger brews a curse, and second Eduardo flips sides like a double agent. Critical inspection of his own thoughts raises the flood gates pouring in curiosity – as to why Vitriolic had kidnapped Miley. Answers are like a hot shower, which neither of them has, so before jumping to conclusions, sticking to finding safety and shelter becomes their priority.

Tyler opens the door to the Stop Shop but before they enter, he looks behind them to ensure all is safe, or at least for now. The distance they have walked secures in their minds that they have gotten away from harm. With all that just occurred nothing is definite, Eduardo's trickery certified that reality. And his deception sub-consciously brings Tyler to begin an investigation of his own. There is little self-discrediting due to the fact his focus is aiming to hit a pattern. Figuring out what moves Eduardo played on him exactly will explicate how far out of the loop they truly are.

Darkness can take away your sight, but deception is in darkness, and that can collapse your reality.

He pulls some wet dollar bills from his pocket and a phone soaked with a blank screen. "Crap, my phone is broken. Where is your phone?" He asks Miley. However, her hand bag is not at her side, which means neither is her phone. Calling for help is ideal, yet Tyler has not actually factored in who he is intending to call. Teri finding out that Miley and Tyler are together and that her daughter was almost killed by some angry dandelions, would most likely set her into a rage. One reason will be for Miley's disobedience and her second reason just for principal.

The clerk behind the counter is an elderly man, face full of hair and a head without a strand. He is sitting on a stool watching TV in black and white picture. It is an old TV with a hanger as the antenna and two knobs for tuning channels. A name tag is visible but the letters are not. And, he is not really watching the TV so much as the TV's fuzzy screen is watching him.

"Sir, do you have a phone we can use?"

He does not respond eyes remaining glued to the screen that flutters in and out of picture. Tyler asks again, "Excuse me sir..." And the old man jumps in fear as if they are ghost.

"Sorry sir, do you have a phone we can use."

He replies, "Give me a heart attack will you. It is in the back but I cannot let you go back there. You kids look like hell." If only he knew the half of it, they felt like they had been through hell for but just minutes ago.

Miley steps forward, "Sir this is an emergency, we need to use your phone."

"We just need to make a call that's it," Tyler says. But the man has an unsure look. The gas station was the only stop on the road and he is not overly fond of strangers, especially teenage kids who typically stop in and shop lift knowing he is beyond his running years. However, they do not fit the profile of teens that usually enter for mischievous purposes. Most teens are wearing hooded jackets and scatter about the store without speaking. Because they spoke first his sympathetic side moves into play.

"What is going on with you two? And why are your clothes wet, a bit late to be taking a swim I'll say," the old man says.

Tyler takes a deep breath and says, "Sir you would not believe us if we told you. We don't want to cause any trouble we just really need to use your phone." The door opens and a bell at the top jingles as a man with a hooded trench walks in. He walks to the back aisle and stops. Pretending to observe some small car utensils, the man peaks from the darkness of his hood. Noticing quickly, the clerk reaches below the counter for his gun, he does not raise it but applies a comfortable grip just in case.

"Can I help you sir," he asks looking towards the man. The lights in the store flicker as the man turns to their direction. Miley turns around and as she does the man lifts his head. His face has strange markings, hieroglyphs like that of the side of the mansion. Tyler notices quickly and issues warning, "Don't worry about it sir, we are leaving." Before they can budge, the hooded man teleports, and then he reappears behind the counter.

"No one is leaving," he says in a fierce tone.

Grabbing his gun, the elderly man raises it in attempt to shoot. Not quick enough, the hooded man grabs the barrel of the gun with his hands and with ease shoves the handle back into the clerk's head. Blood splatters onto the TV and window as his lifeless body drops to the floor. Miley screams and Tyler grabs her hand racing out of the door. It is the first time she has ever seen anyone die. From the movies and hearing about it, it was nothing compared to what she saw. Her expression runs cold and the fear building up her side is breaking down her ability to remain emotionally stable.

They burst through the door causing the bell to jingle uncontrollably; running to the street no one is around and they are surely alone, yet the sounds of silence keeps them company until one lamp post standing tall – providing light – flickers before bursting and shattering glass all over them. Tyler throws his arm and shoulder over her to shield her from falling shards. Nothing can be seen but the remains of what used to be a well sourced light bulb losing the energy to stay bright.

"I said no one is leaving," his voice echoes from the darkness, and the area becomes totally pitch black. They can see nothing and Tyler says quickly, "Miley get behind me." The man does not look like Vitriolic and neither Savatir nor Eduardo, but his movements and manipulation of physics insinuates he is of their covenant. But Tyler assures himself he must be a demon.

Tyler begins thinking of every possible reaction to something jumping out at them, from the gloomy picture they are facing. Whether he had been skilled in martial arts or even had a gun, nothing currently is going to make a strong defense against a force they cannot see. Still he preserves his innovation directing his confidence to many *what if* circumstances, and even then, all that can be wrong, will be wrong.

A dark feeling overcomes them and their skin begins to feel an immense heat. "Where did he go," Miley asks squeezing Tyler's hand as if she is in labor. "I don't know I cannot see."

Fear is like tiny insects crawling over their skin. They want to run but where to is the mystery, and not to mention it will create attention if the demon is someone to fret over. In an instant, headlights appear to their left turning into the station. Speeding like a bullet, a truck rushes towards them and they throw their hands up blinded by the headlights. “What is it now?” Tyler has little faith that anyone speeding that fast is here to put 20 on pump 6. And at that, plans to stop for coffee and lemon pie.

The demon reappears reaching his hand to grab Tyler, and his fingers just centimeters away, are not close enough. Only inches away from smashing into them, the truck shoots pass them spinning its rear around a pump station like some drifting track car, and then it collides with the demon’s body throwing him back into the store window. As glass shatters and a loud crash rumbles the street, the truck stops next to them and the back door pops open.

"Get in the truck," a man shouts wearing a flannel shirt and trucker hat. His eyes are bright blue and skin as clean and clear as a new born. While they know nothing of this man, it is better to get in than impugn his command. Without a third thought, they look at each other and determine safety is not something they rather question, and then they jump in the truck and slam the door shut.

Pulling off, Miley looks out of the back window and the

demon thrust his hand forward. An incredible force surges through the vehicle bursting all the windows. The power is so explosive it lifts the back tires of the vehicle. Glass falls all over them as they lie in the backseat and the driver yells, "Stay down," swerving back into the road and speeding off into the distance.

Minutes to go - part 18

Story time

On a dark road driving to who knows where, Tyler looks up to see nothing is tailing them or chasing after them. A thought of relief rest in his mind but he is very much in preparation to expect anything from this stranger. Who he is does not matter more than understanding what they just went through. Whether or not Miley and Tyler can accept the truth, death is still chasing after them. Something dark and still confusing is stalking their ability to think of anything else they can consider life. However, this is real and Tyler begins to accept it, Miley on the other hand is fighting fear with disbelief.

Miley brushes glass off of her shoulder and legs before staring into Tyler's eyes. Her look of fear and confusion insists Tyler explains. Yet, he has nothing to say, at least not much that can already baffle them more than they already know. Truthfully, Tyler knows just as much as Miley and just as less to explain what is going on. As Tyler looks down into the seat unable to piece together anything yet, he then remembers what his old mentor in high school, Mr. Hurt used to tell him, “If you don't know, ask.” And then Tyler directs his attention to the driver.

"Who are you man?" Tyler asks.

The man – eyes forward shouts, "I said stay down."

Miley tucks back into the seat but Tyler wants answers and refuses to remain in the dark. He shouts, "Stop the damn truck," and the man replies, "I cannot do that, unless you want to die."

"DIE? Are crazy, you are going to kill us?" Tyler asks in desperation to know.

He slows down and says, "If I were going to kill you, you'd be dead already. I do not kill people. Now stay down."

As bad as Tyler wants to refuse, the man did save their lives, and, his questions are not at the moment going to get answered. Not while the man is speeding down the road to a destination they know not where. Miley feels far from home and too far for personal comfort to set in. She had traveled but only once or twice in her life and that also supports her reason for wanting to go on her college tour. Yet, this is no college tour and it is not a vacation. It is a busted SUV with no music playing and a driver without a name given to comfort their curiosity. Tyler is more receptive to the conflicts of the night but he also refuses – in Miley's presence – to show fear.

Actually, in some way even with near death experiences taunting them, he has his concerns also focusing on showing anything that can regain Miley's attention. If that means being brave, Tyler might just run through fire if he thinks she is watching. Some may find it silly to put away the recent events for emotions that have no current receptacle. Miley is not thinking about Tyler or how he feels, but Tyler knows and because her reactions are so foreign to him, he feels pledged to return to her heart. While she stares into her lap, attempting to avoid looking at anything that can remind her she is in this situation, he stares at her. He admires her hair and ears, eyes and nose, and her soft lips. And in that moment he envisions kissing her. In that moment, her love for him still exists, for now.

Hours later...

A sunray is piercing into the passenger window and opening Miley's eyes like blinds turned north. Tyler is still sleep and snoring with his arm around her, she lifts her head from his chest and in the distance she hears chatter. But first, she looks at him and realizes she had fallen asleep in a position that can resemble what does not exist. Her feelings for Tyler are not completely gone, but she does not love him, and that is hard to portray when falling asleep on his chest like a lover expects his love to do, happens.

Strong voices, voices of men are heard in the background and outside of the truck. The tone of voices is deep enough to influence her to wake Tyler.

"Tyler, get up!"

He shrugs and remains unbothered. Miley balls a fist and plants a heavy pound into his chest, "Tyler, wake the hell up."

Uncomfortably positioned, he leans up cracking his neck and limbs. They hear laughter and Miley looks to the ignition but the keys are gone. She begins searching around the front of the vehicle but nothing. Just broken glass and dirty papers lie in the seats.

"Looking for something?" The man says leaning into the right side front passenger window.

Miley screams while Tyler jumps up and out of the vehicle. Tyler is not much of a fighter but he will fight and certainly knows how, only not with his fist. Tyler is a very creative soul, using anything he can to his advantage. Hand full of broken glass, he throws it towards the man's eyes. An almost brilliant move, until he waves his hand over sending the glass in another direction. It looks just like magic, but more persuasively performed with genuine gesture.

"Who are you, and what do you want?"

"I save your lives and you bark at me? My, the gratitude is beyond appreciated," he says, "Nonetheless, I am Simon Peter."

Tyler confused looks to Miley and she shrugs her shoulders clueless as well. He has a hunch but the name is so particular yet rare, he is inclined to ask.

"Simon...Peter, like one of the twelve apostles?" The man smiles and replies, "Not like, is, is one of the twelve apostles."

"No way."

"Way man."

Disbelief is a natural reaction, but for the craziness that occurred last night – and being in the white room with Dawson, Tyler sees no reason to be in doubt. Miley cannot say the same, and so she does not, but her curiosity has been piqued. Stepping out of the truck and onto the dirt, her legs have multiple abrasions. Simon Peter hurries to assist her. Taking her hand, he helps her stand on her two. Miley's leg is sliced up pretty bad and will need attention soon. Simon's eyes grow in surprise as he sees the marks on her shoulder, amazed he asks, "How did you get that?"

"I," she pauses and sighs deeply, "I do not know, it is just there. I have always had it."

Peter let his curiosity rest for now, but the look on his face strikes a dire interest. Tyler hurries over and supports her weight on her right side. They begin walking through tall wheat's and as they do, the laughter increases in the distance. Coming through, they see two men standing holding rifles, they are bigger and buff. One is wearing a white shirt and the other a navy blue polo. Behind them is a house beat to hell and barely standing but from the drapes in the windows, occupied for living. An old black couch with patches of duct tape over the cushions and the armrest, sits on the front porch. Simon Peter and Tyler walk Miley pass the two men and seat her on the couch. She grunts as she sinks into her seat feeling the discomfort in her behind.

"Who are they?"

The man in the blue polo spits and says, "Why don't you ask us?" And then he cocks his gun.

Tyler may not have been the best hand-to-hand fighter, but he certainly is not a coward. He walks over, not close enough to invade and create discomfort but enough to be heard and comprehended. "Who are you?" He says looking him straight in the eyes. In a way, he does not and will not be punk'd in front of Miley, but also as a man, he does not take kindly to being challenged to a pissing contest.

"Kids got melons," the man in the white t-shirt says. He turns to his right and reaches in a cooler pulling out a beer. Placing the bottleneck in between the trigger and the handle, he snaps open the beer with one easy pull. Surprisingly the gun does not go off due to a history of repetitious skill. Simon Peter walks out beside Tyler and begins to make introductions. Pointing to the man in the blue shirt, "That is Andrew, my older brother. And over there," pointing to the man in the white shirt, "that is Phillip of Bethesda."

Tyler cracks a smile and turns in circles, his hands gesturing he has come to another hunch he must speak on. "So wait, wait he is Phillip, Phillip of Bethesda. And, he his Andrew your older brother, and you," closing his hands together and facing them towards Simon, "you are Simon Peter. Is this a coincidence or are you all serious?"

Andrew steps over lowering his rifle to his side, "Look boy, I'm glad you read your bible but here is a news flash, if you are here with us it is because you have saw something. You have seen what gets swept under the rug, the stories people hide in books, and whether you choose to believe it, it's us. And you are here because it is meant to be."

The way he said meant to be causes Tyler to chase around some thoughts. Still smiling, he paces back and forth and walks over to Miley plopping on the couch, resting his elbows onto his knees. Miley perplexed asks, "What is it?"

He stops smiling as his hunch becomes factual evidence and the scattered pieces of events become reality. Instead, before declaring what he feels to be true, true – Tyler allows his thoughts to inquire more reasoning.

"Okay, back at the hospital something happened. I mean it is explainable but unexplainable. I met God. Well, not met him, but he talked to me, oh and Dawson too. He told us to go on with him and back at the mansion, back when that guy was trying to hurt you. I said it, what God told us and that is when the light came," Tyler explains.

Looking at Tyler, Miley is processing his experience. Miley is a believer but more like the sinner who only believes after they sin really badly. In a way, she is not the ideal representation of a Christian.

"Well I am glad it worked," she says. Andrew wiping down his gun states, "It is called faith. Faith worked."

Simon Peter walks over and stands just at the edge of the porch. He knows Miley and Tyler have no idea what they are up against or have been through.

"When a force of evil is present, fear fuels it. Disbelief and lack of courage is responsible for the darkness that seeps into the energy, almost like how Carbon Dioxide blends with Oxygen. Faith however, faith can be a weapon against the darkness. It can be used at any time and if strong enough, it can eliminate the existence of any evil presence. The light you saw was the beginning of a casting," Simon explains.

Tyler attentive and paired with the information is soaking up Simon's explanation. However, Miley has her thoughts preoccupied with other sights. Like Andrew and Phillip who stood tall and very buff. Andrew has blue eyes as well and long hair to his shoulders and his face is covered with a well groomed five o'clock shadow. Phillip is cleaner but has long hair as well tied up and pulled back. His goatee is shaped up but thick with hair. Her eyes are embracing lustful desires and indecent thoughts.

"Casting?" Tyler questions.

Simon replies in confidence, "Yes, like that of our instructions given in the book of Matthew. Demons, evil, sickened bodies and more we have been giving the power – through faith, by Jesus to cast them all out."

Unable to stop smiling, Tyler almost feels joy. But only for seconds, before he is turning towards Miley, observing her gazing upon Andrew and Phillip. Tyler's smile drops like a quarter off a cliff. Simon observes as well but reserves his words. Tyler removes himself from the couch and walks to the far end of the porch psychologically dismissing himself from disturbing views. He leans on the rusting banister and then turns around, "So what is really going on? Why is some lunatic trying to kill me over a tiger I did not even technically kill?"

Simon speaks, "I have heard of your bravery, it is admirable and your selfless act is highly recognized by us, however, you are not up against a lunatic, and that tiger was not just an animal. It was a demon." Tyler is not shy of this tale so he begins to cover what he knows, "I know, it is something about Ziga and being protected by dark spirits." Simon's eyes grow, he knows they know little but had no idea they knew of Ziga. The name being spoken turns the eye of Andrew and Phillip, who even being a few meters away heard the reference. Miley regains focus as the two men approach and returns to the discussion.

"What is Ziga?" She asks.

Simon pulls a small notebook from his back pocket and holds it in hand. He then says, "Ziga is the unmentioned ancient demon legion. A secret society of demons not even Satan himself knows of." Or so they thought, but as of late secrets are blossoming.

Tyler steps fast, "What? As bad ass as that sounds it is actually kind of hard to believe," and Miley follows, "and creepy."

Nonetheless, it is true and Simon has not even begun to inform them of the more unsettling news. Miley and Tyler are stumbling into something very big and dangerous, a situation far more deleterious to their lives than an animal attack, and being a human sacrifice. In the meantime, Tyler embraces their seclusion. For now, their lives are not being threatened. And regardless of how weird it feels to be stationed outside a busted looking shack, with three men claiming to be disciples, mentally it feels safe. And that is good enough for Miley and Tyler to bank on. The absence of normality is safe enough to accept when abnormality replaces reality of the sane.

Minutes to go - Part 19

History Class

Simon begins flipping through pages of his notebook and pin points his index finger on a particular page. The word ***Ziga*** is written in old English, and beneath the word are pictures of monsters with long sharp teeth and horns and some with more limbs than others. The group is huddling around a fire and in the center is an ox head that has been placed on the body of a man. In the picture, also are men with hoods like that of the man back at the gas station, with markings on their arms and face.

"Ziga hunts for doorways. It is their purpose we believe." says Simon.

Tyler a bit confused asks, "If they are not even known to Satan, then who gave them a purpose?" Andrew butts in, "They did," and Simon continues to explain, "Not every evil spirit has the same plans. Not every demon follows behind Satan. What he seeks is a minor goal compared to what the Ziga are after." The question does not need to be asked, however to be sure, Miley speaks on her need to know.

"What are they after?"

A silence sets in, Andrew looks at Phillip and he looks back, and then they both look to Simon, as he is the only one who should answer her question. Simon Peter looks to the ground and then out into the wheat field. The information he is about to deliver he knows he has to tell, and yet he does not quite race to speak as something bothers him. A look of high concern takes his face and then he speaks, "Ziga are after the key."

Tyler and Miley respond simultaneously, "The key to what?"

Stepping up onto the porch, Phillip walks past Simon Peter looking him dead in the eye, and then he looks to the pair and says, "The..." Miley impedes and says, "Key to Heaven."

Peter asks with no hesitation, "How do you know that?" A lie before the truth is spoken out of shame to share the actual facts, "It is hard to explain but I was warned."

"When, how, and by who?" Peter demands to know.

"I was at restaurant and," feeling silly to share but she continues, "a dead girl or ghost told me before I went to the concert." Tyler stunned replies, "You went to the concert?"

He feels the warmth of loneliness wrap his body. "Wow, I am glad I did not go."

"Why would you, you do not like stuff like that." Tyler responds, "Pete invited me, why do you care?"

Her face struck with absence of life, "Tyler, what are you talking about?" His words are making no sense to her. A truth is about to shatter his world, and something about him mentioning the name invites a scary taunt. She shakes her head confused and replies, "Tyler you should not play like that, and Pete did not invite you. This is not funny."

But, Tyler is as sincere as ever. He meant what he said but to hear it from him makes Miley uncomfortable. The words, Pete's name being mentioned, it all doesn't fit. She cringed as he asks her, "What is wrong with you?"

"Tyler... Pete is dead. You know that he died a year ago in a car accident.

Darkness shades his eyes and emptiness is throughout his body. Tyler cannot fathom how he forgot and neither can she. Things are getting really dark, darker than ever before. He knows for sure it was Pete that called him. His voice is still vividly playing in his head. *How?* He thought begging his inner self-conscious for answers.

Had he put Pete's tragic death out of his mind, or had this been some strange paranormal act. Needless to say, Miley is right. Pete had been dead for at least a years pass. Simon Peter invokes his insight, "Ziga is behind it all."

A strong assumption, although not truly conceived with confidence. Phillip, sterner begins digging into the significant matter at hand. "We do not have time for this Peter. We need to act now before they locate the key."

Unable to hold in their instant shock, they both shout, "What!" Tyler then asks, "Wait so there is a key to heaven, like an actual tool that unlocks a door to heaven? Oh wow." As he begins to get dramatic throwing his hands outward, and Miley squints her eyes in ponder. She lowers her head and takes a thought – flipping her hair out of her face. It sinks in, the clues begin to pair up and Miley has figured it out.

Miley stands to her feet and throws her hands out, "I do not believe it," she looks to Simon Peter and shakes her head left to right as she comes to her disapproving realization, "You lost the key didn't you? I saw the way he looked at you."

Lying is not an option even if the secret is out, but a more frightening reality, Miley is right. Simon Peter had lost the key. Walking into the house, Phillip shakes his head in disappointment. Simon knows his wrong, but more importantly he knows his mission. While things are beginning to clear up, one thing is still foggy.

"They key is lost, but it is not actually a key as it is a person. A pure soul, kind, generous, and loving but a soul responsible for unlocking the gates upon death is truly the key. For some reason I can no longer see the key. It, he or she, gives off energy. But, I cannot find them, and it's been like this for five months now." Peter explicated with a sulking impression.

"So how do we play a role in this, why was the sacrifice necessary?" Tyler asks.

If great minds truly think alike, Miley and Tyler already have an idea of why they may have been selected as sacrifices. However, nothing is more pure to the mind than clarity and they both are in a desperate need to get as much a grip on things as possible. They both are still emotionally going through differences. The distance they are keeping between each other verifies they have hidden tension, tension tucked away like a shirt behind a three-piece suit. Coming to a conclusion could be fairly easy but Tyler is not about to push aside his feelings, not even to be the bigger person.

Vitriolic delivered a heavy blow back at the mansion. His words while cruel – and in Tyler's mind still true, allows Tyler to understand how emotionally removed Miley is. Bringing up the topic at this moment might not end well, but it is Tyler and when he has the need to know, he asks.

Looking to Miley and standing up, "Why is it I am not good enough for you?"

"Tyler this is not the time," she says rubbing her legs. He should stop here, but again it is Tyler, "If not now, never so we might as well talk now. I mean with our entire history and you plan this undercover escape from Los Tyler mission, which in turn includes ditching the hell out of me. Your grief practically put me in Eduardo's car." She sighs and replies, "Why were you in his car?"

"BECAUSE I WAS DRIVING, SPEEDING THROUGH THE CITY, AND THAT SHIT FELT GOOD," Tyler says grumbling some extra words.

Her hand flips and she replies, "What is your problem, you are so randomly weird."

While his outburst is indeed sudden, his heart is still hurting trying to find an outlet for what he misunderstands. Having feelings for Miley is not a typical cycle of teens that fall in love and fall out because it is life. Truth is, Miley did love Tyler, but she had never envisioned loving him longer than she did. "Weird? You don't just hold in feelings, you let people know what's up instead of tying the noose around their legs. And after it is connected to a bandwagon of dissatisfaction let them go," Tyler explains.

"Tyler I lost interest, it just happened. I cannot help that," his frustration builds, "Are you kidding me? You can help that by having a damn reason other than I lost interest. Eduardo and Vitriolic called you on that. What you did and were doing was heartless," says Tyler.

Confusion is reaching a peak, Miley has no other explanation she cares to share. Caring about how Tyler feels matters but her intentions was never to stay, and sadly Tyler is coming to that speculation. Andrew is just watching them argue like a real time soap opera, his arms crossed and smirking, he patiently enjoys their conflict. The sky is getting darker, clouds look like smoke from exhaust pipes, and the wheat's begin to feel the push of a small wind. Miley begins crying, mostly out of guilt but secondly due to regret. Her tears are not flooding her face but even one drop is enough to visually avow her frustration.

She lifts her head and looks to Tyler, "I'm sorry but I just never wanted what you want Tyler. I'm not like you, and I'm not ready to commit my time to limitation. I'm young, and I should be able to have options and be able to go places and not have to stress the thought that I am leaving someone behind because I love them. You are not a bad person, but I just do not want that restriction."

Reality is like a piano slipping from the pulleys, and Tyler's world happens to be the unfortunate by-stander in the falling path. Miley has every right to want what she does, and while Tyler and his perception remain inseparable, understanding how she feels is not all that unfeasible. Psychologically, Tyler is well aware of her free will to venture off into life, feeling the relief of locks unsnapping from the emotional cuffs around the wrist of our hearts. Miley's past is full of attention, constant boosting arrogance in her personality through the overly expressed compliments she receives.

Tyler on the other hand, is not so much interested. He actually has awkward encounters with others more than finding connections worth putting effort into valuing. This supports his current hold on his perception of what Miley means in his life. Unfortunately, no matter what point of view he advertises for sympathy, her opinion and decision still deserves respect.

"You know, I know we are young and I know that you have options, but using age and the ability to be porcupine is a bit over exerted. I mean people act like meeting the wrong people is all that good, like falling for someone who looks at your lips more than your smile is worth lying about how you feel," Tyler says almost entering a rant. But, Miley shorts that effort with a very stern opposition, "Who lied to you Tyler?"

He walks closer to her and his eyes widen as he says, "You did Miley, you are still inviting me over, kissing, hugging, and talking about a bunch of sweet shit you don't even have a value in anymore."

She stands up insensible to the pain in her leg and replies, "Because, I did not know how to tell you what I was feeling, that is not lying. I was not lying about the truth, I was..." Andrew chuckles as he pardons their quarrel with his snide comment, "Hiding it?"

Like a stone cold killer the look in her eyes beams at Andrew and he immediately walks off. Passing Tyler, he extends his hand balled into a fist and Tyler extends his as they meet for a quick fist pound – solidifying Tyler has every bit of justification in being upset. Their gesture turns Miley around and she begins to walk off. Simon's eyebrows raise in disarrange, Tyler looks down at her leg, and Andrew – almost in the door – double takes glancing at her leg as well. The three gather at the center of the porch, Miley stops walking and turns back around to see the three of them staring at her with owl eyes in the mid of night.

"What?" She says – her tone a lot louder and forceful.

Tyler points to her leg and Simon steps forward and asks, "What happened to your wounds?" She looks at her leg and sees her abrasions have vanished and there is not any blood residue. Much can be speculated but immediately Tyler walks from between the two men and turns to them inquiring the more peculiar interest. "Wait... Why are you two surprised?"

Phillip walks out of the house and looks up at the sky, he then turns to them and raises an eyebrow, "Am I missing out on something?" He asks.

They all turn around and Simon points to Miley's leg, "Her wounds, they have vanished away without casting or healing." Phillip unimpressed replies, "Because she is a Deagel."

Simon replies on cue, "Are you sure?"
"One of the men called me that back at the mansion," Miley interjects.

He nods his head up and down, and then Simon makes a mental connection of the puzzling thoughts, "But I have seen," he pauses and turns to Miley, "Show them, show them the markings."

Miley a bit uncomfortable still subdues, she shows the scars using her thumb to slowly remove her jacket revealing her soldier. Andrew and Phillip are both gazing in awe. Phillip then says, "The Mark," and Simon steps closer walking around her. "I knew it when I first seen it, but she cannot be Sekhmet's descendant."

Confidence moves in Phillip's words like a snake over satin, "But she is and she is of Vexel and Sekhmet. Their secret affair, yet when she turned away from God he cursed her offspring with a dark mark." Simon, hovers his hands over her shoulders replies, "Amazing. This is so rare, an actual Deagel child."

Tyler gains confusion no quicker than Simon raises amaze, "Wait, I'm a firm believer in awesomeness, but I thought– who are these people? God marked her?" Tyler says.

Indeed a good speculation, especially for men claiming to be the followers of Christ. Phillip knows all about the history of "before" Bible.

"God is the creator of all things, and that includes all things before and after man. We are not the first and we will not be the last. There is one true God, but God did create more than man. Man has gotten carried away with religions and false practices; however their information is in some cases an accurate study," says Simon.

Phillip looks to the sky again, he then gazes at the clouds as the sky transforms from prune-orange to solid smoke. "We'd better head in," he says fixing his fingers around his belt.

Entering the shack, the entire exterior could have been camouflaged in ugly, as the inside is well maintenance. Six recliners gather around a fire pit, and around the base of the fire pit are bibles and Rosemarie's. Nearly the entire room from the floor to the walls and ceiling are hardwood. Six windows are on the first level; and along the wall pictures are of all the miracles Jesus performed. The living room is magnificent, and antiques and relics rest in the corners of the house and near the staircase. Miley walks in with her eyes mesmerized by the dream catchers decorating the ceiling.

They all sit down and Andrew cracks open another beer, and then slurp down the beverage like a slave with his dry lips beneath a fountain. The house has a very delicate setting, yet their topic to soon enter the conversation is unfortunately unsettling. Tyler raises the foot of the recliner and leans back. "Feeling at home?" Phillip questions.

"I don't have these at home, so no," replies Tyler drowning his body into the chair.

Miley leans forward and puts one hand in the other, she then crosses her legs and breaks the awkward silence after Tyler's remarks with pending questions, "Who is Sekhmet? And how am I her granddaughter?"

Phillip sits up in eager interest to answer, "Sekhmet is the Egyptian warrior goddess of healing or, just another powerful angel. She was also a lioness and a solar deity, which, is how she met Vexel when her father Ra met with him in secret against God's will. You are not her granddaughter, you are her direct child. A Deagel is one born of an angel and a demon."

Tyler as always inquisitive, asks, "Angels can have children? Wicked."

Shocking fact, but Phillip confirms, "Not until her, because during Vexel's affair with Sekhmet, she betrayed God's love by having relations with a demon, who is Vexel." Andrew crushing his beer can in his hand with one grip cuts in a name, "Vexel, the demon spirit of vexation, which means you have some angry juice cloaked in your system."

Miley shook asks, "I have power?"

Phillip still gazing upon her mark responds, "More than you can imagine."

No need for second-guessing, Tyler heard Andrew crystal. There is a demon of vexation and Miley is the child of Sekhmet and Vexel. His head riddles with all sorts of thoughts, mostly he conceived the idea that all in the room have gathered, Miley's parent is also a demon. The tone in the room is set by their facial expressions and as everyone but Miley ponders her involvement in this mess. *Does Ziga even know?* Phillip wonders, and if they do know, how are they planning her role to be played? Miley is strikingly fierce when she wants to be, Tyler only caught glimpses of those moments when her anger had been expressed. Yet, she did have her moments– and in these moments Teri had taught her to be her calmest.

Keep calm...

Miley begins to reflect on a moment when she was younger.

She was sitting in her sixth grade classroom, and as she was admiring the posters on the wall that reflected motivation, and then a paper ball hit her in the back of her head. It was her first day class and at a new middle school. Teri was at the teacher's desk sharing a laugh with Mrs. Palmer whose daughter was also starting the sixth grade. Her name was Brittany. Miley turned around and seen Brittany seated directly behind her. Two seats to the left were two girls giggling and one girl pointed to Brittany. Unaware of whom threw what Miley stood up and walked to Brittany's desk. Brittany did not feel intimidated by Miley balling her fist and grinding her teeth. Instead she laughed and the girls seated two seats over said, "Not so pretty now." Miley then banged on Brittany's desk so hard that the posters on the wall fell to the ground. The boom dropped a class window and Teri turned around rushing over to Miley. She grabbed her shoulders and asked, "What is wrong?"

Teri looked to her side and on the floor was a paper ball. Miley shouted, "She threw this at my head," pointing to Brittany. In her defense she yelled back, "No I did not." Miley banged on the desk again and the sound shook everything that could feel the vibration of her fist shoot through the desk into the floor. Teri pulled Miley outside of the classroom and looked her right into the eyes. She lowered her head and then brought her undivided back as her mother said, "Miley, you already know what I am about to say," Miley looked off towards the lockers and then looked back at Teri and replied, "Anger makes you vulnerable and people can control you when you are vulnerable."

The fire in the pit flashes stronger and Miley regains consciousness to the group. Tyler well relaxed, is staring at the ceiling dwelling on the pieces to this sudden puzzle of darkness. He then turns his head and says, "So does your mother know this?" And Miley looks off as she begins to ask herself the same question.

Minutes to go - part 20

Time to go

Nothing is more disturbing than knowing you are the gene holder of a healing warrior angel, and as well, a leader of infuriating souls. However, Miley polishes the idea as her eyes observe her scars from her shoulder to her underarm. A freight train in their brain is hauling inquiries as she uncrosses her legs and begins rubbing her hands over her shoulder, "But how do you know all of this just from my birth mark?" She asks.

A more concerning question to her is whether Teri knows about her history. And, if she does, then that means Teri is not her real mother. Such a thought she prefers to store away for now, although the inclination to inquire is tingling at her curiosity.

"After God learned of the deception, he banished Sekhment from her rule turning her human, and while pregnant, God placed his hand onto her gestating stomach. He marked her first-born and any born – after and under the bloodline with the black mark," answered Phillip.

Tyler looks at Miley and as he does she looks away, almost feeling judgment run out of his eyes and into hers. "What happened to Vexel?"

Smirking, Phillip replies, "Well, God imprisoned Vexel in the center of the earth, much like Lucifer in hell, for eternity."

Thoughts become answers as Tyler realizes how information connects. Miley is the child of both good and evil, but more importantly she has power. How much power is the question and as well what she will do with it when she accepts the fact. As much as Miley wants to break out into a rage, she thinks of Dill. Her younger brother loves her and so does Teri, who raised her like she was her own. Hate cannot develop over her love for her family.

"You said the key is missing, why do Ziga want it?" Miley asks. But Tyler can answer that question; his life was almost taken for the one reason Ziga needs the Key.

"They are trying to break into heaven or something." Tyler says.

A loud crash immediately sounds outside the house. Andrew jumps up and grabs his shotgun covetous for action. Tyler, Simon, and Phillip rise to their feet as well fixating their line of sight onto the door way. The front door is still open and the screen door is slapping against the door seal steadily. Darkness is like a bad energy and everyone in the room begins to feel the heating sorrow like steam in a sauna. Giving eye to Simon, who nods his head, Andrew moves toward the door. He readies his gun, stock in shoulder and barrel straight and aiming. His gun is made of oak on the stock and fore stock, and a sterling silver shines from the action bar to the rib and barrel. On the receiver, read the scripture:

"Though I walk in the midst of trouble, you preserve my life; you stretch out your hand against the wrath of my enemies, and your right hand delivers me."

Psalm 138:7

Andrew cocks his gun and slowly opens the screen door with the muzzle. Simon turns around and darts for the back door. Approaching it, he reaches to check the knob and a crackling sound is heard outside of the door. He stops, back peddles slowly and his hand goes behind his back and up under his shirt. He removes a thirteen-inch blade, holding it firm in hand. Dust blows beneath the door onto the floor around his boots. They all are silent and waiting. Darkness is the feeling of sadness and anxiety – filling the room like a vent pumping heat throughout a home.

Suddenly the back door burst open like a bomb detonated on the other side. The demon from the gas station is standing in the doorway and raises his head to show his bloody face. "Wicken," Simon says grimacing.

He swings for Simon's head and Simon leans left avoiding what would have been a straight jab to the face. Simon grabs his arm with one hand and swings the blade with the other, intending to slice across his stomach. But Wicken anticipates the move, and he spins under Simons forearm turning his joints attempting to break Simon's arm in one sharp angle. Wicken is quick but Simon is stronger, and because of that Simon grabs him by the chest throwing him over the counter top into the kitchen. Kitchenware smashes onto the ground as he lands on the sink and rolls to the floor.

Tyler looks to Phillip asking, "Shouldn't we help him?"

Phillip never looks back and says, "He can handle himself," and then Andrew yells, "GET DOWN," as a black ball of energy surges through the front door just missing Andrew's skull.

The ball of energy forms the shape of a man standing behind Miley. It is another demon, and just as furious. Tyler shouts, "No," as the man removes a curvy blade from the sleeve of his hooded robe. Quicker than rainfall, Tyler maneuvers around the chairs and charges the man, spearing his body towards him. Tackling him to the ground, Tyler's face molds an angry expression. While Miley and he shared differences in emotion, his passion for her remains alive and evident as he raises his fist. Just before he sends his blow, the man pushes Tyler off of him, sending Tyler soaring into the wall side along the stairwell. Smashing into the wall, Tyler falls unconscious lying on the floor. He will not be getting up right away after such a powerful impact. The demon then rises to his feet and stares at Miley with no other intent in his eyes but to attack. Fear becomes her blemish as she freezes in place scared into a motionless reaction. Her hands begin shaking and she quivers in terror knowing his next move is surely a deadly strike.

Just before the man budges, Andrew says, "Not today," as his shotgun goes off only an inch away from the demon's head.

Blood splatters and a bright light flashes as the demon's head explodes and his body vanishes into thin air. Miley covered in blood screams in shock after witnessing the brutal kill shot. Glass can then be heard shattering in the kitchen. Simon has Wicken by his robe and thrusting heavy blows into his face. He tosses the blade to Phillip who catches it by the handle. Wicken using all the strength he can muscle pushes away from Simon's grasp like a rock in a slingshot.

Free from grip, Wicken flips backwards over the chair and lands before Miley. His head raises and his eyes glow orange placing sight onto her. He reaches forward, his hand burning in blue flames and intending to catch Miley in his grasp. Before a finger touches her, he roars in pain as Phillip shoves the blade into his ribs. Turning the blade into his side, Phillip recites a phrase, "In the name of Jesus Christ I cast you out of this world," and he removes the blade sending Wicken to the floor bursting into black ash.

"Is everyone okay?" Simon Peter asks breathing deeply.

Stunned in fear Miley does not respond or budge. Andrew runs over to Tyler who is still lying on the floor looking lifeless and beat. He picks Tyler up and carries him over to the chair and placing him onto it. "Kid are you okay?"

Tyler does not respond. Andrew looks to Phillip for help, but he looks to Simon unsure. Approaching Tyler, Simon stands over him and lays his hand upon him. He then says, "In the name on Jesus Christ, you are healed."

Tyler jumps up gasping for air, standing he says, "What the hell just happened?" Miley is still staring at the spot where Wicken fell and perished. Her heart is beating like a steam engine, and she then looks up at them all and faints.

"We have to get them out of here, Andrew can you take them home?" Simon asks. Andrew shrugs his shoulders and replies, "Alright."

Back home

Back in Randallstown, a squad car strolls up the block slowly admiring the environment. The street is quiet and empty. After the attack many of her neighbors have become public recluse. Although police make a decent effort to secure their street, the idea something bad did happen can also mean it can happen, again.

The officer analyzes Andrew's vehicle, but seeing Tyler in the back seat through the back window. He nods his head and Tyler nods back assuring all is safe. His acceptance in the community is truly paying off.

Pulling up to Miley's house, Andrew turns to the back seat and says, "You two cannot stay here long, they will be back." Tyler shoves Miley by the shoulder waking her up. "Miley, we are at your house."

She places her hand on her head and sends her fingers through her hair. Unclear thoughts rush through her mind as well as a headache she suffers from falling to the floor. Tyler reaches to grab her hand but she balls a fist and pulls her hand back. Even though he showed great concern for her, all that she has learned is keeping her from trusting anyone, or letting anyone in at the moment. On top of the fact her distancing demeanor remains to prevent any misconceptions on Tyler's behalf. He then asks, "Are you okay?"

"I am fine Tyler, just let me out."

He opens the door and gets out, and extending his hand to help her out of the vehicle, she ignores his effort and steps out on her own. Deeply confused, he cannot understand why she is behaving so negative towards him, but still he keeps his distance and places his hands into his pockets. She begins walking to the door and Tyler starts to follow, "No, don't. I mean I'm okay, I need to be alone."

It can be difficult to understand her motives and even more her ability to turn off her emotions towards Tyler in the snap of a finger. It appears to him that her feelings were fading long before their encounter with the tiger. Inside, he feels more concerned with how she became the way she is more than her being that way. Tyler immediately begins taking full responsibility, "Listen I am sorry, whatever I did that made this," lowering his head trying to gather his words, "...so wrong."

She sighs and replies while walking to her door, "It is not your fault, and I just need to be alone right now, good bye Tyler."

He exhales and looks to the sky as if the clouds would drop an answer like a tear of rain. Regardless of her stating the fault is not his, having no control over losing someone you love is a reality you assume responsibility of. Especially, when you cannot turn off how much you care. But Miley honestly has more significant concerns, like what she has learned about her mark. As she walks inside, Tyler gazes upon as if she is still standing at her doorstep. It was there they both stood many nights before. He would kiss her and stand before her gazing into her eyes with the deepest heart felt passion.

"Shit happens kid, let's roll," yells an insensible Andrew.

Tyler replies, "It is not that easy. Sometimes I feel like to be loved is to be a burden."

Tyler gets into the vehicle and slams the door. "Easy kid, Beyonze' didn't eighty six your love life," Tyler cracks a smirk, "You named this truck after a pop star?" Andrew squint his eyes and grinds his teeth, "You know, they say don't judge a book by its cover, I say judge a man by his truck."

"But this truck is horrible, and I been meaning to ask how is it that you all are disciples but have guns and drink beer?"

Starting the truck, he looks at Tyler still squinting, "Kid are you a saint? '*Surely there is not a righteous man on earth who does good and never sins. Ecclesiastes 7:20.*' No one is perfect not even us."

A good question Tyler asked, but Andrew referring to the word to support habits, known to man as bad habits, is not acceptable. Although, who is Tyler to judge? After all he does not have the cleanest track record for staying out trouble. He reconsiders his thoughts and determines that a bigger issue is at hand, and then he begins weighing his options.

At the moment, he does not have many, or so it feels that way. With Vitriolic out looking for them and Eduardo knowing where he lives, going home is a sure way to guarantee death. Although, he is not so sure that is the purpose they have for him. If Ziga truly wanted Tyler dead, they could have pursued that interest back at the mansion.

"What's next? I do not know what to do or where to go. Eduardo knows where I live," says Tyler.

Eyes locked on the road, Andrew raises an eyebrow and replies, "and who is that?"

His jaw drops and his nerves quiver beneath his skin, how deceptive is Eduardo that not even Andrew knew of him? Before he raises his next question, he assumes that Eduardo is probably unknown to him, and furthermore he slouches into the seat tilting his head back in thought. With all the information he has learned, could the disciples be just as deceptive as Eduardo. Tyler acknowledges the fact they never announced where they stand or what their intentions are in the situation. Assuming is never the greatest choice in discovering the answers to anything. Yet, it is safe to assume after witnessing Simon Peter beat the crap out of that demon. If Andrew, Phillip, or Simon wanted to do them harm, it would have been less than an effort to do so.

Nothing is sure as far as what is next but Tyler understands the situation even as hard as it is emotionally fathoming the details. If they are telling the truth, the key to heaven is greater than any concern man can ever have. Most daunting is the thought Tyler has about Ziga retrieving it. What would a secret society of demons do with a device like that? Invade heaven, the idea sounds impossible but even the thought of the idea itself, is enough to make him wonder in fear.

Minutes to go - part 21

Anytime now

Miley throws her clothes into a bag and looks at her posters of New York. She is above age to go out on her own and ready to relocate, and not just from Tyler but the entire situation. Her intentions to leave had been well in thought after Tyler's injury. In a way, she had seen him at the time as dead weight. Looking out of her window she envisions the conversation she has to have with her mother, and then she blinks snapping back into reality, knowing that there is no way she can tell Teri that she is leaving for New York. Not to mention the thought crosses her mind that Teri may not even her real mother. It is that thought, or Miley can consider that Teri is some ancient angelic walking relic.

She shakes her head and smirks, as the thought itself sounds idiosyncratic.

There is one person she can call, so she picks up her house phone and dials a number. As the phone rings she stares at the picture by her bedside. It is a picture of Dill and her at the park with baseball gear on. Miley did not play sports but she dressed up in the uniform that day to encourage Dill to give it a shot. It was a big moment because Dill was recluse and frets the very idea of actively being around other kids.

Talking him up, Dill walks into her room and stops as she turns around "Are you okay?" He asks. She hangs up the phone and sits on the bed, and Dill walks over to the bed and takes a plop down. "I'm okay, I just been through a lot," she says looking off into the corner of the room.

Dill looks at her arm and bruises are faint but still visible. "What happened? Did the man with the horns hurt you and Tyler?"

Miley's eyes pop like kernels in intense heat, "What man Dill?" she asks imagining the worst after what she has just experienced. Had Dill seen something, or someone? If so, how has he been so emotionally removed for a six year old; it is expected at such an age to fear being exposed to any demon or creature. Yet, nothing about Dill's presentation insinuates fear or worry. Dill's reaction is less of what is expected and that makes Miley worry about what exactly he might have been exposed to.

He replies, "The man that was at the house, the one with Tyler." She ponders a thought and then returns to inquiring, "Why did you say with the horns?"

Fiddling his fingers, he lowers his head and withdraws, but Miley has to inquire more. She needs to reassure herself that Dill is talking about Eduardo, and if he is, then her worries of relocation are far less significant.

Miley slips her hand into Dill's and asks, "Dill, what did you see?"

Turning his face into shyness, Dill almost restricts his tongue from speaking, but a look of concern on Miley's face even a six year old can read.

"The man had horns and an ugly face with really big teeth," he says looking into Miley's eyes. Miley straightens up and releases Dill's hand as the thought of his description is over taking her current reality. Demons, sacrifice, apostles... *Is it real or am I hallucinating and everything that occurred was just my dream being taken far too deep into reality?* She closes her eyes and zones out, tuning out the sounds and any thought of what just occurred. Reality can sometimes bite, which if it does then it has its mouth full at the moment.

Silence set in and the darkness behind her eyes becomes a beachfront with tides brushing up against the shore. She can feel the sand between her toes and wiggles them into each grain to capture the feeling. The sky has absent clouds but a bright sun shining like a lighthouse in the mid of night. Looking up at the sky, she sighs and then she lowers her head to look upon the beach. In the distance she sees a man, and he is standing yards away. Nothing about his appearance can be recognized but a black coat. The image of his face is darkened but as she stares he approaches and his image becomes clearer. Floating over the shore like a smooth breeze, the sky darkens and a chill runs up her spine like a cold wind. Without blinking, his image vanishes. Looking left to right she can see nothing beyond, and just like that she is alone on the beach. Only the sound of the tides flows into her ears.

Until, warm hands press against her exposed shoulders. In a delicate white dress she stands, eyes closing as the palms of the free hands glide along her arm. Fingers slip into hers and grip her hand firmly, and then she feels a chin sink into her lower neck as lips graze her ear. Then words whisper in, "I know what you are..."

Her eyes pop open and she turns around to see Vitriolic who burst into flames at sight. Miley's face loses color and a cold blue fills her skin. The moon disappears and the cool breeze becomes an intense amount of heat brutally sourcing the environment. Rocks begin to crumble and lightning strikes multiple times over throughout the sky. Her heart begins to beat like a bass drummer and her hands begin shaking like a wind compass caught in a breeze.

"Miley... MILEY," Dill shouts once more.

She jumps as if ice-cold hands rubbed her wrong. Dill jumps back as well in reaction to her sudden movement. He jumps up and volts for the door but Miley stands, "Dill no, I am sorry." Stopping before his exit, he stands at the door awaiting her next words, which if not affectionate will confirm his fearful desire to leave.

She hugs him and says, "I love you. I am just going through something and need to clear my head. Everything is messed up."

"Where's Tyler?"

She pauses, any implication assuring Tyler's absence will be longer than just a few days and Dill will become upset instantly. Her words are chosen carefully, but also before speaking, she looks out of her window as she determines if her words should be truthful. Would it matter if she lies, how would Dill know the truth? It is not like it is Dawson; it is just Tyler– a friend who happened to come around a lot. Miley thought over her excuses, none seem to be honest but also no matter how attached Dill is to Tyler, she figures he will eventually grow older and get over it. A misconception many adults make about their children, as they assume because a child is a child their memory is poor.

Miley turns to Dill and replies, "Tyler had to move Dill, he moved back to school so he can get a better job." As Miley says it, she looks off and leaves eye contact. Her words even sound unbelievable, or at least she feels like they are being as though she no longer feels any significance for Tyler emotionally. Dill opens the door and leaves the room. As Miley goes to shut the door behind him, Teri's small hands create the loudest silence-breaking double knock on the other side of the door. Her head peaks in and her fingers wrap around the door slowly pushing it back. After entering she takes one look around and places her hand under her chin and then scratches her head.

"Are you going somewhere like yesterday?"

"Tyler and I just got into it and I am going to Amiyah's house," she says grabbing her sweater and tossing it into her duffle bag. Teri walks around her suitcase and raises an eyebrow at her room, which is pretty messy. Clothes are scattered everywhere, shoes and heels are laid out like a yard sale, and her laptop is hidden beneath old cell phones and electronics.

Teri inquires, "Miley you are not usually this," pinching a wrinkled shirt in between her fingers, "unorganized. Are you sure you are okay?"

Miley folding clothes replies, "Am I sure? Mom you never asked the first time," and Teri shrugs her shoulders saying, "I mean I figured if it is about you and Tyler, you know how you feel and how to deal with y'all situation."

Calling her mother feels distant, it scares her more at the thought she has been living her entire life amongst a possible stranger. However, Miley is not yet ready to address the situation in fear of the truth, or, a lie.

She stops folding immediately and her face tightens as she says bold, "We have no situation. Actually," Miley drops everything and walks over to her desk and takes a seat, "Mom, why did you just kick Tyler out like that? You love him."

Teri replies, "I do like Tyler, but I love my children, and tiger or no tiger, that man creeps me out. I don't know what is going on, but I know that my family will be safe from what and whoever." Her explanation is fair, but Miley can sense something, she is not quite sure yet, of what it is. Her mother starts picking up her clothes and cleaning her room. Whenever Teri begins to clean, it is a clear sign she has something on her mind she is trying to avoid discussing. Miley picked up on this when Dawson and Teri would share their differences in the basement of the house, assuming no one could hear them.

Once, Teri cleaned out the garage because she and Dawson almost got into it over his complaints about her cooking dinner. She stopped cooking for Dawson because he spent too many nights out late, and would stumble in the house drunk expecting leftovers in the fridge.

"Mom, I know when you start cleaning it means you are avoiding the topic," Miley says. Teri stops picking up clothes and mimics stone, motionless but in thought as she closes her eyes and reopens them to say, "Miley I have something to tell you, it is about your father."

A horn honks outside and Miley stands to look out of the window, it is her cab. Her phone rings and she answers,

"I'll be right out. Mom I have to go, I'll call you when I get to Amiyah's house."

There is a hunch to where this conversation can lead, but again Miley fears the truth too much to dwell into the topic. If she can avoid hearing her mother tell her the truth about her past, and her mark, it may help her remain sane. Or at least for a manageable amount of time, which can sooth the wounds made by questionable truths.

She grabs her bags and heads downstairs. Teri remains in the room and watches from the window as her daughter enters the cab and closes the door. Taillights turn on, as the cab rolls off removing her from what would have been an awkward situation. She sighs and clinches Miley's sweater in her grasp, Miley's cold heart towards the absence of her father prevents her from having interest in the topic of his history. Although Teri wishes she could have explained, in a way, she is happy she did not have to but it is imperative that at some point she share. Teri turns around and Miley's bedroom door is partially open and Dill is standing in the opening.

"Dill..." Teri says and then the door opens all the way revealing Eduardo standing behind him.

Later

Pulling up to Amiyah's apartment, the cab stops. Miley picks up her phone to call, and she pays the cabby before grabbing her bags then exiting the vehicle. She has a thought in mind of stepping out onto the sidewalk in front of NYU. A smirk left quick as she begins walking up to the complex door. Miley reaches for the handle and the loudest boom she has ever heard erupts into the air. She turns around and a black SUV has smashed into the back of the cab, sending it into a parked car and flipping over. People rush out of their apartments to speculate in a matter of seconds. As a crowd gathers, the parked car explodes sending a ball of fire into the air as orange flames light the sky.

Everyone is pushed onto their backsides by the force of the blast. Miley ducks down and debris scatters everywhere around her. Amiyah rushing outside, and behind her Thomas, jumping down the stairs.

"Hey, what's going on?" Mac shouts from the sidewalk about thirty feet out.

He is facing the accident and holding a bag of chips and soda he just purchased from the store. He had left about 20 minutes ago before Miley arrived. Mac, now in a rock stars t-shirt with jeans tight as a pirates noose. Even for what appears to be an offside character, Mac's true colors paint the scene when he begins speeding over to the cab.

Reaching it, he begins to pull the man from out of the passenger side of the vehicle. He struggles to shift his weight as the man begins to fade in and out of consciousness. Amiyah turns to Thomas who is staring and instructs him, "Go help him," and Thomas hesitates. One of his feet moves forward but the other is not about to follow the leader. Before letting his fear show in his actions, he reveals his cowardliness in speech, "He is as good as dead, and I am not going out there."

"You have to be kidding me?" Miley says to Thomas who sighs and looks to the ground authenticating his look of shame.

Amiyah screams, "Mac, watch out!"

A telephone pole begins to crack like glass hit by a heavy stone. The sound in sync with their eyes confirms the palpable outlook, which is that pole is going to snap directly onto the cab and crush Mac and the driver. Miley refuses to be a witness and races over to the scene. From where she took off, it feels like more than enough time to help, but before she can make the curb, a loud snap ruptures the suspense of onlookers. Everyone gasps as they anticipate what is irreversibly coming.

Her left foot hit the street and her right foot is just leaving the sidewalk, but as close as she could get is as far as she needs to be. The pole towering over them comes down like an elevator when the break snaps. Mac is still yanking the man from the seat and he almost has him out. He has his arms underneath the driver's armpits and begins back peddling away from the cab. But, the driver becomes conscious again, he panics beginning to shake and wobble screaming, "Oh my God, oh my God."

Mac stops back peddling as the driver becomes far too heavy and flimsy to grasp, if only he would stop moving Mac can get a grip. Finally he secures him in a hold wrapping his arms around the driver's torso, but before he continues to peddle backwards he looks up. Motionless and without a holler or sound of fear, and within two seconds Mac's clear view of the sky is removed by a massive darkness.

A thundering boom silences the witnesses around the scene. The entire complex becomes an abandoned island, as silence is the bass line. Orange is the color that takes the vision of everyone who cannot blink after what they have just seen. Another explosion let out shaking the area as the transformer and fire combust. Miley is thrown several feet back and lands onto the grass ten feet or more from where Amiyah and Thomas are standing.

She cannot hear a thing, and as she leans up she sees Amiyah rushing over falling to the ground. Her lips are moving but her words cannot be heard. She then turns her head to the left and near the burning wreckage are two people, a man and a woman. They both are wearing black t-shirts and black pants, and staring directly at Miley. Her vision is a bit blurry so she cannot make out their faces all that well. One blink and they begin pointing at her, and a flash of fire waves before removing their presence from sight. Standing to her feet she sees that no one is visible in the flames, and for a moment she is quite unsure if she had seen anyone at all.

This is the second time Miley has seen death in her life, but this time it is far more different and difficult. Mac was young and not entirely as lame as she thought him to be after witnessing his heroic act, or shall we say, attempt. A feeling arrives and it is not regret but more like misunderstanding. Mac has lost his life over what, some drunk or lazy driver? At first it does not make sense why everything even occurred. Strange thoughts almost left her mind but like hands approached by fire she brought them back. Miley may have been conflicted with thoughts about her life but she has not gone crazy, not yet. The images of the two people she seen becomes a bit more vivid. "*Demons,*" she said to herself for reassurance. She then turns to Amiyah and request her something of her, "Give me your car keys."

"Where are you going?" Amiyah asks concerned.

Truth is, Miley is heading home but she will not say. Subconsciously she knows who the man and women is, or she has an idea but either way she knows what it means. Suddenly she reflects on their image and the picture clears more. Like windshield wipers removing staining rain, the image of their eyes is recollected with detail. She sees their faces again, staring boldly at her, and then she notices their eyes are ruby red, sharp teeth, and slashes on their cheeks like they had been digging into their own skin.

A feeling takes control of her and without question she grabs Amiyah's keys and runs to her car fearful of the worst anticipation. It never dawned on her that Eduardo had been to her house, and the day he warned them he evidently had sought out their location. She must go home, and her fingers begin shaking in fear of the thoughts her mind begins to produce. Worry sets like the sun and darkens her bright thoughts of an escape. She may be leaving the city, but it will not be tonight or anytime soon.

Tires burn rubber on the street and the car drifts into the direction of her home, as she speeds off in fear for her family.

Minutes to go – part 22

Just like before

As bad as it feels to be helpless, Tyler has to accept that is exactly what he is. Yet, it becomes a better thought to acknowledge the fact of what he is, rather than finding confidence in helping others, in order to redeem his esteem. Being as though technically branding a smile on the face of others has long been a hobby and gift of his. Mostly, Tyler spent his time comforting others because he knew not how to comfort himself. Or what he found comfort in he rarely acquired and enjoyed. At the moment, he thought about the reality of his actions, the reminder of his poor decisions, which he allowed alongside his emotions to remove the ability of willingly seeking joy.

Andrew admires his deep thoughts as he leans against the wall head low pretending to mind his own. However, being able to read the minds of others are gifts the disciples utilized, especially Andrew who reflects deeply on the situations he once started but never finished. If you are wondering what that means, yes you are right. Andrew was once in love just as Tyler and accurately just as young.

Long ago...

John the Baptist had just finished preaching the gospel, and a crowd grew around him as his words captivated the minds of those who relinquished their ears. He preached on, "Give up your ways, turn from your wickedness. Live not as a fool for the wages of sin are death. God is the father, Jesus is the Christ, stand with me and follow thy name into salvation," he had eyes round and nearly leaping from their sockets as their ears brought in the wisdom. The land for miles was silent under the tone of John's voice, spearing his beliefs through the openness of the area. Not one soul present dare begged to differ, not the way John spoke and surely not with the affirmation in his voice. All but one was attentive and without distraction.

A woman, with green eyes and hair long lying upon her shoulders like a child rocked to rest and comfort, was gazing upon. She was smaller than most of them, but not invisible as she had to be the most beautiful woman eyes could lay sight onto. But her beauty was beneath the recognition of anyone out there. Everyone was listening to John but she had not allowed her ears to remain more open than her eyes. Beside John was standing Andrew, looking young and just as attentive as the crowd, yet admiring how much of their attention John had captured, his eyes looked over the crowd in amazement. From face to face he had seen what could be described as the most stunning effects of God's wisdom being taught through John.

As he looked upon, his head was turning eyes going from one person to the next, and then his eyes stopped. His neck stiffened and his breathing even ceased action for about five seconds. Five seconds that became the longest identification of something special. Andrew saw the woman looking at him, gazing with no intent to break focus even if the sun fell to the ground and darkened the sky. Still, she would gaze upon and for a moment it is as if her green eyes lit up and shined a direct line of sight to Andrew.

John had begun praying over the people one by one. As he did so, Andrew could not allow the sixth second to be one he did not move on. Move he did, towards her from off the rock, which he stood and into the crowd he gazed. Moving through, everyone's eyes were closed and their hands rose in praise. He ducked beneath the arms of one man while using his hand to part through the others standing. The woman being so small, he could not see her from the ground, still he moved throughout the crowd determined to find his admirer. Time began to feel longer than expected and he had not identified her face. For a moment, he stopped and turned his head left to right taking his eyes in each direction. Not one resemblance could he find, but he returned to movement and continued to search, as the contact they made with their vision inspired the type of curiosity you do not let stray into unanswered time.

Just as he began to turn around and make way back, a hand grasped his forearm. He looks down and sees her and she is as beautiful up close as she was from a far. A stunning stare turns into words, "I am Andrew, what is your name?" he asked taking her hand into his.

"I am Illyssia. You are a beautiful man," she said placing her hand along the side of his face. Her smile came prior to his reply, "And you are a beautiful woman." She removed her hand and placed it over his as she held her other. Looking upon him she said, "I want to walk with you, not just today but tomorrow and through time. Will you lead me? Can I come with you as you preach the gospel?"

Andrew turns to look at John who is laying a praying hand on the people. Turning back around without another thought he said, "Yes," and he took her hand.

In their travels, she kept Andrew mentally strong, his heart was always encouraged and open. They prayed together just as much as they walked together. Roads they walked upon began to become their path into a passionate future. At times, Andrew would carry Illyssia just to keep her feet from tiring, and as well to show his strength. He was indeed a strong man and she a loving woman, and their bond appeared spiritually inseparable.

There is no time to consider emotions, as history is not as significant as life, and saving many lives today. Or is it, either way Tyler has become disconnected with reality. His dreams are creating this barricade constructed of emotions, which Tyler is refusing to take down. Young love is always the most difficult to handle, to tolerate, and to understand. You are introduced to a room of new feelings and definitions for them are strangers with masks on greeting you with hugs and toast to good times. This party seems to last as long as time does but only until another presence is made. Someone else walks through the door, and as they do, someone hands you a mask instructing you to put it on. And then they invite you to greet their new guest just as they greeted you. Andrew's flash back made Tyler's discomfort understandable. But, it does not make it a priority.

Love always feels new when it is really just the grand greeting. A big introduction, which will only last about as long as it takes for the next person to enter the room and stand into the spotlight hoisted above the door. You feel like the life of the party and as soon as you lose that feeling, you spend your entire duration of the party trying to get it back.

Tyler is putting on a show when he should be enjoying himself, and the moment– while it last. So much confusion is on his mind, and only to be faced with the harsh markings of a curse. If there actually is a curse, Tyler begins to think as he reflects now on Eduardo's behavior. Quite deceptive and puzzling but nonetheless all puzzles have a pattern. All Tyler needs to do is understand his pattern and he can figure out what is really going on. Regardless of the fact Simon gave them a heads up, there still remains many grey areas. Areas where questions are unanswered as time begins to tick while they search for something they do not know how to find.

"We have to hurry up," Andrew says looking to his watch strapped around his left wrist. It is a sports watch, and likely no more than thirty dollars but the way he admires it and postures his arm, you would suspect it might have cost a pretty penny.

They are in a department store located just outside the inner city. Shopping at Gunner mall was not an option. There are too many opportunities for Ziga to make a move. In order to avoid skeptical behavior, they drove out of the area so Tyler can buy some clothes. He had been in his drenched clothes since the other night. At this point, he needs to at least feel fresh.

Even the idea of buying new clothes trips him out. To think that from some crazy animal attack to not even being able to go home, his mental sulking becomes his daunting realization. Tyler turns to Andrew and shouts, "Miley!"

"Let it go kid," Andrew says placing one hand on his waist and facing his other towards Tyler.

But this is not a love bite to the dome piece; Tyler actually realizes exactly what he should have caught onto immediately after leaving the disciples 007 hide out. "When Eduardo came to warn us about the curse, he came to Miley's house first. We dropped Miley off at home. We have to go back," he urges.

Andrew is a bit too dull with his response as he replies, "That was hours ago, and she is probably dead." A rock cannot be more heartless. You would think Andrew will lighten up a bit, but he does not. His emotionless blows and stick to the script ideology, steers his reasoning skills. Andrew does not feel the need to place anyone or anything over his purpose. Miley may have been a Daegel, but her involvement as far as Andrew is concerned, is insignificant.

"You do not know that. Do not say that because you do not know that. We have to go back."

"Kid hurry up and get your clothes, we are on a timed schedule. We cannot go back there." They can go back but secretly Tyler's passion is bringing back some memories about how Andrew once behaved for Illyssia. But if he is not going to choose to understand, Tyler is about to make an attempt to force his hand.

Tyler steps forward and looks him square in the eye as his seriousness cannot be mistaken, "We are going back because this is not about just her. People are going to get hurt. If what I experienced at the mansion is anything like what is going to be coming after them, we have got to go back there and save them. It is not their burden and not their fault."

Their eyes do not break focus, and next Andrew sighs looking off into the store. He is thinking and then sucks his teeth looking back at Tyler. Something changes his mind, whether it is Tyler's Hulk stare down or having some sense of care, Andrew replies, "This is stupid, actually it is got damn stupid but we will go back to check only. And if they are okay, no stepping in or Family Matters Urkle business. We leave and get on the road."

He stares back squinting saying, "You watch Family Matters?" Andrew tightens his face and shakes his head left to right as he says, "Shut the hell up kid," and then turns around walking off.

Tyler throws a black jacket over his shoulders and rips the tag from the sleeve. Before rushing off, he looks into the mirror and admires his black V-neck shirt, black cargo pants, and black boots. Something about his appearance made him feel like a bad ass and like he is ready to fight, which is momentarily until he thinks a little longer on it and realizes he is mocking Andrew's demeanor.

Andrew is on the phone, and he looks over his shoulder every couple of seconds and then continues to mumble. While it strikes Tyler as suspicious, he is not prepared to address him on the gesture. Instead, he waits until he ends the call and follows him outside and into the parking lot.

Time to go

Outside the store at the car, footsteps creep up on Tyler as he stands at the passenger door of the SUV. He turns around and sees a man who is beyond dealing with the struggle. His pants are ripped all over and he has on three coats with a winter hat and it is about seventy-nine degrees out. Shoes, if that is what you can even call them have holes in them and dirt all around the sole.

Scratching behind his ear and through his nappy beard he says to Tyler, "Hey young man, hey young man. Do you have any spare change, I am hungry I just want to get something to eat?"

Tyler begins patting his pockets playing the role of *I will try to pretend I have it.* But, Tyler does not have a dollar and truthfully neither does he have any change to spare.

"Sorry about that sir, but I do not have a thing."
"Come on. You didn't spend your last on those nice clothes now did you? I just need a dollar or two."
"Sir, I am sorry but if I had it I would definitely give it to you."

Security for the strip mall drives by and the man ducks his head intending to shadow himself from their sight. As they roll about two cars up he lifts his head and drops his shoulders, giving off the impression he may not be particularly fond of the officers presence. He tucks his lip and blows out into a sigh.

"Son, if you do not have any spare change, can I least get a lift, I seem to have lost my keys..." and before another word is spoken the driver side door flies open and Andrew begins pacing around the back of the car. He walks up to the man and pulls a handgun pointing the barrel directly at his forehead.

A sour face he has as he smiles and says, "Now Andrew that is not what Jesus would do?" Andrew winks and replies, "That's why I will."

A single gunshot echoes and the man falls to the ground with blood soaking his hat and running like a stream through the cracks of the concrete. Mall security spins around the lot and returns to the area. An officer jumps out of his vehicle and removes his pistol.

Tyler shouts, "Whoa! Why did you do that? What are you doing?" And Andrew, who refuses to explain himself, raises his hand over the man's body and says, "In the name of Jesus the Christ, I cast you out of this world."

Finishing his last word to recite the command, an officer raises his gun and takes form. Legs perpendicular, trained posture and a firm grip as he locks his aim onto Andrew requesting his obedience.

"Drop your weapon and get on the ground."

He looks from over his right shoulder as the officer goes for his radio on his shoulder to request back-up. As soon as his arm left his hand to support his aim with the gun, Andrew moves so quick the officer blinks and he reappears on his side. He grabs the gun and turns his wrist like a doorknob, the officer let out a scream unlike anything human. A voice of torment rages in pain and then Andrew grabs his neck squeezing just enough to keep him controlled.

Muscles in his arm are flexing as a visual description of how tight his grip is on the officer, or, what appears to be an officer. His eyes roll back into his head and shuffle a new set of eyes in view. They are ruby red and his teeth become a tarter yellow.

"We will retrieve the key," the demon says and as he speaks his finger rises pointing in Tyler's direction, and then he continues, "The boy will die and Heaven will be ours, Hail Ziga."

Turning to look at Tyler, Andrew's thoughts entice a riddle. Information has been undisclosed as he feels like the demons know something the disciples do not, or he does not. His focus goes back to the demon and he throws his hand up to its face and recites, "In the name of Jesus the Christ, I cast you out of this world," and the demon fades into black ash.

Sirens sound nearby, and Tyler is standing with his thoughts skydiving from his eye sockets using his eyes as parachutes, finding that the seriousness of this situation is far deeper. The demons are getting closer and Andrew can feel it.

"Get in," he instructs Tyler with a sense of urgency. Tyler does not question his command, he gets in and they back out only to see two cop cars pulling into the parking lot. Andrew throws his weight into the wheel turning right, and they leave smoke rising from the street as they drive out of there.

A car entering their column refuses to stop causing them to swerve into the flowerbed separating the car columns. Lucky for them, Andrew has faith in his truck as he hits the gas sending the tires over the curb and running through the dirt. Inching by the stubborn driver of the other vehicle, they barely make it pass.

Unfortunately, the seconds it took to make that move allows the cops to locate them. Their engines indicate the chase is on, and also causes Andrew to make some very risky moves. Tyler grabs his seatbelt but struggles to click it in as they shoot out into the street swerving into and in front of traffic. A small car darts pass their right side and only a foot away from side swiping their vehicle. Another car speeds up beside them and as Tyler looks over he sees the driver's eyes are ruby red and her smile revealing some horrible looking teeth.

"Strap in," he tells Tyler who finally hears the click preventing his life from flying through the front windshield. They swerve through cars left lane to right lane, and as they do Andrew suddenly receives a phone call. He lets go of the wheel and reaches into his pocket to get his flip phone. The look on Tyler's face may have instantly placed him in a graveyard. At the speed they are going, one bad move will result in their death and that will result in the end of this book.

Tyler does not want that, so he reaches for the wheel to steer. Andrew flips open his phone and answers the call while grabbing the wheel back and maneuvering the vehicle from the lane where a car has stopped at the light. Red lights usually mean stop but in this moment Andrew hit the accelerator as if he is stepping on a roach. Cars honk and brake hard as they jolt pass a SUV whose side mirror snaps off making contact with their taillights. The SUV spins out of control and smashes into the first cop's vehicle, sending it into an abandoned store.

Andrew smiles and says, "One down," and then he regains focus onto the road.

Snap is the sound of Andrew closing the phone and placing two hands onto the wheel making a hard left throwing one hand over the other. A cop car spins the corner directly behind them and it is officially a car chase. Sirens and engines fill the city streets, and next the cop car pulls fast up on the passenger side. It is another demon, and this time he extends his arm out of the window while smoothly moving the car closer.

Glass shatters as the demon fires a shot into the truck. Tyler grabs the side of the door and braces himself. Leaning forward, Andrew extends his arm over to the passenger window and throws his hand up. Brakes scratch the cylinders as the cars slow down avoiding what would have been a casting. Another shot goes into the vehicle from the back window and it is apparent he is aiming for Tyler.

"C'mon there's two people in the car," Tyler shouts as a bullet hits the headrest he is ducking beneath.

"Kid he doesn't care"

"What are we going to do and where are we going?" Tyler asks still finding cover beneath the headrest.

"Phillip called, says Pete wants us to meet him at Destiny's Gate."

"What the hell is that?" he asks but ducking again as another gunshot is sent into the back seat. The cop car whips around them and tries to speed up in front.

Andrew shouts, "Hold on," grabbing the wheel with two hands as he uses the front right side of their truck to tap the left tail end of the cop car. Glass smashes from the lights on the cars colliding, and the cop car rips to the left flipping over a parked vehicle. Andrew puts the truck in reverse and speeds backwards braking at the wreckage.

Tyler unsure of whether to be amazed or frightened leans his upper torso out of the passenger window, looking over the roof. Andrew takes a hard look at the cop and blood is dripping from his head and glass is puncturing his face. His eyes are closed and for Andrew that is good enough. Screeching beneath the tires smoke shadows the street and they roll off making a hard right onto another block escaping the chase.

Minutes To Go - part 23

Destiny's Gate

Nothing says death like a graveyard, or the rate of speed Andrew is going down the high way. After a few turns and a long drive down a county road, they arrive at a graveyard. Andrew and Tyler step out of the vehicle and before them there is a stone archway. The sky resembles a smoke grey ash, reflecting only moonlight towards them.

Walking pass tombstones the moon lights the sky like a ceiling lamp. Andrew is still in deep thought, and he strides without deviation as he battles with integrity and redemption. In his mind, he is calculating how long it has been since he seen Illyssia, and nothing about Tyler's connection to Miley seems foreign anymore. And honestly, it never did but Andrew hides his yogurt side fair. His love is channeled into rage and his desires invoking pain, Andrew made good use of his abilities, he has to or else he will be too broken to serve.

"There it is," he says picking up his head.

"I do not see them," and as his words question the unseen, they walk into a force field that is protecting the Gate's location. On the outside of the shield it appears to just be tombstone after tombstone, but inside is a tomb with

Egyptian markings all over it and a cross at the steeple. Walking inside, they run over to Simon Peter who is at the tombs door waving his hand left to right above his head. Prayer is a practice but also a key itself. Peter reaches into his collar and pulls out a small necklace with a miniature vase connected.

"What is that?" Tyler asks. And Phillip, who from out of nowhere is suddenly standing next to him says, "It is his deepest and most holy prayers to Christ. Only that can open the Gate."

An inquisitive Tyler desires to know more, as his faith is little by little becoming a factor in these life-threatening moments. Which is in fact, when most of us find the time to put our faith in God– during those uncontrollable life-changing times. And then Tyler begins to reflect on his life before the attack. For a moment he questions his past, and then he riddles himself with the question, *"When did I need God before?"*

Phillip says, "All the time and every time."

Tyler struck with shock looks at him as if his mind is an ocean for fishing. His escape at the mansion feels and seems unreal but Tyler cannot deny any longer. He mumbles, "God," and as he does the doors at Destiny's Gate unlock. Tyler smiles and Peter as well, and then Phillip shouts, "Peter!"

A smile gone far too quick as a blade enters his side and Eduardo shoves Peter into the tomb. Quickly he walks in and grabs the door closing it behind them. Andrew draws his weapon and Phillip races for the door only to be cut off by Vitriolic, who appears with Miley in his grasp once again. He is wearing a leather glove and holding a bible to her neck like a knife. Smirking he says, "Hello fellas, and Phillip."

Ziga has the upper hand again.

Minutes To Go - part 24

Tick Tock

Vitriolic stands before the tomb and issues one warning all but Phillip fears. Nothing is more threatening than the word itself being used as a weapon for terror, and as striking as it is to know that one demon has the boldness to actually use it. That is what everyone else thought except for Phillip, who dared him to make a move with the bible in his hand. "You have ten seconds to drop the book and the girl."

A certain feeling takes the atmosphere. It is darker than what any of them have felt for centuries. Vitriolic then opens into his speech, "Century after century of solitude and you find that your freedom is in jeopardy on this night. It is here where you and your Christ will experience the undeniable irrevocable conceptuality. Your world is no longer yours and neither is your God's reign over it. Remind yourselves disciples that there is and always has been one purpose for your existence, to protect the people who believe in your God. Ziga has no fear of your kind and hardly a reason to fret now."

Andrew cocks his handgun and steps forward saying, "If you and your boy band need something or someone to be afraid of, I have both for you right here."

"You have nothing for me to fear...but I have something for you to fear and that is the soul of Illyssia, which has been burning like a hog over a pit of fire since the day your eyes last witnessed her miserable," and he drops a punch line that actually hits, "and foolish sacrifice."

"Shut up, she is not there," Andrew replies bug-eyed. Truly he is unsure but hopes for an answered prayer. But Vitriolic is stalling and Andrew begins to play into his deception. Yet, Vitriolic is not one to bluff, as he is famous for keeping his word no matter what side it stands on. Unlike most demons that sour every deal they can for a soul, Vitriolic is enticed by his renounced threats. As much faith as Andrew has, a part of him might have been convinced that she is in hell. And he can sense it, which led to Vitriolic's next taunt.

"Her flesh has fallen from her corpse more times than a soul on earth finds J daddy. Now back to you," he says locking his sight onto Tyler and as he does Tyler fearlessly replies, "You have nothing to say neither to me nor for me."

The thought of Miley being harmed alleviates his rage and dismisses his fear. Cruel thoughts begin to enter his mind like a thief sneaking into an open window. Tyler can see a blade slicing across Miley's throat and her body dropping to the ground on top of another corpse, which is also hers. And then he sees it again, another Miley having her throat sliced and dropping onto what looks like a tower of bodies bleeding eternally. "Stop it. Get out of my head." Vitriolic chuckles and says, "NO, not until I get what I want."

Just the thought of seeing her die is like a fire set on his skull, and his hands rise to his head gripping tight. He drops to one knee and begins screaming in agony. The odds are not in their favor, Phillip can make a move but not without risking Miley's life. Trigger-happy Andrew can fire off a few shots but he knows the demon will just throw Miley in front of the bullets. No need to sugar coat, because this situation has no advantages for them as they are at a loss.

In the tomb

Cod webs decorate the corners of the room and many books are piled upon a desk to the left side, and atop it many quills and a map. The stone of the structure is old and cracks every few minutes or two, and while the floor is tiled marble it looks as if it were recently installed. Candles are lit around a coffin made of pure silver, a bit dusty but pure. On the cover of the coffin is a scripture, and Peter leaning on it begins to read it aloud.

"Ephesians 6:10-18

The Whole Armor of God

Finally, be strong in the Lord and in the strength of his might. Put on the whole armor of God, that you may be able to stand against the schemes of the devil. For we do not wrestle against flesh and blood, but against the rulers, against the authorities, against the cosmic powers over this present darkness, against the spiritual forces of evil in the heavenly places. Therefore take up the whole armor of God, that you may be able to withstand in the evil day, and having done all, to stand firm. Stand therefore, having fastened on the belt of truth, and having put on the breastplate of righteousness, and, as shoes for your feet, having put on the readiness given by the gospel of peace. In all circumstances take up the shield of faith, with which you can extinguish all the flaming darts of the evil one; and take the helmet of salvation, and the sword of the Spirit, which is the word of God, praying at all times in the Spirit, with all prayer and supplication. To that end keep alert with all perseverance, making supplication for all the saints."

After reciting the scripture Peter falls to the floor holding his side, he is grimacing in pain. Sliding backwards as Eduardo is admiring the eloquent structure, and he takes his stand, "You are as foolish as your purpose."

Confidence plays a greater role in deception, as it is the contributing factor to convincing your enemy that you have the advantage. Eduardo begins to play upon his wit, "Are you not a fool yourself? If not more a coward without loyalty. We only want freedom, our world is becoming overcrowded and for some time we have been seeking out some new property. Who'd knew Savatir would stumble upon God's big secret. And the space, oh I told Savatir he should take up Realty because the man's got a gift."

Peter spits out blood and says, "You will never find the key and you will never make it to the gates of heaven."

With his finger on his chin and elbow over his hand he says, "Peter, still denying the truth? Stop it. No roosters crowing in this room. But, there is death playing a fine tune." Peter coughs and groans as a pain grows within him.

Eduardo exhales and continues, "Well not Mozart but an assonance nonetheless. Either way let us not waste time bickering threats and mild insults. The key is here and we both know it, where specifically Peter I expect you to tell me."

Tyler may have been fresh to Eduardo's deviant manipulating tactics but Peter is not. Giving up the key is not all that is to the deal, and after all, even he has no idea why Ziga has an interest in a teenage boy. Peter sits up against the back wall and grumbles, and then he asks, "What does all this have to do with the boy?"

Wrapping one hand in the other and glowing with deception he replies, "You mean Tyler, well we wouldn't be much of a secret society if we did not keep secrets Peter. Speaking of secrets, could you," he grabs a candle from off the ledge and kneels down to Peter, and then he places the flame to his wound, "tell me where that key is, or how to get into the coffin – where I'm guessing with a lack of hidden compartments is probably the only place it is."

Peter tightens his fist embracing the pain rather than allowing it to weaken him. Slapping the candle from Eduardo's hand he then says, "For everything there is a season, and a time for every matter under heaven:

A time to be born and a time to die;

A time to plant, and a time to pluck up what is planted;

A time to kill and a time to heal;

A time to break down, and a time to build up;" and Eduardo cuts him off in speech finishing the scripture, "a time to weep, and a time to laugh;

A time to mourn and a time to dance;

A time to cast away stones and a time to gather stones together;

A time to embrace, and a time to refrain from embracing;

A time to seek and a time to lose;

A time to keep, and a time to cast away;

A time to tear, and a time to sew;

A time to keep silence and a time to speak;

A time to love, and a time to hate;

A time for war, and a time for peace."

"A demon... that can speak the word," Peter says.

Eduardo turns around with his eyes burning orange and shouts, "ONLY TO PROVE IT WRONG. DO NOT WASTE MY TIME WITH FAITH, I NEED WHAT'S IN THAT COFFIN PETER." The entire room rumbles and candles fall to the floor. Peter is losing blood and is hardly conscious, and even if he decided to fight back it will be a waste of a dying effort. And suddenly he has a vision:

"Come with us as we see to it that Jesus of Nazarene undergoes speculation as do all who speak of grace and

glory by those other than whom we already serve." Jesus was led to the priest and as they guided him Peter was many feet away. Jesus looked over his shoulder not so much to look back but to let him know, he was aware his presence was not by his side. Peter fret at the sight in his mind and did not dare out of concern come to see it through that he walked with Jesus instead of behind him. As they came to the front of the courtyard, the priests requested that the son of God speak in hope they would find crime in his speech. But as Jesus spoke nothing became evidence for foul intentions. As the priests gathered and received not that what the sought, Jesus turned to Peter and as he did, Peter looked to the ground. Shame had overtaken his presence and his eyes never looked back to his leader."

Peter's eyes are closing and with little to no energy he whispers, "Jesus the Christ, I once feared my walk with you, and have refused you, but you have never refused me. Today, God the father, I will not make the same mistake. In the name of Jesus the Christ, give me strength," and a light within him surges through his body like a city grid after a black out.

Peter stands to his feet and Eduardo swings for his ribs. Blocking the shot, he grabs his wrist and throws his left arm away from him, Eduardo – with his right hand, jabs but Peter ducks beneath. He wraps one hand around his right arm while using his left to grasp the back of his neck. His knee drives ninety degrees into his rib cage again and again until Eduardo uses both of his hands to block a fourth attempt, which would have cracked his ribs in half. Peter's physical strength had left with his wound, but his strength in faith is all he needs and he knows it.

Eduardo pushes away sliding back to the front of the coffin, "Faith will not save you." His words are still spoken with confidence but unable to move Peter into doubt. He rushes him faking a jab to his left side and sending a strike to his right. Peter leans to the right avoiding his blow and chops him in the sternum before shoving the bare side of his hand upward and into his face. Falling back he slams into the door but also bounces back in retaliation by spinning around Peter's straight jab. An elbow to the lower back and he sends him to his knees. He turns opposite side connecting with a low kick to his stomach tossing Peter onto the ground.

"Before I kill you, give me what I want. I am reasonable and if you do I may spare you for a favor," Eduardo implies walking around Peter who appears to be down for the count. Not yet and not now because Peter grabs the base of a candle that fell and swings it like a shackle clipping him by the shin. Flipping onto his feet, Peter cocks back and sends a forceful jab to Eduardo's jaw. The desk cracks into two as Eduardo crashes through it. Peter wraps his arms around his neck securing a chock hold.

"What does Ziga want with the boy?"

"And because you think I fear death I will tell you?"

Peter tightens his grip – likely if he squeezes any harder he can snap his neck, and Eduardo gasping for air squeals out his words, "Alright...I will...tell...you." Peter loosens his grip to allow him to talk but not enough for him to feel confident in making an attempt to escape.

Eduardo is still who he is known to be even at a disadvantage. No moment can be an opportunity for him, because if he can, he will weasel his way out with any resource available. After maintaining a tight grip for about a few more seconds, Eduardo is ready to talk. He wastes no words and comes straight out with it, "The boy, Tyler is the key."

Instant perplexing of thoughts trying to bridge over mysterious waters spins the world in Peters mind. But, so sure of what he knows, he cannot allow himself to be convinced. After all– this is Eduardo, a well-known delirious yet analytical and intellectual trickster. Peter cannot do it and in his mind he knows he will not believe him, and then his grip retightens around his neck. Here arrives the moment where if you have any last words, you drop syllables, which is exactly what Eduardo does.

"This..." Eduardo barely sucking in oxygen "is the truth Peter." Peter rings his neck to the left showing off his strength. Yet, Eduardo speaks again, and for a man near death he might lie to save his life but to live – even if just seconds longer, he may also tell the truth.

"This is true," a voice says behind them.

Peter let go of Eduardo and slowly turns around unsure of what to expect. He has a hunch and if so joy may fill his heart quicker than the sun has ever filled the sky. After turning completely around, he sees Paul looking back at him with those steel blue eyes. Peter cannot believe it, and his eyes fill with a tear as the sight of his brother in Christ alleviates his hope. Paul left Peter in charge of the Apostle Fighters, and he had left long ago without further words or instruction but only two words, "God called." There is no sense in explaining, but Peter also has curiosity. The Key's location has always been only known to him, and as well how is it that Paul has arrived? A sudden misanthropic look, but trust helps Peter uncap his words sharing his misunderstanding.

"Brother, did God not trust me alone? I couldn't have lost the key, it was removed."

Paul replies, "He trust you, but he would never leave a powerful tool in the knowledge of one man. The key was placed into the boy. His death is their way through." Peter looks around as so many thoughts are brushing over his head like bristles, "I do not understand it is my responsibility to keep it safe. I never sold a word neither unstitched a thought."

It is so difficult to comprehend, and in his mind he questions most if God has lost, or had lost, his trust in him. And, even worst he questions if God never trusted him to begin with. Nonetheless, questions never subtracted from his faith. A diligent servant and most renounced for great acts, still Paul has an expression on his face that takes away life in one glimpse. Peter notices but to question his brother would be criminally disloyal. Frustration is withheld inside one single lingering thought and he asks, "Brother, why are you here?"

His hand goes to his shoulder and he replies, "Because I need you to open the coffin."

He would never question Paul, not once in his life has he ever questioned Paul, but at this moment he has no choice. "I cannot do that brother," says Peter who places his hand onto Paul's hand.

Candles begin to blow out around the room one by one. Three are left lit and begin burning the wax rapidly. Peter slides Paul's hand from off of his shoulders and asks him again, "Why are you here?"

"Brother, open the coffin," he says moving closer towards him. Peter does not step back and after a second of silence Paul says, "In the end, you will understand your destiny is greater than your purpose."

Peter's eye gape open and his lower jaw hang from his

face. His chest pokes forward as blood begins to stain his shirt. He looks down and a blade is piercing through his breastplate. Paul takes Peter's hand and places it onto the coffin. The coffin illuminates and the sounds of locks snapping release some combination of security.

The top of the coffin slowly raises open and in it is a staff. There is more pain in Paul holding his hand than the knife in his chest. Funny how trust works, you can always rely on someone until, well you can't. But what worst a betrayal than your own war leader removing you from the fight, and at that before a demon?

Paul still holding Peter up whispers in his ear, "You will learn in the end my brother, you will learn in the end," and he lays gently his body to the floor. He looks straight and sees Eduardo standing there. A sharp stare and he breaks sight to stand up and look back into the coffin. Eduardo mumbles, "The Staff of Moses."

Minutes To Go - part 25

Clocks started...

Rain begins to pour outside and the grass beneath their feet turns mushy. Andrew refuses to stand there and be as useless as a mop on a beach. Phillip knows well that any move made will likely result in the death of Miley. Yet, he can neither allow Vitriolic to feel as though his way is all that will stand for tonight, or that her life is as valuable to them that they cannot spare it. As Tyler's feet begin to sink into the mud, he palms the side of his skull with one hand and braces himself from falling by placing his other onto a tombstone. Reoccurring pain is like a merry-go-round spinning counterclockwise at 100mph.

"This will not go on much longer," says Phillip.

A promise guaranteed by emotions but not perceptual capability. Phillip knows they have no upper hand. One move, no matter how stupid or skilled is going to result in someone getting killed. Evil has a way of taking bad and churning it into worst. A grin opens the floor for him and he responds, "It will not, not much longer and this will all be over. And, you all will be dead." A cracking noise is heard, a force has just met a solid structure from the look on Tyler's face, and rain begins falling onto an invisible sphere that is shielding him.

Another cracking sound and they each look to him and see his fingers gripping tightly into the tombstone. Small chunks of stone fall to the ground and the pain in his mind is now awakening something. Phillip is in total shock but he is not alone, Vitriolic cannot understand what is going on and does not like to be the one to wonder unknowingly. This misunderstanding brews fear within the demon.

"What is this?" he asks, and his head looks up to the sky as lightening begins to form and thunder roars like a beast after a kill.

Tyler's eyes fill with light and he begins to wobble as he attempts to walk towards them. Stumbling left and then right he picks himself up only to stumble again. He passes Andrew and he is speechless as he looks into Tyler's eyes admiring a light that only has one sure resemblance. Tyler a few feet from Vitriolic drops to his knees, and then he lowers his head and the light disappears. It is dark and wet again as rain crashes onto his head.

Vitriolic, while sure of much is very unwelcoming to this unforeseen and sudden act. Fear breaches the walls of his confidence and shatters the glass casing around his authority.

"What is wrong with him? What is going on?" He is confused and shook up.

Whether he wants to deny it or not, any and every demon knows that light. A hard thought to receive is how such a light is coming from some teenage nobody. Fear and misunderstanding begin to speak. "Tell him to get up and back up or she will have a closer walk with JC, and I mean that in the literal sense."

Phillip begins to step away and back up from Vitriolic. While clueless as well, the light is nothing to question or second-guess. Just as he steps forward, light shoots out of Tyler's eyes like a laser beam into Vitriolic's sight. He removes his hands from Miley and his arms stretch out to his side. His body begins to fill with light and he screams so loud tombstones burst into rubble. Beams of light cover his entire body and extend from his head into the sky.

A force of energy spears back through the tunnel of light into his head and his entire body is decimated. Tyler falls onto the grass and the rain stops like someone snapped. Phillip runs over to grab Miley and as he does her body turns to black smoke and fades into the air. It is an illusion. Vitriolic never had her in his grasp. Andrew rolls Tyler over and shakes him by the shoulders. They have a hunch about what has occurred but speaking on it seems, even for them, a bit over exaggerating.

"Tyler, wake up kid," Andrew says shaking him some more.

His eyes are closed and his body is as loose as a wet noodle. Unfortunately for Tyler's face, Andrew is not the gentle type. He slaps him and shouts, "Wake up dammit," and Tyler jumps up and shouts, "Whoa, whoa, whoa," causing Phillip to run over and help Andrew contain him.

"You are okay, you are okay. Tyler calm down."
"What happened? Miley?"

"She was never here," Phillip says.
"What?" Tyler asks bewildered.

"Tyler she was never here. Vitriolic was using an illusion." He stands up with the assistance of Andrew pulling him to his feet. "Where is he? Where is Peter?"

As he said his name, the doors to the tomb open. Phillip and Andrew turn to see Peter lying on the ground near the coffin. They pace over and as they enter the tomb they stop short unable to grasp the reality of what their eyes can see. The coffin is completely empty and the room is smashed up, but most painfully recognized is Peter with a look none other than death upon his face. His lifeless body has bruises and a bloodstain in the center of his shirt. They roll him over to his back and as they do beneath him is the map that was on the desk. Peter exhales suddenly and they both aid his last breath.

"Peter, what happened?"

He can barely move but with his last ability he touches the map with his finger and the lines, numbers, labels, and unseen locations illuminate. Peter says, "Take the map," he coughs hard and in agony saying, "This is bigger than we thought. Hurry...there is not much time. The boy..." his words fade as his life exits and his body shatters into particles of white orbs.

Andrew and Phillip watch as their leader vanishes into the afterlife. A question raises concern, as they look at the coffin unsure of its contents. Sadness wreaked and soaked their hearts like a towel thrown into a pool. Peter is dead, and someone killed him. They knew that as soon as they seen his body, but another major concern was still at hand.

Tyler is standing in the doorway and asks, "What is going on?"

Both Andrew and Phillip lower their heads feeling the depression that runs in the stream of life from the river of death. Questions shift the tectonic plates in their heads, and a mental earthquake shakes up their world as they look at the map with intuition. Illuminating lines are connecting to three locations. They read:

Destiny's Gate, Baltimore MD

Sword of the Baptist, New Orleans Louisiana

Tomb of Resurrection, Wyoming

Leaning over their shoulders, Tyler asks, "What is all this?" And Phillip replies, "These are the locations of the weapons of the father. His eyes stress in shock, "Weapons of the father? That just does not sound good and just using context clues here but would the father happen to be God?"

"Yes," Phillip says placing his hands onto his own face and sighing deeply.

Andrew stands tall searches around the room for further clues. He sees foot prints near the top of the coffin and proceeds to check them out. Steps were made in blood, which most likely came from Peter bleeding out. Observing the size and tread of the sole he walks around the coffin and looks for the most recent set of prints around the door. After careful analysis, he concludes one set belongs to Eduardo and the other set belongs to Peter. Just as he reasons out continuing his search, he looks down at Tyler's feet and he is standing inside a set of prints far bigger than his own. "Don't move!"

"Okay, geeze I'm stone."

"Phillip, over here," Andrew request his attention take notice to the prints. "There was a third man in the room," he says. Phillip stands and points to Tyler and says, "Move him," and Andrew places his hands underneath Tyler's armpits and picks him up moving him out of the footprints.

"Really, is this necessary? I can walk, I have legs."

"This is not right. What is going on? What was in the coffin?" Andrew asks placing Tyler down beside him.

Phillip lays the map onto the coffin top and begins to breakdown his speculation of this situation, "Ziga has the Staff of Moses. Peter is dead and we have no idea where the key is. Peter would have never told Eduardo even if he knew." Tyler intercedes, "Why did we come here in the first place?"

Andrew says, "For the map."

Phillip takes lead, "This is Hermes Map, but only Peter could have read it."

Tyler folds his arms and asks, "I am sorry did you say Hermes? As in Greek," increasing his tone of voice, "MYTHOLOGY?" Sarcasm has never failed Tyler's act of evading the sounds of ignorance. A stressed in thought Phillip replies, "Yes, yes Tyler Hermes. Now, what he just did was let us know Ziga's next move. And we have to beat them to it."

Tyler asks. "What are they planning?"

A good question, and also a question Peter may have had an answer for. While his death is unfortunate, he did not make it a loss. It takes Phillip a few seconds but then his fingers run through his hair and he brightens the darkness in his mind. Like a link snapping into place with another, Phillip goes out on a hunch but strong assumption.

"We have to hurry. Peter your death was not in vain," he says and then looks to Andrew and Tyler explaining, "They have been throwing us off this entire time. This was never about the key. Or, just about the key," he takes his index finger and goes across the map, "Andrew remember our project in New Orleans," asking Andrew who nods his head and smiles. Phillip made it his business to emphasize on the experience. Tyler new much from his American history class back in school. Only reason he paid attention in class was due to a young lady he could not take his eyes off of. She was into history like a bug collector fascinates over insects. Tyler knew getting to know history would enable him to make a big impression if ever she granted him the opportunity to speak.

Having some recollection of the biblical timetables causes him to question Phillips story about New Orleans.

Minutes To Go - Part 26

60 years ago

New Orleans, Louisiana

A trumpet played soul into the concrete and a combination of piano keys moved the joyful feet of the people. Fancy shoes and heels moved about as the music binds their spirit with the will to dance. All smiles under the rope of lights hanging from street railings, and above the street were bulbs crossing from window to window; keeping the glowing smile on one young lady who twisted and twirled as her beaded necklace spun around her neck. All the women had seven to ten hoop bracelets dangling from their wrist. Pearl earrings sat in their ears above a mixture of complexions. Light, dark, brown, and more varieties of skin color jumped and sang along in unity. Race was insignificant as a concern and truly there were no concerns for anyone. Especially, not the men who wore tuxedos and luxury defined suits with a bow tie resting in the center of their collards. The energy was flowing like a water main busted from out of the band.

Patterned stone made the streets, and tables and chairs decorated the sidewalks. Open doors to every establishment as the theme for the night was "All welcome," and when they said all, they may not have meant it– had they known who took their welcome as an invitation.

Two men walk into a tavern, and no, this is not the start to some bad joke. Their suits are pin striped and black to the cuff link. Hair slick back and a top hat titled to the side, they walked with a groove as they made their way to the bar. Reaching it, two ladies already present smiled and begin to flirt with gestures. Working their magic, as some would say, as women in this small tavern had no intention other than a lucky night to knock off the wealthy men who walked in. But they were smart enough to not have played their game, so one of them said, "Excuse me ladies," as they parted the two girls and took their serious demeanor's to the bartenders attention.

"Two White Russians," one of them said to the bartender and he nods back confirming the request. And then a stylish toned voice identifies them, "Andrew and Phillip, I'd of thought Heaven would of kept you two on post at the gates. Yet, to my surprise here you are in my little ole town. What calls for the occasion?"

Phillip, with a clean shave and a smile that can put the night away turned around– and as he did, Andrew turned as well to see John standing before them. Andrew opens his arms and John moves in as they hug smiling at the sight of each other. John then extends his hand to Phillip and they shake in respect. Many people were in attendance and the dance floor begins to move to the pace of the music.

"It is good to see you brother," Andrew said as he turned to grab their drinks.

John extended his invitation to leave the noisy atmosphere, "Come, and let us talk in my office."

The door opens and an epic sight is revealed. A nine-drawer file cabinet sat in the left corner and a tall lamp with four bulbs in the far right. Pictures of John and many people decorated the right wall while licenses and other certificates were on the other. There was a rug laid from the door to just underneath the legs of the desk. On the rug was a unique picture of a man resting with lions in a den. His desk was large and organized and everything was in place as if nothing on the desk had ever been used. Two chairs sat before the desk and as John walked by he said, "Sit," going behind the desk and standing at the window flipping a single blind with his index finger to look out.

Phillip crosses his leg and holds his glass in hand, "We have reason to believe Ziga has business here." As if they insulted John he turned quickly and his face took appall. "Ziga is not in my city."

Disbelief set in like seeds in soil, as John did not feel that Ziga had the audacity to make a presence, and at that made a slip pass his resources. Demons were heavily about the city but Ziga, Ziga moved in a manner so discrete John's working eyes and ears had not noticed. John at the time had no idea Ziga's movements were like the distinction of their order, a secret. These demons took moving in silence to an entire new level. They are never seen, never heard of, and even after their presence had been rumored before, never proven to have created the chaos they are responsible for. But nonetheless, Ziga was in the city and Andrew and Phillip would not be there if they had not.

"John, I assure you God did not reassemble us to chase false trails. Ziga is here," Phillip said. Andrew had taken

his drink back in one gulp and leaned forward to lift his voice. "John, brother, before I walked with Christ I walked with you. I trusted your word without concern and even with it. Ziga is here. Trust me." John did not take kindly to his warning but also he could not shrew it off as some over exaggerated combination of words.

Whether John could have accepted it, regardless when Ziga makes a move it is so beneath the soil, by the time your shovel touches the dirt the roots of their deception have grown. A hard knock on the door sounded and the three gave their attention with caution. The knock was foreign to Phillip and Andrew but John, he knew the knock well. "Come in."

A man in a white suit with a black tie and a scar down the side of his cheek walked in and in his grasp the collar of a man in a fancy suit with silver shining all over. He threw him to the floor while still clutching a bag in hand. Attention to John he said, "Sir, we have a problem."

"Evidently so," John replied as he walked from behind his desk and grabbed rosemary that was resting like an ornament.

The man continued to explain, "We found this idiot in the lower chambers. He tripped the alarm and had this in his possession," and he pulled from a bag a sword. The sight of the sword made Andrew and Phillip stand to their feet. Andrew rushed over and grabbed the man by the shoulders of is jacket and punched him directly in the nose.

"What are your plans?" Andrew asked cocking his fist back again.

The man squinted as his nose began to run blood and replied in his Irish accent, "I do not know what you are talking about." Andrew hit him in the gut and he coughed as if he were having an asthma attack.

Phillip then spoke, "We know you are with Ziga, why were you trying to steal the Sword of the Baptist?"

He denied any affiliation, "I have not a clue of what you are referring to. I am a common thief lad." John remained silent for two reasons. One, he had no clue how Ziga had made it this close to his establishment, and secondly, what interest Ziga had with his sword. Phillip and Andrew had a hunch however, but for the moment beating the answer out of the man was their first approach.

"What is your name?"

"George"

"Well George, we know you are a demon so drop the human act, and we also know Ziga is in the city, or else we would not be here." Still in the grip of Andrew, George tried to move a bit but unable he just continued to speak, "Fellas, I do not know what Ziga is, and if you are after whoever for whatever, you're beating the crap out of the wrong guy. No doubt you boys are off your mark ye?"

Phillip slapped Andrew on the shoulder and said, "Send him packing," and Andrew released him extending his hand to his forehead. He gave but a second for George to come clean but the man played his cards and tried to call his bluff.

Andrew began to recite, "In the name of..." and George wept for mercy, "NO! No do not. I won't go back."

John stepped up and said, "Well that did not take much."

"I cannot tell you what I do not know. I do not know what is the purpose of my theft I was only ordered to retrieve it," George said. Phillip believed him but Andrew did not and because he did not his fist sent another blow into his rib cage. George fell and John intercedes, "You know not why you steal but you steal? And what you almost stole you would have been rewarded what?"

George replied, "A place in Heaven."

They all looked quizzical and could not believe the statement made by a demon. Questions are like rain drops and they fell heavy in the office. A demon who seeks a place by the father, it made no sense. Ziga is a demonic society with nothing but evil brewing one disaster after another. But a demon, seeking heaven, no batter could have swung at that curve ball. John looked to a particular picture on the wall, and it was a man standing with a sword in Spartan armor.

George caught his glare and acted on it, "That is it, isn't it mate?"

Before Andrew and Phillip could catch a clue George kicked backwards – sending John's guard to the wall. Andrew swung but he ducked beneath and gave him a knee to the thigh and spun around his right side. Phillip less physical removed his golden 38. Revolver and fired three shots. George swerved left as the first bullet went by and slid right then back left dodging the other two. His face met the barrel of the gun and before Phillip could fire another shot, George waved his left arm knocking Phillips right arm from aim. He then gave him a strong shove into the chest and met John at the picture.

His face was filled with evil and determination, "I need that," he said and John stepped aside and said, "Take it," and so George tried. He felt all over the picture and could not figure out how to remove the sword. John then grabbed his cane from the side of his desk and he stabbed him in the back right through the spinal cord leaving him minutes to tell a lie. The cane glowed like a star and transitioned into a sword about 32 inches long. And then John removed the sword and George fell to the ground on his back. Phillip and Andrew got up and rushed over. John kneeled down and performed another trick, "This is the sword you seek, in my hand and I can use it to spare you of all your sins and you will be sent to heaven. But first, I need you to tell me how is it you believed you could make it without it?"

George grumbled and coughed up blood as he replied, "I know the sword is useless unless swung by you but Ziga has found a weapon, your sword will help create it. The Key to heaven." George's eyes closed and his last words were, "I told you what I know, now send me off."

John said, "As you wish," and stood to his feet. He winded his sword and as it began to glow he threw it down between his neck and skull decapitating George completely. His body burst into black mist and his head as well.

Andrew asked, "Can you really send him to heaven with that thing?" John grabbed a handkerchief and wiped his blade clean as he responded, "No, he is going to back to hell."

Phillip wanted to know more, "What is this weapon?"

"There is a rumor."
"What rumor."

"That binding the Sword of the Baptist, The Staff of Moses, and the Spear that pierced Christ side with the Key will create a tool capable of blocking out God's sight of the world." Andrew fret and as did Phillip, even the thought of such a device brings devastation to mind. Not to mention how did Ziga know of such weapons and the apostles had not. John did not entertain rumors as hard facts tend to satisfy his questions, and not speculations based upon coincidence. They could take no second-guessing, because if Ziga is up to something they have their leads and must act on them immediately.

" We must go. If Ziga has made an attempt to retrieve the sword they are making attempts at others relicts. John you keep that safe," Phillip said.

John shook his hand and said, "They will never be this close again. Farewell my brothers." He hugged Andrew and watched as they left out with their acquired knowledge.

As they left he stood at his desk and looked beyond his window. Out and up at the sky he gazed seeing all the stars that gave him hope. But, in his eyes were concerns. He thought to himself the worst fear for mankind. A weapon so terrifying that God used it during the times of Noah. John frets at the stories but he worried more for Andrew and Phillip, who he knew might be chasing a false rumor.

Tyler looks upon them both and says, "Wait, so what is the weapon?" They ignore his question and then Andrew comes to a startling thought, "Where is gate to Vexel's cage?" Phillip grabs the map and shouts, "Shit."

Tyler still waiting for an answer converts his curiosity. Andrew shoves him by the shoulder and says, "Come on kid we have to go."

"Where?" Tyler inquires.

Phillip says, "To get Miley."

He cannot understand what made her so significant just of recently but if finally his concerns are being taken into consideration, he is with the plan. Even with Phillip failing to elucidate on the sudden urgency to check on Miley, which Tyler feels a bit entitled to know of – being as though he has a closer relationship with her. Trust must play a role and for Tyler, who is unable to define what he is going through, now would be the time to start making your decisions on faith.

But then Tyler as much as he wanted to do both – inquires on but also does not ask of his encounters with Eduardo. His manipulation helps him realize how easily he can be moved using his emotions as a device. In a way, Andrew and Phillip being recluse with what information they know, helps Tyler appreciate the fact he is not being lied to. The way he sees it, lies are not told out of silence, or are they?

The plot thickens and from one concern, to about three more. Ziga is making fast moves and that makes Tyler think for a second *we always seem to be behind.* Did they? Or are they just in the right place at the right time. That is kind of how manipulation works right; you have to be where someone needs you to be in order for him or her to move you mentally or physically.

Tyler has a hunch, one with a topic of particular interest. Miley just became priority number one. Andrew not but hours ago deviated from even checking up on her. In the midst of the insane driving and gunfire, Tyler failed to remind Andrew of his destination, that is, unless he lied. This is highly likely, as they have shown him nothing but stern commitment to this cause.

Neither of them questioned Peter's death further than discovering the map. It makes Tyler begin to question their motives. Someone had killed Peter. And the way he handled the demon back at the shack, it almost seemed impossible to believe Eduardo had taken him out. If he did, just the mere thought of Peter's death makes Tyler shimmer.

Questions are still piling, but Tyler feels reluctant to begin a game of Q&A.

Minutes To Go - Part 27

Burning down faith

Miley watches as her home enrages in flames. Fire burns as if the entire house is a forest, spreading to the roof – flames sprouting from the chimney and windows. Debris with fire attached falls from the smoke cloud filling the dark morning sky. Police sirens are heard in the distance and not far behind – fire trucks. The fire shines in her iris and her body is as still as stone. Without blinking, a tear drops from her eye and rushes down her face like snow in an avalanche.

She looks up to see falling before her is a picture partly burning. It is a picture, or what remains of a picture, of Dill, Miley, and Teri. Catching the picture by the corner she stares expressionless thinking to herself of the moment they took it. And then, she drops it watching it float to the ground, much like a leaf at the break of autumn.

A cop runs over and asks, "Are you okay?" Miley remains speechless – gazing upon the flames. As the officer begins talking and making gestures, she is in a trance set off from social interaction, and also shut off from actually embracing the living.

Andrew and Tyler pull up to the scene nearly taking out a barrier as police begin to seal off the scene. Hopping out of the vehicle, they begin running over. An officer steps in front of them and begins to enforce his authority. Before he can release a word, Andrew raises his index finger and waves it left to right over his head. The officer stops in mid-speech and stares blank.

He then says, "This way come on," and begins taking them through the fire trucks and squad cars. A bit manipulative, but Andrew is not the type of man who likes being presented with limitations. Tyler can see Miley standing on the curb. The officer is still trying to talk to her but she remains unresponsive. The pain she feels is so deep, her heart could be bottomless. She is unable to even think of any other thought. Every wave of intense heat makes her nerves rattle beneath her skin. Teri and Dill are either in that burning wreck, or they are missing.

"MILEY," Tyler shouts rushing over. She breaks focus and turns to him. "They are gone..."

Tyler looks at the house and his eyes widen in fear. The words hit like an eighteen wheeler and he looks to Andrew taking in the evidence of Ziga's efforts, which are apparently any means necessary. A moment captured by silence as Andrew lowers his head and Tyler stands unsure of his next gesture. There is something he can do, but neither Phillip nor Andrew would approve. A rescue mission is not as imperative as finding the key, but if only they knew they had already found it.

"We have to..." before Tyler can complete a thought, Andrew takes a bold stand and intercedes, "No." Tyler thinks to ask again, but his entire body language is giving off this irrevocable position of choice.

However Andrew feels about what option Tyler thinks

they have, he wants no parts. Arms crossing and looking to the ground and then back up, he is still insinuating his solidness. Not to mention Andrew is a big man, so not only does he look like he cannot be moved, he actually cannot.

Tyler walks in a small but quick circle and says, "Come on man, this is her family."

A car pulling up and slamming on the brakes can be heard from the distance. Car doors slam shut and within seconds, running through the crowd of officers and firemen is Dawson. He stops to see what creates a boiling hurt in his eyes. His home, at least what he still thought it to be, is burning down. Before his sour heart can tear, Dawson regains composure. As much as he would like to resurface some despairing remnants, he prioritizes and begins looking searching for a clue to start his investigation. Fire fighters are running throughout the scene and preparing to put the fire out. Through the crowd, Dawson spots Miley, and she is still standing motionless and without a sign of hope. This is not a lead he can imagine useful, but the sight of her removes his priorities as a cop. Instead, he develops an intermittent fervent side.

Making his way over, he sees Tyler and Andrew but he overpasses their presence momentarily. Even though he is not Miley's biological father, it is in his best interest to act like something he has never been to her. Passing them both he approaches Miley and places his hand on her shoulder. She shrugs back and Dawson's hand drops immediately. A bit of resistance is shown by her due to the circumstances of their current situation.

"It's okay Miley, it is okay. Tell me what happened?" A sharp look tells her story more than words can delegate. The reflection of fire burns in her eyes and Dawson knows the look better than anyone else.

He replaces his hands on her shoulders and gives her a stare only sincerity makes, "This is not your fault. Whatever happened, you will not blame it on yourself. I won't let you so don't try. If you want to blame someone blame me."

Tyler looks upon them expecting Miley to break out into a rage – hitting Dawson and taking him up on his offer. Even Dawson braces for impact unsure of what her reaction will be. Yet, the complete opposite breaks into reality as her reaction is lunging over hugging Dawson. She hugs him so tight you would have never known he was never there. As uncommon as her reaction is, nothing about it seems completely unwelcomed for the moment. Whether Teri is truly Miley's mother may be up for question. Right now, she misses her mother and her little brother, which makes the comfort welcomed in their absence.

In this moment, Tyler had seen something worth fighting for, even if Miley's heart is no longer his. Dawson who has spent years out of the picture is embracing her with tears rolling down his face. He is displaying a desire that kept him always prepared to walk back into their lives. The distance does not matter and neither does the bad communication, or, his constant destructive behavior. Nothing matters right now but the fact he is doing what he can do.

Andrew looks upon them and hides his ability to sympathize with Miley behind his steel expression. But something is not right and Andrew can feel it. He lifts from off of the car and takes notice to a particular detail. It is because of this one interesting fact his action alarm triggers. Phillip appears from behind a squad car and gives Andrew a look no one can mistake. Andrew looks at Tyler and then looks to Dawson. The back of Dawson's neck bears a black marking, a significant marking that indicates only one thing.

Just as the love in sight brought peace to a horrific visual, Dawson's skin begins to mutate. His face begins remolding, and his skin– like slim drools from his shape and size. A crude laugh is heard and Miley lifts her head from Dawson's chest. A pale face with black markings crossing over the nose and flaming orange eyes appear. A dress shirt and slacks transitions into a red and black suit, with a black handkerchief in his chest pocket, black tie and shirt, and black shoes. It is Vitiolic, how– is the question but it is too late to even ask. Tyler waste no time for charades again. He jets over with his fingers tight into a fist. Anger is guiding his desire to remove Vitriolic from their realm. Tyler's violent pursuit is fearless and fueled by an act of retribution.

"You bastards!"

Although it is only Vitriolic present, Tyler's rant speaks for the entire clan of evil insurgents. Moving quicker than ever before, he tosses his body into a straight jab that connects with his evil foe. Thunder cracks as his fist collides with Vitriolic's face. No longer than a second is all it took for him to teleport. He reappears on top of a squad car and everyone gives attention to him. His presence dispersed energy of ruin and darkness. Everyone feels an intense wave of despair and grief.

Officers begin to sulk and weep, and firemen drop their instruments and look to the ground with irreplaceable dysphoria.

Confident and angry Vitriolic makes his threats public and direct, "You, boy will die," and then looking to Andrew and Phillip he continues, "and you disciples fail to realize," he shouts with a force strong enough to break all the windows on the cars and nearby homes," YOU CANNOT SAVE ANYONE!"

The sky begins to display an orange flavor as the clouds reflect the light of the sun rising. An early morning is approaching, but darkness still resonated in the area. Vitriolic begin his rage infected act with no mercy. Four police cars rise into the air and begin to spin counterclockwise. Tyler looks at him and sees the evil burning in his iris like wood in the middle of a bon-fire.

"Stop," Miley says crying. Her mark begins to stain her skin painfully. The evil is attempting to propagate what Miley has residing beneath her smooth skin.

Standing like a King on hill, he shows his foul looking teeth and replies in a gruesome tone, "Never."

The destruction commences. Four homes surrounding Miley's burning casa are about to feel something so sinister. Rotating of the vehicles stops, and he throws his hand in the direction of four homes, which sends the squad cars crashing into the homes causing a massive explosion.

Out of one house a man comes running through his front door with fire surrounding his body. He falls to his knees as the six occupants from the other homes come sprinting out. Their bodies are burning with raging flames. The sight of their skin being reduced to nothing but crispy flakes of flesh, encourages Andrew to unlock his spiritual beast.

Vitriolic teleports to the street and flips a fire truck in the direction of an elderly couple standing in their front lawn. They disappear behind the truck barreling back into the flames and smashing a hole into the front door. A woman and her infant stumble out onto their lawn but luck or a miracle turns her fate. Cops take charge out of fear after recovering from their bewilderment.

Gunshots begin firing in his direction but he teleports over to one cop and snaps his finger, snapping the officer's neck like a twig underneath a field boot. Phillip appears in front of Vitriolic with every intention to stop the madness. He grabs this dark monster by the neck before he cans teleport again.

"This ends now." Phillip instructed.
"Yes, yes it does," Vitriolic replies stirring up all the energy he can harness.

An ambulance engines revs up and speeds off into the direction of the other officers. Andrew speeds over like a flash of light and grabs one officer by his arm, he then grasps another by his collar, and before he can get to the last man. The ambulance runs him clean over smashing into a parked car.

Pushing the ambulance off of his legs he looks to his left and right to see the two men he had just saved are bleeding at the skull and dying. The third officer starts shooting at Phillip and Vitriolic. He does not care who the aggressors are, he just knows neither of the two are patrons of Randallstown.

Thrown over a car by Phillip while evading gunfire, Vitriolic crashes onto the roof of a car crushing the frame completely. Phillip spins out of the way of the gunshots and ducks behind a car on the other side of the street. Miley and Tyler are looking at what truly resembles a war zone. Demons begin to appear rising from out of the ground. Black robes and sunflower yellow eyes are attacking anyone and everyone.

If hope is a dollar, they are down to their last buck. Morning begins to flow in and as daylight breaks showing the deaths of several people. Two of the deaths are Miley's neighbor Mr. Cantwell lying with his wife in the walk way. Miley watches as their bodies are burning to a crisp. Flames consume their corpses and the stench fills the air.

A feeling removes her from her natural state of thinking. Pain fills her bones and rage pumps through her arteries. She begins hyperventilating and her hair begins to rise from off her shoulders like static is running through her body. A demon appears in front of them with three more demons at her side, and eyes just as red and full of evil as his.

Brakes scratching the metal enter the environment, and Dawson and Benny Booter hop out of an unmarked squad car. They see the men in black robes thrusting their claws into civilians and shredding through their flesh. The two cops waste no time letting their guns off. Benny a sharp shot, aims with precision and nails two demons in the chest. They do not go down. Dawson fires shots off at another demon, and just as quick as his 12 gauge shotgun took the evil beings from their feet, they rise up and the bullets push themselves from out of their bodies.

"What the hell?" Dawson says.

Benny shouts, "This isn't working sir."

Andrew rushes over and Benny aims for him, he implies his cooperation quickly, "Don't shoot. Trust me," and just as he speaks a demon leaps into the air. Andrew catches him in mid-air by the neck. He places his hand over the demons forehead and recites a casting, "In the name of Jesus," and light burst from his hand turning the demon to black ash.

Dawson's jaw drops and his eyes become fixated on Andrew. He cannot believe what he just witnessed. His eyes reveal his perplexity on the actuality of Andrews act. Benny is appalled as well but a bit more receptive to the mystery. Andrew cannot wait for introductions and there is no time to explain. Demons are terrorizing the block. Five home owners had already been killed. Their families are fighting for their lives as demons taunt and chase them.

"Here, this will help," he says to Dawson and Benny as he places his hands onto the barrel of their weapons. "Lord, bless these devices that through your power we are strong."

A strobe of light flows over their weapons and Andrew shouts, "Now shoot!"

Another demon moving fast as wind teleports in and out of Benny's aim. Benny is waving his gun left to right trying to pin a shot, but he cannot. However, his intuitive nature takes on a hunch. He aims his gun to the left as the demon teleports right. Anticipating his move to the right the demon teleports back left, but Benny jerks his gun right and aims it hard left sending off a single shot to the head.

Black ash appears as the bullet makes contact. This is nothing like he ever experienced. Death is all around them and immediately Benny notices two bodies lying in a front lawn, and the house behind is next to Miley's ongoing burning home. He jets over and a pain breaks his ability to focus on the chaos. Standing over his grandparent's dead corpses, he drops to his knees and grabs his grandfather's mutilated hand. A single tear sheds and hurt exits as anger and vengeance creeps in instantaneously.

The hurt is fuelling Miley's heart to do something she never imagined possible. An insurmountable barrier of energy rotates around her. Tyler concerned, steps up and she waves him down to the ground without ever touching him. Pain creates a grueling desire for retaliation. Ziga is awakening a darkness that had been beneath the surface like roots in soil. Nothing makes her feel worse than realizing that evil had been festering inside her.

Dawson is on the other side of a flipped over fire truck. He can see what used to be his home burning out, but he cannot see Miley as of yet. Chaos is taking over the street, and either something is burning, blowing up, or being shot as Ziga continues releasing its fury. So much energy rushes through Miley it causes her to lose her balance.

Her eyes turn pure white and from the heavens lightning strikes like spears thrown from Spartans. Making contact with everything, no one is safe from her wrath. Lightning hits a squad car and it explodes on contact.

Another bolt strikes a tree nearby and a branch drops onto a demons body. Vitriolic deflects the strikes waving them off but his demons are decimated as black ash burst around him. As cars are struck, trash cans hit, and even solid concrete breaking upon contact. Tyler looks up and sees the woman hovering over her baby with her body trying to protect her only child. He jumps up and begins running in her direction fearless of the lightning striking him into nothingness.

A bolt almost smashes into him but he steps to the side and continues sprinting toward the woman and her helpless child. Vitriolic appears in front of him and swings for his head but Tyler – athletic and quick – ducks beneath and spins around his entire body. As he makes his way around he never stops running toward the woman. There had been so much death this dark morning, he refuses to see anyone else be harmed, especially an infant.

This seems like a foolish moment to sympathize, but Tyler has no expectation of witnessing a child die. Even as he is sprinting towards them, he has a short reflection of his own child hood. Being alone for nearly most of his days and struggling to understand why. A portion of his determination is entitled to make sure this child will also have a parent. Unlike he did, so many days and nights over and over.

Miley finally ends her rage and comes back to her normal self. Her hair falls to her shoulders and her eyes regain its natural color. No doubt her behavior was more demon like but could she accept that. As she is looking around at the damage, her hands are shaking at her ability to cause such destruction. It may be possible to conclude she caused more environmental damage than Ziga. Her abilities are freshly used.

A last effort to save a life is in pursuit, and as Tyler reaches the woman he grabs the child carefully. To have never held a child in his life, Tyler looks as if he might of acquired experience before. He then uses his hand to assist the woman who has a bloody gash in her leg. She can stand but it will be painful to tolerate. Tyler understands this but his concerns are for their lives. Just as his hand reaches for hers, Vitriolic shoots a force of energy in their direction sending Tyler into the air and many feet away crashing onto the grass. The impact of the fall looked like refrigerator dropping from the sky.

Evil fills his face and as he watches Tyler land. He smiles in comfort at his ability to have caused total chaos. In the sights of everyone, it appears that Ziga claimed another life. This life is worth their wild enough to vanish – leaving death as a verb for memory. Fires are burning and split wires dangling from light post, and beneath them bodies of Benny Booter's comrades. The sight is awful but he has received his first taste of true violence, although in a form far from any police officers training.

Dawson and Benny make their way around the debris and see the true destruction. Hell can easily become a metaphor as fires burn around the environment. It is definite, Ziga had only shown them a preview of their diabolical efforts. Vitriolic looks upon them in confidence assuring himself they all are defeated. And then, he looks to Phillip and Andrew before vanishing in his accomplishment. A smirk seals in the confidence in his actions. But his main goal, the piece to the puzzle that needed to be placed into position, is Tyler.

Death is a constant in the process of living. It happens all around but for Andrew and Phillip nothing breaks them more than trying and failing. They are God's most trusted soldiers in earth's realm and they were selected for a reason, but this morning that reason has been challenged. Depression is a storm and rain drops are falling along with the confidence in their mission.

The apostles know Tyler is dead. A fall like that cannot be survived, even Vitriolic knew as he removed himself from the calamity. Inquisitions are brewing in Dawson's head. Before he remains confused, he needs answers.

Dawson approaches Andrew and asks, "Who are you?"

Andrew looks at Phillip, and the moment is taken with silence. Introductions had already been impeded by a tragic battle with the demons. However, they know now or later, they will have to explain. The two glance over at Tyler and before their depression truly set, a sight recovers them from a second of gloom.

Regardless of what they all thought, reality is painting a picture they can vividly see the message within. They are many steps behind and they have wasted more than enough time putting together the pieces. Eduardo played his hand well, Savatir has vanished across the country, and Vitriolic refuses to die. As Ziga gains another advantage, more demons are coming out of hiding. More obstacles lie ahead for each and every one of them but faith is a powerful tool. And, at the moment Ziga is using it far more effectively than Phillip or Andrew.

Peter is dead and although his spirit is in heaven, the rain falling like stones onto the concrete affirms he is not resting peacefully. The fight is on, the clock has started and survival is no longer the only objective. Evil wants to dance and the floor is open.

Minutes To Go - Part 28

Final chapter

The rain is cold but the humidity is high. Phillip with crossing his arms and legs watches as cars roll by their failed effort to save many lives. A trunk full of artillery and a bible in hand Andrew looks down to the street watching blood run in the water pass his boots.

Before sadness set in the atmosphere, the woman comes to and looks off for her child. She jumps to her feet and Andrew takes notice, as does Benny, Dawson, and Phillip. Mud stains her clothes and as her fingers press into the grass, a mother's instincts raise her from the ground even wounded.

In the grass – again, Tyler lies on the lawn of Miley's charred home and with hands covering his eyes. His arms are holding something and he begins to feel the rain hit his face as his eyes open. Death has not captured him yet as the apostles feared. The hands remove and it is the woman's baby. No more than a year old, the baby resting on his chest is smiling alive and well. A voice in the distance screams up the block, "MY BABY!"

Andrew and Phillip look up and over, and they watch the woman run over to Tyler falling to the ground taking the baby from his arms. She looks at him and joy is not a word with enough value to describe how she feels. Tears blend on her skin with the rain and just as she smiles the rain stops.

"Thank you, oh my gosh thank you so much," she says hugging her baby and staring at Tyler in a manner so graceful. He nods his head up and down and replies, "Not gosh, God."

His head falls back into the wet grass and before he can rest his eyes again, his name is spoken.

"Tyler," and his head raises to see Miley walking up the sidewalk towards him. Her shirt is ripped and her face is full of dark marks from smoke flashes. Drenched in rain, she smiles removing any doubt of her ability to care about him. Although he sees her smile, he also understands that it is his life she is grateful to witness the survival of and not their love.

Even though love fuels her concern, it fuels his as well. Faith has been restored and the apostles begin to feel their favor turn.

They say before you go to war, learn your enemy. After tracking Ziga for centuries it became hard to understand their gutless acts of violence. But as the lady holds her baby they watch as the one who saved the day is not them but an inexperienced teenager. A young man is beginning to believe in his purpose, and even after his inability to accept a broken heart. Like a hammer hitting a nail, Andrew and Phillip realize their true purpose on this mission. Saving man is not the goal; the goal is to help mankind save each other. Tyler's selfless act brings revelation and promise to that perception.

The sound of footsteps squashing mud in grass turn his head to his left where he sees Phillip's hand extending in his direction. Andrew walks from behind him and extends his hand as well showing a brute look of confidence in the boy they are protecting. Tyler takes their hands and as they lock in grip Phillip says,

"Ephesians 6:10-13

The Whole Armor of God

Finally, be strong in the Lord and in the strength of his might. Put on the whole armor of God, that you may be able to stand against the schemes of the devil. For we do not wrestle against flesh and blood, but against the rulers, against the authorities, against the cosmic powers over this present darkness, against the spiritual forces of evil in the heavenly places. Therefore take up the whole armor of God, that you may be able to withstand in the evil day, and having done all, to stand firm."

Benny extends his curiosity again, this time expecting an answer, "Not to interrupt," he says still in shock about the death of his grandparents. "Who are you?"

Tyler looks to Benny and to Dawson, he then smiles and says, "Apostles, they are the apostles."

Miley smiles and wants to greet him but she shoulders him off as he steps closer. Vitriolic's act compromised her ability to feel trust. Especially in Dawson's direction where she questioned trusting him for many years. Phillip looks to the sky and then he checks his watch. Andrew takes a quick peek at his watch and then looks at them all to reassure the fact of the hour.

"The clocks started, and Ziga has shown us how far they will go to see their plans through. We don't have much time to figure this out. Tyler," Phillip says then turning to Miley, "Miley, this is real. You don't have to stay, but we cannot protect you if you go."

Andrew steps forward cocking his handgun, "Times a ticking, so we need you to choose now." Tyler looks to Miley, she looks at Dawson and he takes a second to process the unknown. "What is going on, do I even want to know?"

Phillip steps forward and says, "Those men you were shooting at, the ones that would not go down. They were demons from hell. They are not the worst of their kind but their leaders are. If we do not act now, you and your kind will have more to face than protecting your town."

Benny with a hardened stare does not care about who the men are, he wants revenge. "What can I do to help?" Andrew steps forward, "Are you sure? These are not just demons, these are demons who have been created for one purpose and that purpose only to be completed."

Fear has no place in Benny's blood or bones, he is ready. His grandparents were all he had left. And in his mind, he must at least honor their death with some effort to seek vengeance. Dawson has taken favor in Benny for his good service. If Benny is going to elect himself for battle, he is not going to let him go alone. After all, most of his officers serving Randallstown are lying in the street, lifeless.

Dawson reflects on his moment in the white room. He knows that this is not pure coincidence. He looks at Tyler and Tyler nods his head to the left, insinuating that he at least take consideration of what is going on. He wants to father Miley, but he hardly has the strength. Dawson too knows of a secret or two, and just as Teri does, he carries a burden in words that can place more distance between Miley and his relationship. For now, the thought rest away. His gut says trust them, as he remembers God's words in the white room, "*Go on with me and do not forget I am here.*"

"Just explain everything later, right now I need to call in and get this area cleaned up." Dawson says confirming his acceptance of the mysterious. And now, there is one last answer before their departure. It is true, the apostles cannot wait any longer, and they need an answer now. Ziga has acquired the Staff of Moses and having just one of God's weapons is one too many.

Phillip approaches Miley and Tyler, "What's it going to be?" They both smile, and what seems to be a moment of appreciation for each other, is more of a removal of fear. They looked deep into Tyler's eyes, and they can see it. The courage inside his heart is pumping out into his destined soul. The apostles do not know of Tyler's true purpose, but they know now, he is ready. He has accepted the responsibility his future may tie him to.

As Tyler is pulled to his feet, Andrew places his hand on his shoulder and smiling he says, "Come, we have work to do."

"You loving yourself, trusting yourself, and forgiving yourself...
Is your best chance at surviving this."

- Andrew

Cori D. Coleman

So a little about me that I would like to share...

I hate the idea of race. You are not white, black, Hispanic, or whatever label they gave you. You are what your name is. Don't settle for less, I won't.

Ps. I love tacos.

19103054R00155

Made in the USA
Middletown, DE
04 April 2015